JACK KEROUAC'S CONFESSION

Robert O'Brian
New York City 2011

This book is a work of fiction. All characters and events are a product of the author's imagination. Any similarity to real persons, living or dead, is purely coincidental.

Copyright © 2009 by Robert O'Brian

All rights reserved, including the right of reproduction in whole or in part in any form.

To the Memory of My Mother
and of My Sister

"The true mission of art is to provide a bridge between the living and the dead."— Rudolf Steiner

PART I: THE TONIC CHORD

Song for the Lady

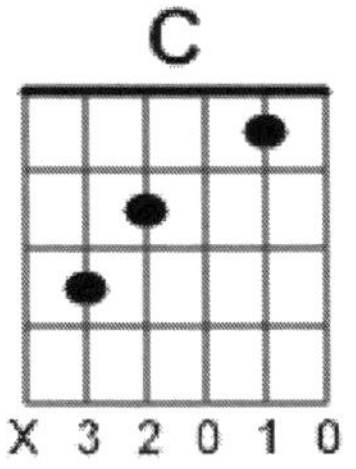

ONE

Gabby

"She said, 'I know what it's like to be dead.'"—John Lennon

It was when the last Kennedy brother was dying, Ted Kennedy, it was April or May, can't remember, and I was strangely aroused, staring at a magnetic spring moon at twilight just after the senator was diagnosed with brain cancer, not long after I returned home from Lowell, Massachusetts where I'd heard Jack Kerouac's confession—aroused because there's nothing more seductive than leaving town.

Nothing.

Except, maybe, the moon.

If what some call daylight's cradle, the crescent moon, were to wax and grow until it became the head and snow-white hair of somebody, you'd think it'd be Teddy Kennedy's head or maybe an aged Kerouac's, but the truth is, the metallic spring moon reminded me of Gabrielle Moses, my friend Joshua Moses's mother, because I began to see, maybe with an inner eye, a faint image of the woman bathing in the crepuscule as I stood there—no, actually, I thought of Joshua or had an image of Joshua's mustachioed face as he spoke, his squeaky voice lowered a step, about his mother whom he called 'Ma,' never 'Mom' nor 'Mommy;' who lay dying somewhere just off the Jericho Turnpike on Long Island, dying of progressive supranuclear palsy, PSP, a horrifying, muscle-destroying disease that's usually misdiagnosed as Parkinson's but, in any event, erodes all control over bodily functions, all mobility, even eyesight. When I last saw Gabby, she was totally blind and her skin looked as if it'd been savaged by barbed wire. She couldn't even scratch her nose. Was like she'd been buried alive. Trapped inside her skull. Imprisoned by the moon.

"You and I have a bond between us," Josh had said to me a number of times over the years and by this, he meant we'd always be blood brothers of a sort because we both had bedded Dustin Hoffman's girlfriend—not at the same time—back in school, when Christina was an 18-year-old freshman with crimped blonde hair and Swedish blue eyes, as blue as suicide. She was outrageous even then, played the dumb blonde at times, the helpless virgin at others, wore red velvet and white lace over her long and thin but not angular body. Looked like Claudia Schiffer. One spring day, I met her in Manhattan and she was wearing a Cub Scout uniform—blue cap and shorts, knee socks—and braids and asked me to be snotty to her and I complied. Wouldn't you? Have complied? Hers was a kind of child-like sexuality, masochism notwithstanding; she had that high voice, not quite a deer-in-the-headlights look, more of an I-can't-believe-people-would-do-that sort of naïve appeal to her. Christina left Buffalo after only one year to model in the city, to cohabit with Dustin Hoffman who was between marriages, and to become a fashion tycoon, pioneering and marketing some shoulder pad innovation for women which made her a fortune in the Reagan years. Dumb like a fox. Today, you can see her on YouTube selling her line of clothes, that high-pitched baby voice now damn near an aggressive merchant's *basso profondo*. Still pretty, though. Still blonde. Lips like fat red worms.

“I have no residual feelings for Christina,” Joshua used to say. “I mean, there are things about her that are not exactly healthy. She never asked me to be mean to her, but telling you to throw her down on the concrete so she could get all scratchy as she put it and demanding that you rip off her panties out on the campus podium and stick it in her and practically strapping you down so she could suck you out in the open in the middle of the night is a little too funky for me.”

“She told you that?”

“No. You did.”

“Me?”

“Yeh. Years ago. I had no presumptions about blonde *shikseh* women but in the end, Christina was like a soulless blue-eyed Aryan to me, willing to destroy marriages, friendships, invade the Sudetenland of domestic bliss if she needed to. She called me just after Miriam and I were married and wanted to meet up, but I said ‘no.’ Okay, we did meet once and she was all over me in the back of a cab but she stopped calling when Miriam got pregnant with Ellie. Christina was some kind of born-again Christian, too, or a Scandinavian Protestant with the A-frame house and the Bible, then they moved to that mansion, her parents did, in one of the five towns on Long Island. Crazy chick. But you and I wouldn’t have become friends had it not been for her, I don’t think. It’s like you’re part of the family and it all goes back to Christina.” Joshua paused and gave me a grave almost angry look under his big black specs and Melvyn Douglas mustache. “Do you want to go see my moth*ah*?”

I nodded that I would and the two of us climbed into JoMo's van—maybe it was a year ago when I was down for a visit—and drove to the Taconic, crossed the Whitestone Bridge, got on to the Cross Island, then to the Long Island Expressway which, dotted with only a few cars, reminded me of a soiled dinner table after a Thanksgiving feast. If you'd known Gabby, you'd have loved her, too; she smiled easily and was beautifully proportioned. Gutsy. Smart. Argumentative. Expressive blue eyes—Saint *Louis* blue—would raise her fist at her kids when irritated; on the phone, for instance. She wasn't above suing restaurants or bus drivers when she felt it was her right. When Moses and Blau, another school friend, were held up for a night at the airport in Montreal upon returning from London, sophomore year of college, Gabrielle got on the phone.

"You *sheep*!" she screamed at Joshua whom she called 'Jay.' "Tell those bastards to put you up in a hotel with dinner or we'll see them in court! I don't fucking care who they are or what kind of operation they have! Tell them to do right by you or I'm calling my lawyer!"

The boys got the hotel room with dinner and breakfast in the morning. Must have been years, decades ago, when I went over to the Moses home in Jericho without Joshua, to watch *The Godfather* and hugged Gabby at her mahogany red front door and sort of fell in love with her; self-conscious because I was certain that Gabby felt the tumescence when we embraced, thought hardened into fact. There were times I didn't hesitate to say that I loved Gabby more than I loved her son.

"So, you making any money yet?" she used to say with an inquisitive look that stung like thorny briars. Her hair was the brassy goldish, almost sunset orange that middle-aged women of that time opted for. Gabby had quit smoking sometime in the 1980s, but her voice was still raspy and smoky. Sexy, but she never put it on, never played belle-of-the-ball or sex-starved housewife. No knowing looks or double *entendres.* Gabby preferred candor. It was indicative, you might say, that Mrs. Moses said just before getting sick—before she started screaming at parties and bar mitzvahs, 'I want to die! Oh, God, I can't take this anymore, I want to die!'—that Franklin and Eleanor Roosevelt had 'no relationship.' She didn't say they had no sexual relationship—and obviously Franklin and Eleanor had a great partnership—Gabby said that they had 'no relationship.' Period. Don't you find that deliciously indicative? Sort of perfect? Her passion and knowingness; the stark sensation of drowning in emotion, the pity beyond all telling, evoked, conjured almost casually by one diamond-like expression of all time's loss and longing?

No relationship.

The pity of love.

"*Oy*," Gabby'd say to me, "you've been going to school for years now, *bubi*, when are you going to settle down and get married? You love children. What's the matter? What happened to that girl you were seeing? The one with the big, brown eyes? Was she the lawyer? No, that was the other one. The blonde. I should have been a lawyer, you know I could have been a lawyer, another Ruth Bader Ginsb*oig* if I'd just gone to Cornell like I was supposed to but those were the days when you got married out of high school. Sometimes, I think

Harry and I shouldn't have married so young, may no unkind word be said of him. And Harry should have been free, too. He should have been a musician, a pro. He loved his jazz and clarinet and played for me on our second date. 'Frenesi,' 'Begin the Beguine,' 'I'm Confessin' that I Love You,' he was really something. My cousin Cecile said that if Harry had stayed single, he would have been Jason Robards in *A Thousand Clowns*.

"'That's Harry,' Cecile would say, 'Jason Robards in *A Thousand Clowns*.'"

"You know, guilt is a good thing," Gabby continued, chest heaving like the morning tide, invisible cigarette in hand. "Guilt is good. It inspires you to do good things. Look at the civil rights movement. What about the labor unions? Lots of good things come from guilt, am I mistaken? I don't want to come on too strong or make you feel guilty, but I think you should get a good job, find a nice g*oil* and get married and have a family. How long are you going to wait? You're not going to be young forever. I have arthritis. I know. Getting old is no fun and you have to be young to raise a family. The world hurts, *boysha*. I have arthritis. I know."

I enjoyed needling Joshua through Gabrielle, provoking her with statements her only son had made.

"Gabby," I began, "the other day, Jay and I were talking about the U.N. or something and at one point, your son said, 'wait. Who is Albert Schweitzer? Of course, I know his name but I don't really know what he did.'" JoMo is a bit of a polymath, but there are lapses. Gaps.

Gabby took the bait and immediately turned to Joshua. We were sitting in their pastel-colored

Long Beach summer condo. “Who is Albert Schweitzer?!” she repeated, her voice rising like a police siren. “Who is Albert Schweit*ZAH*!? He was a preacher and an organ player who went to medical school at thirty like your sister, Shira, then went to Africa to inoculate thousands of people. Children, too. He was also one of the greatest interpreters of Bach ever known. He was one of the greatest humanitarians of all time, may God strike me dead if I lie. Reverence for life. That was his thing. Reverence for life. What are they teaching at those colleges? Is this what we spent all our money on? So, you could be ignorant? Who is Albert Schweitzer? Oh, my God, I’m going to have a stroke!”

But Gabby didn’t have a stroke. She lay dying off the Jericho Turnpike of an unmentionable disease; a mass of putrescent mortality that sees and feels nothing.

Unless . . .

TWO

Babylon
(Queen of My Song)

"Your depression comes from your insolence and your refusal to praise."—Rumi

Since returning from Lowell, Massachusetts, where I heard Jack Kerouac's confession and got my horns and sanity back, I've been trying to elevate my writing, elevate all expression, actually, to a form of praise because first of all, your depression comes from your insolence and your refusal to praise and, second, praise for the ideal of the eternal feminine, for the Lady, is probably the best way to transform the earth into a work of art.

That's our job here. That's all my argument.

When you sing praises to the Lady—and I'm thinking of Gabby as I write this—you begin to feel as though something like golden blood runs through the veins of the earth, no toxic sentiment about it.

Make the world a work of Art.

For *Her*.

Revise it.

The world hurts.

While I've never been what anyone would call an abject failure with women—I idolize them too much to be a complete failure, I worship the French braids and shiny lipstick, their wisdom, the peek-a-boo outfits, the clinging sweaters, the lace, the ensellure, the striving in the eyes, their hidden strength, their desire, Claudette Colbert's chest heaving up and down as Gable takes off his shirt, their eternity, their genius, their tongues—I'm more than willing to believe that the Messiah waits to be born inside the belly of a great lady—while not abject, I've been, clearly, a failure at romance and partnering which is to say, a failure at love. I have no sense of it, love that is, and I've sabotaged and ruined every one of my love relationships with infidelity, jealousy, neglect or just plain ordinary meanness.

Jealousy, of course, is the worst: ***where is she? I called at 8:00 and there was no answer but she said she'd be back before eight, so why isn't she back? Did she go out for drinks with Alvin? She says Alvin's gay but who really knows? At parties, she chats with one guy for half an hour. Why half an hour? A little flirting is okay, but thirty minutes by the guacamole going psss, psss, psss with the same man is an affront. An insult. If you're going to have an affair, have one and let me go but I am not going to wait around by the phone or at a party and be consumed by this interior monologue, by this diabolical inner accuser.*** And it does consume and torment you, worse than Hawthorne's bosom serpent. *Oh, how it gnaws at me. It gnaws at me . . .* I couldn't get out of bed for days because Lyla, a Southern belle-of-the-ball, refused to stop lunching with a red-headed yuppie law student. Lyla had a heart condition and I was actually happy that she had to be hospitalized for a day because that meant she wouldn't be going out for lunch with the redheaded yuppie. Esmé, too. She had some problem with her thyroid and I rejoiced privately because the condition briefly curtailed her social life.

This was way beyond schadenfreude. This was Love, right?

"Strumpet! Whore!" I could almost hear myself bellow like the Moor, commanding armies and navies of jealousy but, alas, never my own heart. And as for being mean, I once yelled at Margo, one of the kindest women in the world, yelled at the top of my lungs because she was late for dinner. We stood on the Bowery near Bleecker Street, outside a Thai restaurant on a cool spring evening, and I yelled and carried on like one of the Bowery characters, then told Margo she could spend Friday night alone if she were going to continue having 'an attitude' and The Lady's ghost just disappeared like smoke through an open window. Why wouldn't she? Anger, like alcohol, attracts people at first, goddesses, too, then, finally, repels them, and I'd become repellent in so many ways. La Betty Noir.

"Look," good friend Blau once advised, his eyes like black olives resting on white cloth, "you don't have to actually look her up and down, you know what I mean? Not up and down and up and down, staring at her belt. It's kind of a giveaway, Slick. Too easy . . ."

And I cheated, oh God, cheated and lied. I'd call Esmé from a phone booth on Central Park West and say 'I'm working the late shift at Fried, Frank and Shriver, dearest. I'll call ya tomorrow' or from my flat in Astoria, with Tatiana in the middle room—I'd shut the door and place another long-distance call with pine needles and love nectar drying on my neck. Pre-cell phone days. Eventually, all parties would find out, in fact, that's how I wanted it so as to avoid the commitment and so on. Leonard Cohen said "I have decided to seek beauty the way other men return to the religion of their fathers" but you won't always find beauty, passion and love in the same embrace, so, it was easier if the women I knew were alcoholic and not all together because then I could make my case to Esmé, protest that we aren't getting along, not in *that* way, and, oh, I'm being unfairly treated and need comfort and passion and that's why I'm going over to the Upper West Side twice a week to lay with a drop-dead-on-her-face drunk and so on and so forth. When you're desperate like this, when it's not about love (***love*?**), when it's not about two hearts and the innocence is kind of hidden, no vulnerability, then—

BEHOLD!

It really is the vanity of vanities and a striving after wind, even if she has silk bikini panties and smells like cream and rose petals and it won't be about the truth, rocking, sweating, calling out to God, it'll be about my garden idol smashing against hers, *my* marble hard flesh, *my* machine powered blood, *my* triumph, not hers—PULL DOWN THY VANITY, I say—and see, usually, she was out in a few hours anyway, out, asleep, drunk and after two days or so, I'd take the serpentine train up the serpentine Hudson River, back to Mount Kisco to stay with the Moses family, then drive west across the state to resume a ghost deception, to lie essentially, and smile because although all is vanitas and a striving after wind and hurt and perfidy rule the world, *my* marble idol vanity is ever faithful and never lies to me, but it wasn't always this way, wasn't always this corrupt:

GARDEN OF EDEN

Lovers

With their clothes
Off

Unashamed.

You don't lust after flowers, doncha know.

"There is a truism that makes me angry," I said to Blau, "that a man enjoys nothing more than a catfight, two girls pulling each other's hair out. Not true. One of the most attractive things about women is their own appreciation of the feminine, their support for each other, and if that sounds banal, their language, then. That language women have."

I accuse you of being a woman. Do you understand the severity of this charge?

Good friend Blau once joked that every year, women get together at the Woman's Convention and work out more strategies to fuck over men.

(You have to admit: it's funny. Just picture it.)

I began substitute teaching after moving back to western New York from the Big Apple, when preparations were being made for the Iraqi War.

"Well, it looks like they're going to bomb the hell out of Iraq again," I'd said to Blau over the phone.

"Babylon," said Blau. "They're going to decimate Babylon. The old Babylon, the original Babylon."

And while the oak leaf clusters, the epaulettes and the pin-striped suits got ready to destroy or, rather, completely loot and plunder ol' Babylon, the mind wandered from one of the old musty schoolrooms, back to my own Babylonian past, to my old neighborhood, back to a kind of Babylonian idolatry, to my greatest failure, to a buffoonery so profound, one can only see it as sublime, as something beyond even the imaginations of the stars. My brother won't admit it now, but way back, the two of us were crazy stupid in love with a little grape-skinned Jewish girl with long curly hair when we were kids outside Buffalo, New York—obsessed would be the word, I dreamed that she would love me and that I would save her from the Nazis in my old man's '76 Pontiac Catalina. To paraphrase Thomas Wolfe in *Look Homeward, Angel*, she was wine in my blood, a music in my heart. I was the star, she was the crescent. My brother and I watched as the little girl searched for crayfish in the muddy ponds before the suburbs were finished and when she became a woman, I dreamed of her nakedness and her scent, in fact, could almost taste her, then, years later, I saw her in Manhattan and got her address and sent her poems and prose, her curly hair was cut short and I swear she was even more lovely than I'd remembered. Now, this was a muse lady. Maud Gonne. Sœur Thérèse. Regal. Unattainable. Goddess of the Hunt. Smokin' hot.

My brother moved away and says he forgot all about her but I took my guitar and harps and sang at her window in Brooklyn, sent her letter after desperate letter, mailed her an old shopworn book of Robert Burns' poems with dried rose petals and then, one day, saw her picture in *The New York*

Daily News because as it turns out, the grape-skinned Jewish girl is Condi Rice's niece and she was at some reception in her honor wearing big hoop earrings and, of course, I was desolate for now my chances of winning her had become even slimmer and, still, I sent her letters and sang "Summertime" over the phone for her and wrote things like "your skin literally takes my breath away and makes me tremble not in fear, though, because I would kiss every inch of it until you, too, were left trembling and breathless" and other treacle that is, frankly, embarrassing to relate now because in the 21st century, you're not supposed to have emotions anymore (not really), but later I prayed on my knees that she burned all of the letters and poems I'd sent to that Brooklyn address. Hopefully, she threw them in the fireplace or shredded them with an Ollie North shredder or put them in a perdurable plastic bag and sealed them with a little white twist tie and one hoped she was undercover, too, because when you're getting set to do Babylon, the poet's dreams have no place and every vestige of earthly beauty must be stolen or erased.

(You probably guessed by now that I didn't get the girl.)

THREE

The Right Values
(Ghost Dance)

"The Eternal Feminine draws us forward."—Goethe

One girl I shouldn't have got was Lyla—Lyla with a "y"—who put me through the most humiliating changes of my life; she tormented me, taunted me, tasked and heaped me so that I would have been better off had she roped, gagged and flogged me, so excruciating was the anguish. An armageddon of emotion. God *fuck* her. Eleven years my senior, Lyla was a Southern belle, married and divorced three, four, maybe five times, red glossy lipstick, big round saucer-shaped brown eyes, clear pale skin, thick shoulder-length flamenco brown hair, plu-perfect Michelangelo painted breasts. The Black Madonna. Old Spanish with Spanish eyes. Scot or Scots-Irish, too. Think Hedy Lamarr or Natalie Wood but even more voluptuous and with a southern accent or Ava Gardner in the early days, in *The Killers* most likely, legs crossed, leaned back, strapless gown, blood and fire in one being, all we know of heaven, all we need know of . . . Put it like this: the seductive power of this woman renders unnecessary any dishonest, florid, idealistic description or revision because *there* she is. Or was.

I mean, this is a human possibility. This walks among us. Or is it The Lady?

Many women say that they want a sensitive, caring, soft man who will listen to them and nurture them, who will get in touch with his feminine side but people, women, sometimes deceive themselves. Lyla was almost the reverse. She would tell you that she wanted an old-fashioned man, a man who takes charge, but she would let no man dominate her, not in terms of money—she was big southern estate wealthy—nor in terms of her life decisions. She really was Scarlett O'Hara with a dozen years added to her. Not quite Blanche du Bois yet, Lyla was shrewd, thrifty, intelligent and hardheaded, sort of a belle-of-the-ball feminist, proudly unreconstructed and unrevised, but sharp and fiercely independent, too. The daughter of a physician, Lyla had been a teacher for years and advised me not to follow suit, citing the time she was hit in the head with a pencil thrown at her by one of her music students. Lyla taught music (she was a pianist), math, English, art, just about all of the subjects, and she'd been a successful businesswoman, too. She was studying law with me and had her contracts, torts, malfeasances, misprisions, well-pleaded complaints and civil procedure down cold. She was nobody's fool and her naked breasts, let's call them vivid incarnations of the will to breathe, were more rapturous than anything found in nature, more captivating than the autumn sunset; a Roman feast, as beautiful as justice. A terrible beauty, you might say. Not trying to sound worldly or knowing, but you could not be unimpressed by or casual about her breasts and be human. Salomé would intone breathily that a frightening music emanated from them, from her, but if asked to describe Lyla just after she'd slipped off one of her black lace teddies and laid it beside her big brass bed, neither Gloria Steinem, Naomi Wolf, nor even Michael Musto (or Salomé) could fail to praise Lyla's sumptuous buttermilk breasts or her carnation pink Lord-have-mercy-I-could-die-right-here-and-now hardening nipples. Candor ends paranoia.

I could die right here and now.

"*Ah* ran away from home," she sobbed on our first night out together. "*Ah* want to care for you. *Ah* want to make you happy. I'm loyal and true." That was our first date! Lyla wore a powder-blue zip-up dress and we walked under an umbrella from the car to the pub, her left boob rubbing against my arm and chest as we tried to get cover from the rain. The first kiss: she acts so grateful, like a man had never tried to kiss her before. Lyla's kisses were intoxicating; she gave those thick-tongued sweet strawberry wine kisses—the kind that taste good even with tobacco on the breath—and when I drank deeply at her delta (forgive the indiscretion), when her girlie juice squirted out from her ducts like a fountain of dreams and ambrosia, I got to the origin of uneaseful bittersweet life itself, so I thought; was transported to another place, to another time, to Nefertiti's bedchamber, to the secret chambers of the pyramids; hallucinatory, archetypal, immaculate but we're too sophisticated for all of this now, right? Sex is death, disease, impotence, pharmaceuticals, indistinguishable from money. Sex *kills*.

Right?

Lyla wore garish furs, drove a big black Lincoln town car and, let it be said, you will never meet a woman silky refined or white-trash sleazy who loved to take it in her mouth as much as Lyla. One evening in early September, I was in the passenger seat of her town car and she said "take it out, take it out please" and when she saw the erection, diverting her eyes from traffic for a moment, she let out a weepy mournful, almost animal cry and virtually collapsed with weakness, then reached for the velvety tip of my manhood with her thumb and forefinger, her other hand on the steering wheel.

"Let's stop somewhere down that road," Lyla insisted and quicker than summer lightning, she dove for that thing like it was buried treasure, so eager was she to give old Iron John another lingering French kiss. Just after Thanksgiving, we were watching *It's a Wonderful Life* at Lyla's place and before Bedford Falls could even come to George Bailey's rescue, Lyla became possessed, seized; she was maniacal, mad, working it for dear life, absolutely determined to soldier on with me between her teeth, then she maneuvered everything in just the right way, stopping, starting, then with her fingers, she pressed and released perfectly until the seeds of desire were catapulted on to the red and green of her embroidered Christmas sweater. But the most pathetic part of this seamy tale is that I was in love with her. I was consumed. Trapped. Imprisoned. *I smell you, I touch you, I taste you. Now, I'm your slave.* Graphic sexual detail is not embarrassing to relate, to share with others: it's the emotion that's embarrassing. Who wants to be this vulnerable? Supposed to rule over your emotions and not let them rule you . . .

There was no peace with Lyla, none at all, except when we made love, when we fucked till dawn, scaring away, you might say, even the phantoms of the desperate desperate night, belly to belly, like two worlds touching, when I could feel her coming like a shower of hot snow around my cock and mons pubis. "Pornography is ugly," we used to say. "*This* is beauty." *To be loved, to be loved* . . . I made Lyla the center of my existences, temporal and mythical, made her my soul catcher, the embodiment of every hope and dream. She was, in a way, my creation and also my opiate, my jailer as well as liberator. Was like she was tattooed to my skin. Of course, the jailer, the beast is within; I was my own captor but when the goddess is mewing "I'm trembling, I'm trembling," because you've got the spear of destiny between her taut creamy legs, you don't see it that way and why should you? I was so obsessed with Lyla, I sometimes wanted to *be* her, wanted to know what it would be like to receive. . . what it would be like to be seen by *me*. . . and to stand in front of a gold-encased mirror and gaze at my naked shoulders and breasts. To be ground zero for all that sexuality and femininity. To be seen.

Should I wear my hair back in a ponytail today or wear it down? Is it the glossy red lipstick for today or the clear? How much of my body should I show today? A little of my belly? Just a strip of skin where the blouse fails to meet the belt line? Even though I have millions, I just swoon when a man picks up the check. It's so gallant. How did I get to be so hard-hearted? Nevertheless, being Lyla, you'd wonder about your girls, your two daughters. *Will they be all right? Will they be happy? Will they find the right men to marry? Men who will be servants to their beauty? I love them so. Why are we here anyway? What's our purpose? To love? That must be it.* It's all kind of out of fashion now, *c'est vraï*? This adoration of woman. This idolatry. The mystery behind the silk, the strategies of conquest while pretending to be conquered, the receptive principle . . . *who will fill the empty amphora that is my heart? Who will complete me in a marriage made in heaven?* Until the 19th century, women were known simply as "the Sex;" not the weaker sex or the fair sex, just "the Sex," because women were understood to be the container, for both genders, of romance; women were the caretakers, the guardians of beauty—protecting sexual love and glory, the Truth, from the wild wolves and the too-rough hands of the world, the way a mother protects her child (one reason two straight women can cuddle and French kiss)—and still are, although one sometimes wonders if the PoMo homeland security people will outlaw beauty some day. Yes, I wanted to *be* Lyla in those unfathomably passionate moments. As the song says, I'll be your mirror.

"You're a delicious man," she'd drawl and, of course, I believed her. Who wouldn't? "Sometimes when you speak in class, *ah* listen to you and *ah* just want to rip your clothes off. Such a beautiful boy. Truly, you are my heart . . ."

(Maybe she was telling the truth but, as my old friend Hubert used to say, "the devil will tell you 99 truths. And one lie.")

Lyla grew up in the Baptist church but later become an Episcopalian because this is what all earnest, devout, God-fearing, upwardly mobile Christians do. J.P. Morgan did it, so why not? Tragically, Lyla had assimilated all of the prejudices of her father and of her father's father, all of the awful, soul-destroying, bone-calcifying xenophobia. Racists hopelessly in love with their prejudices, who guard them like diamonds, who literally define themselves by their relationships with the "other." Lily-white frat boys dressing up as gangstas on a Saturday night, for example. Still, there was something about Lyla's passion, that passion you see in the eyes of the brylcreem toupeed evangelists with gold rings on their fingers and in their painted and perfumed coiffed consorts—religious conviction so deep and penetrating that it spills over into the sexual or, perhaps, sexual passion so deep and on fire, it carries over into the religious—that may be redeeming, hucksterism notwithstanding. None of this abstemious monkish asceticism, no "I'm sorry, dear lady, I cannot. I'm a man of God." *Of course* they get caught with hookers in motel rooms. Of course the white supremacist preachers and politicians slip it to their kids' wet nurses and sire illegitimate (not right?) babies that grow up to literally haunt them. It's not just the passion, though, it's the love of the shadow, the lust for repentance, you might say. The hypocrisy is epic yet the passion and even the martyrdom of Elmer Gantry will always be preferable to the dead-cold, cadaverous certainty of the anchorite and the angular righteousness of the secular liberal who also wants to outlaw beauty. Even the cries and yelps of a Tammy Faye Bakker had more soul than the perorations of priests or scientists, or TV anchors for that matter, it's just that those preachers don't want *you* to know that passion, only them, and the racism, of course, is ugly and unbearable. When Lyla said that Dr. King was "despicable and self-serving," I could have strangled her (non-violently, of course) and watched her body become lifeless and limp, cinnamon breath and perfect tits be damned but no one could say she was lukewarm, someone to spew with disgust from the mouth of the apocalypse. She was, in a number of ways, despite all else, the Blessed Magdalene, the fallen lady, or maybe the Ukulele Lady: if a man showed the right kind of interest, she loved him.

But she was unhappy.

Of course.

She was the world.

Like all those who don't atone, Lyla couldn't just sit and ruminate on her real sin, the sin of bigotry; she had to elevate it to a virtue. She couldn't just admit to the sin and say "Yeh, I've got a problem, I'm a bigot, I need to expiate." No. The very thing that kept peace away from Lyla's black widow heart was raised up, elevated to something desirable and virtuous. A shining city in a swamp. It was good, then, that her church was an all-white church because, that way, tradition was maintained and there's the issue of states' rights and blacks don't want to mix with us, anyway, so we're doing them a favor, don't you see, and I don't care about race or color, truth be told, I only care that a man has the right values.

"That's crap," I remember saying to her. "A black man could recite Shakespeare's 116th sonnet, from memory, bake a crème brulé and dance the minuet and you still wouldn't let him into your country club."

"If he had the right values," Lyla insisted. "Oh, yes, we would. If he had the right values."

In spite of it all, though, I really was in love with Lyla and felt that I couldn't live without her. I was helpless. Trapped inside the temple of her heaving femininity and it hurt to see her cry or on the defensive.

"Don't you wag your finger at *me*," she cried, "you can't judge my soul. You can't . . ."

When I told Lyla as we studied criminal procedure that under no circumstances would I consider being anyone's *sixth* husband, she stormed out of the law library and I chased her down the hall and that was when it all began. Or ended, depending upon one's perspective. That's when she started spending quality time with the red-headed yuppie, dilating her brown eyes so that they were even bigger and rounder, playing the part of the coquette with the come hither stare. Loyal and true. The red-headed yuppie was not only at her side at all times, he was in our every conversation. He was such a gentleman, he knew how to dress, he owned some apartments in town, he was well-fixed for cash, he was going to be a great attorney. I was just vulnerable and stupid enough to be affected by this song and dance. I couldn't eat, couldn't sleep, devils filled my head and left me weak and tormented crazy like flesh without blood. What if they go out somewhere and she puts her hand on his while sitting in the car? What if they walk along Ellicott Creek holding hands the way we used to? That was it: just the idea of Lyla holding hands with another man sent me into unspeakable agony, into perdition, bronco on the freeway. Oh, merciful God, what if they *kiss*? KISS??? One night, after finally dozing off, I dreamed that Lyla was sipping a tequila sunrise on some yacht, not with the red-headed yuppie, but with an older, distinguished, well-heeled businessman in a sailor's cap and loafers, no socks, graying temples, chiseled face, a man who commanded other men, who bred horses and owned a vineyard, everything that I am not. *Oh, how it gnaws at me. It gnaws at me . . .* Our conversations became poisoned. Where, at one time, everything I said was charming and insightful, the soul of wit itself, now I could say nothing that wasn't boorish and inappropriate.

"If you're going to be a teacher," Lyla admonished over dinner, "you have to be more subtle. You can't be so open about your judgments. You wanna be a bohemian your whole life? A beatnik? And if you *are* going to practice law, you have to be more thick-skinned. You really are an ingenue. Now, look, that's not how you eat soup. Watch me." She sat upright, composure serious and sober as a judge. "You put your spoon in the soup this way, away from you. Sit up straight. Bring the spoon up to your mouth but don't bend to eat it and never lift up the bowl . . ."

Our dialogues would heat up like a jet engine with Lyla going on about 'the right values.' She didn't care about race, she averred, only about values.

"Oh, my heart, you're going to give me a heart attack," she cried. "You know *ah* have a heart condition. Don't make me have another episode . . ." then we made up and she pleaded with me in a teary whisper as if under duress: "are you going to explode inside of me again? Oh, dearest, when you explode inside of me tonight, have mercy on me. Please, have mercy on my poor heart . . ."

If Lyla sounds vulnerable here or brittle or even a tad silly, I was even worse. Much worse. "Don't you love me?" I asked her about a week later, in tears myself. "Do you love me?" An old-fashioned word, love, but that was the feeling.

"I love everyone," she responded, having regained her powers. "I try to love everyone I meet." I yearned for succor, for true love, romantic love, and suddenly Lyla was Gandhi, was my old friend, Kerouac's favorite, Saint Thérèse de Lisieux, loving the broken heart of the world the way a mom forgives a rowdy kid.

"Don't you know you are killing me?!" I screamed at her. "KILLING ME!!"

"She's a drug," I whined to Blau. "She's heroin. I can't stop. Can't quit."

"There are other drugs," Blau said quietly over the phone.

"No, there aren't," I assured him.

"Can't you just make this woman your fuck buddy and forget about the, you know . . . love and obsession?"

"No, I can't."

Never give all the heart.

Now, this is true, this actually happened, no revision here, no lie, no fiction: the jealousy kept building steadily, kept growing like a weed, like fly larvae on August corn. Lyla knew just how to play me, touching the yuppie's hand when she spoke to him, eating lunch with him near every day, then greeting me at her apartment door at night in her black lace teddy and pink robe. I was beyond miserable and sex was my only respite but, eventually, even passion couldn't keep the black dog away. I wasn't in the garden anymore, but, what's a heaven for, anyway? Our tolerance for each other's differences was vanishing more quickly than the rain forests. Once, I mentioned that Jesus of Nazareth may have been a black man and, much to my surprise, Lyla didn't argue to the contrary.

"But I'd never let a black man touch me," she added, "not even if he were Jesus Christ." Special Southern emphasis on the 'Keeeer-ah-st.; like fat sizzling in the frying pan.

"But, you're a Christian. Devout . . ."

"I know. *Ah* just couldn't. Couldn't. And I could never let my daughters date a man who wasn't white."

"So, you wouldn't let your daughters date Jesus Christ? He's not *good* enough?"

"I didn't say that."

"But you did."

"I don't care about his color. He has to have the right values."

"Wait, I have to get this straight. You wouldn't allow yourself to be touched by Jesus? You don't deny that he was black. Or not white. So, tell me because I don't get it. You're saying that he's not good enough? You wouldn't go out with Jesus Christ?"

"Well," she said completely in earnest, "if he had the right values . . ."

FOUR

Book of Dreams
(North American Book of the Dead)

"Dreaming ties all mankind together."—Jack Kerouac

For nearly a decade, I couldn't shake the black dog of depression because, joined as I was to a tiny and anemic, de-oxygenated phantom self, I was a beast without a dream, without horns, the right kind of horns, without light or gold or genius, without any sense of 'I am,' sleepwalking, close to madness. For years even before the bubble and the Great Recession, I'd felt incompetent and ineffectual. Rootless. Looking for a good and noble career as, clearly, I had failed at everything I'd attempted. Saw my sins and errors collect like drops of hot tar inside a deep and narrow cup, only to be poured over the face and flesh of every emerging sensation, rendering them stillborn. Couldn't even hear the 'right' music, didn't have my ears attuned, couldn't hear the Lady's Song in the lily-whited key of C.

"Really wish I were one of those great men like Newton or Linus Pauling or like Buckminster Fuller or even Allen Ginsberg," I'd say out loud to just about anyone, "who rises early, gets to work quickly in the lab or in the studio or in the garret and with patience and intense concentration, solves problems or produces great works of art, but the truth is, I'm the original feckless fuck-up. It's like concrete lightning. I'm a fuck-up, callow, a ne'er-do-well," I told good friend Blau, "worse than a junkie beatnik. I don't grow plants anymore, don't know the human anatomy well, can't identify flora or fauna, know next to nothing about cars, can't fix leaky pipes, don't breed horses, brew my own beer, collect antiques or build wooden cabinets. I don't know wines and I've never made a wise investment. Have no savings, no retirement and no children. Thomas Jefferson could plant and harvest an acre, break a horse, set a broken leg, argue a case and lead men into battle, but I still struggle to pay the rent. And I am *not* the happiest man alive.

"I'm good at neither poker nor chess, not a mover or a shaker, not politically active, don't make things happen all the time, in fact, I'm so immature, so useless, so ill-equipped to deal with the world, I once thought that I might be a saint, you know, too good for this world like Saint Francis or Michael or Kerouac's own Saint Thérèse of Lisieux, the Little Flower of the Child Jesus Face, but that's impossible, too, because I'm greedy, self-indulgent, perfidious, hot-tempered and envious of others." See Blau now, listening intently behind his jet-black eyes.

"I have an adversarial relationship with just about everybody and everything. Don't even want my friends or family members to succeed too spectacularly. I'm a hanger-on, a wanderer, a wayfarer, a backstabber and a gossip who'll trash anyone once he's out of earshot; a decent conversationalist who can barbecue lamb chops, and show an old schoolmate around Manhattan, other than that, it's a cipher, a leech, a space-filler, a vagabond, a rootless cosmopolitan and my name'll never be scratched into the Book of Life. The Israelis say that a man should be like a cactus, tough and prickly on the outside, sweet and tender on the inside, but I'm just the opposite. Adders with cloven tongues do hiss me into madness. I'm one of the insane, as mad as Naomi."

Blau, a son of the Holocaust, always says that the artist has to be the sane one, particularly in an increasingly insane world.

"The artist has *got* to be the sane one," Blau said to me in Le Figaro or in another Village café. "In an age of fragmentation and neurosis and bankruptcy, the *new* artist has got to be a body in motion; has got to be about sanity, intimacy and completeness."

I always liked that: sanity, intimacy and . . . What was the last one? People thought I was nice because I was sometimes soft-spoken and attentive and appeared to be congenial but I knew I was a mean bastard who rejoiced when I saw old friends from school looking old (even black-maned Blau); I liked it when marriages failed, when wives walked around with that look on their faces, the look that says 'I could have done better, you can see that I got stuck with stupid here' because I was thinking 'maybe she'll notice *me* and give my shredded life meaning and incandescence with fleeting and flirtatious eye contact.' I'd been fired from jobs for falling asleep in the broom closet, for disappearing hours on end; didn't own a suit until I was thirty-five, and I could never finish anything. Took clarinet lessons as a kid but stopped rehearsing, so I split my clarinet reed to avoid playing and even scratched my arm up with chicken wire to get out of performing in a school recital while the nation cried out to be healed on ABC's Movie of the Week. Showed some small promise at football at about ten but never went to practice and got benched. Quit

Junior Achievement after about two days. Got a law degree but never practiced.

Sorry for the self-involvement, but my mind was like the hydra with the heads that keep dividing into two, each thought leading to two more thoughts, like some credit default swap spiral or the sorcerer's apprentice, or a tonic chord, haunted by a shadow subdominant chord that never resolves itself with the lost dominant chord. Was as though I hadn't the conviction to even complete a whole thought at all which is a disaster for anyone trying to live respectably in the pain factory, in the graveyard that you call the world. The corporation. The Clampdown. Often, I'd have, moreover, a sickly Major Major feeling that my voice is too high and thin, has an adolescent or even a foppish timbre; doesn't have the deep, sure resonance you generally hear and want to hear in a man's voice. ("Makes you wanna *hiiiiiide*.") A kazoo in the universal orchestra. A squawk. Above all, I was unfocused and without resolve.

"My life needs an editor!" I wrote in big letters on a yellow pad. "Spontaneous prose?? *Take this story, this life, my cruel heart, just take it. I don't want it anymore . . .*"

And then there were those bastards—you know, of the Fucking Bastards . . . ? What I could never understand about some of my old college mates and former colleagues when I was writing and editing and living in New York City was that *they* had the nice jobs and nice salaries, had the spacious offices in midtown Manhattan with computers, unlimited long-distance, secretaries and their names on the masthead. *They* had the perks, the trips to Las Vegas to see the Tyson fight, the interviews with Keith Richards, lunches with Bowie at the St. Regis Hotel, they took home the premium giveaways, the tapes, the CDs, even state-of-the-art sound equipment. *They* had it all, I thought, and yet they seemed wary of *me*, resentful of my yellow pad and diminishing HORNS and the friggin' $600 per story I got if I was lucky. I was like one of the poor relations. It's like my existence on the planet was a *problem* for them. (Hey, man, just that you're alive, just that you walk the earth, pisses me *off* . . .) They seemed so burdened and unhappy but *I* was the one who had to sneak into the office to steal a desk and a computer, a fax machine or a phone to do an interview or to check up on facts in L.A. Editing. Revising. *I* took the overnight Greyhound bus trips to Jeff Town prison in Jefferson City, Missouri or to Martha's Vineyard, lucky to get some sleep, though we all came up together and I even gave one of them, one of the editors, his big break.

And what was this kingdom they had to protect with Byzantine complexity and secrecy? They were just setting up photo shoots and schmoozing on the phone with publicists anyway, all of which made for an unusually miserable time, the Nineties. The early Oughts, as well. Absolutely miserable. For close to a decade. I'd lost nearly all my power.

Then, everything changed.

Everything.

After I got to Lowell and heard Jack Kerouac's confession.

Listen.

There has to be some mechanism by which one can escape this heinous epidemic of depression and anxiety and, from what I've heard, the Art of

Revision is the most effective one: Change Your Story, Change Your Life. The Greatest of the Arts.

"The road is life," wrote Jack Kerouac who knew better than anyone that a song about leaving town, about the road, about life, can't be the proposition of someone sitting at a desk writing, but of a body and mind in motion; a body and mind revising itself, reversing entropy, and getting *gone*, as he and the jazz players used to say. The body is minute, the unknown is vast. Nothing's more seductive than leaving town.

Going out on the road is like telling a new story, like Neville Goddard's concept of revision: assume the *feeling* of the wish fulfilled and the wish'll come true, even in the face of the Ugly Spirit. The staff of Moses, it seems, is the "secret," the technology of the 21st century. Zero-point energy. The tachyon field. We are what we think about all day. *I am . . .*

"The greatest revelation in my generation," said William James, "is the discovery that human beings, by a change of inner attitude can produce outer changes in harmony with their inner convictions."

Take a sad song and make it better. Dream a better dream. The goddess Revision. Furthermore, I think that when Kerouac said dreaming ties all mankind together, he meant the dead as well as the living: history can be revised and reimagined in the best sense and those who've passed on can be touched by our words and thoughts just as the living are touched by the dead through the written word and in dreams and I'm not just posturing.

"I hope it is true," wrote Kerouac, "that a man can die and yet not only live in others but give them life, and not only life, but that great consciousness of life."

And remember Rudolf Steiner: the purpose of art is to bridge the gulf between the living and the dead. Our thoughts and deeds and dreams are *food* for the departed.

Revision is the key. Atonement is the mode or mood or tone or tune. Like the *kaddish* tuned to another pitch, to A=444. Everybody must atone. Agenbite of inwit. Then again, there's the matter of 'spontaneous bop prosody' and Kerouac's alleged refusal to revise his writing.

"Maybe Kerouac was wrong about this," you might say to yourself, "because you *have* to edit. You can't always be spontaneous and 'never change a word.' You have to revise. Even Bellow talked about 'the revised man.'"

Everybody must atone. Take a sad song and make it *better* . . .

But how?

Allen Ginsberg appeared to me in a dream and said "as time goes on, you'll find that Rumi was right when he said 'your depression comes from your insolence and your refusal to praise,' because underneath every descent into depression, every failure, every frustration, every addiction—somewhere underneath the storm and stress, you'll invariably find a big 'fuck you.'" Allen's voice was low and steady, like a Gregorian chant. "You want to be an exciting person, be excited," he continued, "you want others to notice your beauty, notice their beauty. Bored people are boring people. You can praise anything and everything, not just infinite creation. Kerouac taught me that. You can praise your rose bed, the blue vault of heaven sky, the azaleas, the ocean that seethes and rages like a boiling pan, the laptop, Karl Rove, clipped fingernails by the toilet bowl, the sweat on your asshole, the living and the dead of Babylon, sexless Babylon whose soul is electricity and banks, whose buildings are judgment, whose knee is bent to Baal and Moloch, whose dream song is long-forgotten—praise the Lady, the guitar-shaped Lady!—speak the good word and speak to your angel of things: they don't care about cosmic consciousness, they want to hear about *things*, but in any case, praise, praise, praise, even if you have to lie and revise."

Say 'I am' and the cops and the yuppies fall to the ground . . .

(Aren't you sick of these tepid, paralyzed men, whining about their loneliness and angst and the impenetrability of woman? If she wants you to take her dancing, don't go into a Marxist-Hegelian rant about the shallowness of an unredeemable America the way I used to do, and don't freak out if she steps outside for a smoke like these hornless New Age yahoos. If she wants you to take her dancing, merry gentlemen, what do you do?

You take her dancing.

If she wants to go to that fancy four-star restaurant with the nouvelle, nouveau, what the hell cuisine, no need to inveigh against the wizards of finance and the invisible Babylonian bloodlines, take her to the restaurant and enjoy the red snapper and the Caspian Sea beluga caviar. Dante said that generosity makes the wings of a woman's heart flutter. If she wants you to take her dancing, take her dancing. And if you're worried about the obsequiousness of it all, the possible indignity of too much compassion and cunnilingus—'all that eatin' pussy' said Bukowski, 'it's kind of submissive after a while'—if you're worried that you'll become an icky and uxorious suburbanite, made of copper, horns and balls cut off, remember that revision is the key to happiness and revision is an ancient song and the ancient song's dominant chord is the woman's orgasm. Q.E.D. The Goddess unites the realms of the living and the dead and brings you to sanity. I would draw the line at shopping.)

"You wanna know what getting your horns back is about?" Hubert said back in the Eighties, Hubert who wore at his heart, the fire's center. "It's about one thing: can you say 'I am' in a convincing way?"

Your weaknesses and doubts fall to the floor, but I don't want to fall, not when The Goddess is around, you understand . . . male strength. Performance. This has never tasked nor heaped me in any big way, but I'd become fond of saying, 'there's a reason it's called impotence: you're helpless. There's nothing, absolutely nothing, you can do about it." Not true. *Your depression comes from your* insolence *and your refusal to praise.*

"A man's lack of potency comes from his saying, on some level, 'I will NOT,'" Blau said at his grandparents' Passover seder in the Bronx near the botanical garden. Blau had a lot of hair back then, black and slick like Eddie Munster. Magyar eyes. "I will not praise your magnificent French braid and your white cotton blouse with the embroidery. I will not kiss your lips, nor will I caress and lightly bite your nipples and dip my tongue into your navel. I won't stroke your clit with my thumb and with love as we're thrusting and even after I pull out, when we're resting on our backs. I will not praise the eternal summer of your beauty, the one that doesn't fade. I will not get clean. I will NOT. I refuse to praise the goddess. Won't praise, just whine, whine, whine. It's a choice, Slick. Ya gotta remember that." Blau raises an index finger. "It's a *choice*."

This is what happened to me: I lay in bed with the Brown-Eyed Belle of Saint Mark on a Monday morning before work, before taking the subway from St. Mark's Place in Greenwich Village up to 30 Rockefeller Plaza where I'm working for the magazine. I'm kind of limp. Shagged out. "I fucked her brains out Friday night," I'm saying to myself. "I fucked her Saturday morning, Saturday afternoon; made her come like a fountain, like Al-Fawwara—cascades of water, pyridine, squalene, carbamide, acetic and lactic acid, and alcohol pouring on to her bed—Saturday night, fucked her hard and long on Sunday morning and Sunday night, too. I'm tired," I'm thinking, "I've given enough." Then, it hit me like the queen of spades: Blau was right! On a somewhat conscious level, this red-eyed Beast is saying 'fuck you. I can't be bothered. *I don't* feeeeel *like it . . .* " He who has an ear, let him hear: Your potency, the serpent lifted up in the desert, your ecstatic union with the Goddess is your **natural** state. You have to go out of your way to be limp and ineffectual and alone. 'Gethsemane' means 'semen.' Seeds in the garden.

Do <u>you</u> suffer from resurrectile dysfunction?

The unconscious is virgin, untouched soil waiting to be pricked and seeded by an affirmative thought. Use your horns. Anyway, I was beat some years back. **BEAT**. Unable to praise. Began to cry often. Not boo-hoo-hoo necessarily, but days despondent, lifeless and without color. Out of tune. Years . . . Youthful restlessness impels one to go out on the road at eighteen or so, while the approach of middle-age, with its attendant failures—divorce, debt, disease, depression—bears witness to another yearning; the yearning to remake oneself. I shook in bed and found it difficult to sleep. Trembled. Often, I found myself awake at 3 AM and after an hour of tossing and turning, I'd get out of bed and roam the streets of the Lower East Side. (Loneliness wasn't the issue; it was the fear of loneliness.) New York City is music, one massive composition of thunderous and gentle melodies, and the Lower East Side is a sarabande or The Third Man theme on speed—and I don't even know what a sarabande is—or sometimes a slower *fado* filled with hookers, hustlers, street poets, crack heads and junkies—all dead, now; all ghosts—doing the nod under the neon lights of the Houston Street delis, underneath the early morning stars that, let's say, with more envy than mercy, look down on the soul-moist and iron-hardened flesh that every single day and night marches with goofy Mardi Gras abandon to its ruin and presumed redemption. It's been said that early morning stars listen, too—patiently, like the souls of the dead. They *listen*.

If you were me, you'd recall old women in house dresses with bloodied legs pushing empty shopping carts on Attorney Street, passing drug and gun dealers ("hey, you wanna buy a Night Rider?" was the most interesting pitch you'd hear) as cops stopped their squad cars at select rests and intervals to collect bribes, while Old Howard, a real Lower East Side native in his dull gray T-shirt and Yankee cap—big, tall guy—drunkenly roamed the streets,

Jimmie Rodgers and Gene Autry pouring out of his boom box. Plucking. Yodeling. Counterpoint to both the furious melodies and the languid songs of fate.

"Gene Autry, king o' the cowboys!" you'd hear Howard slur more than once on dreamy and liquid yet symmetrical nights. "King o' the cowboo-oys!"

See now Billy Boy, a Tompkins Square scene maker and hustler, another ghost, crouching in a below-ground tenement stairwell, furtively fastening his black leather pants; Asher, a Jamaican raconteur and pot dealer; Allen Ginsberg in his sleeveless and green down parka, ambling along Second Avenue, stride for stride, with a dirty-blonde-haired cherub boy wearing a denim jacket; Quentin Crisp in his ancient purple jacket, pants and almost-hippie floppy hat, ambling along Second Avenue, stride for stride, with a dirty-blonde-haired cherub boy, same denim jacket; and witness Ilona Klein, once a great copy editor for Condé Nast and an actress, too, who's lived on Ninth Street for decades and is going broke. Writers and wags at Condé say she's a bit desperate now, too.

"Ilona, I thought that was you," I say to her in front of the Chrystie Street garden at about one-thirty in the morning. "How's everything?"

"I'm out of work," she says. Short hair. Voluptuous. Glasses. Shopping bag. Cute and literate. Kitten-like. "I can't pay my bills."

"But, you were the best," I say. "Everyone wanted you."

"Yeh, I know."

"It must be your breasts," I say. An old joke. I touch her right hand. "Remember? You intimidate women and make men nervous."

She laughs. "You're so male. You have such a man's perspective. I was flat until I was seventeen, you know. Flat as a board."

"Flat? You?"

"Yeh. Men's undershirt flat. And I didn't want breasts. I didn't want to menstruate. Who needs it? But now, I'm an F cup." She lights a cigarette.

"F cup?"

"Yeh. I think it's the same as triple D. But I refuse to go to G." She exhales smoke and laughs again. "You know how women are: 'I want that girl's boobs and *that* girl's ass. I want that one's hair.' I need to edit myself. I'll do anything to get work again."

"So, what happened to your acting?" I ask her. "I saw you in a Woody Allen film. You were combing Alan Alda's hair."

"That was so long ago. I mourn those days like the passing of summer." She pauses. "Hey, outlaw," says Ilona slowly. "Did we sleep together? I mean, back then?"

"Yeh, we did."

"Oh." She gazes at the sidewalk. "Was I in love with you?"

"I don't think so."

"Were you in love with me?"

"No. Not really."

"Not even a little?"

FIVE

Joshua

"In all that plays into waking life as dream or sleep, the dead are living."—Rudolf Steiner

Now, listen: Did you know that a man's etheric or elemental or essential or subtle body is female and that a woman's essential or elemental self, her metaphorical self, where she hangs out with the sprites and imps and sylphs and sidhes and genies, the fairy world, is male and that's why the mystery of life and death and heaven and earth and waking and dreaming is the mystery of male and female, doesn't matter if you're straight or gay or transgendered? I'm sitting on my sofa in Queens one day, trying to change my state, heighten my awareness (sanity is a kind of ritual), waiting to hear the answer to a still not-quite-articulated question; a question about life, love, about every kind of ecstasy. Fate. Passion and compassion. I fall into a shallow sleep and that voiceless voice says, very quietly, 'it's finished.' The voice descends. Seems to evaporate. An evanescent pocket of intelligence. Queen Mab. Muse. Boson. A light blanket on the sleeping self; electromagnetic; dream within a dream, yeh, all of that, but I really heard it. It was audible. *It's finished.* No more coughing in ink and thinking just what the others think and wearing the carpet with my shoes. It's finished.

Did I not say 'ye are gods*'*?

Did I not fucking tell *you*?

But, we're far from the Promised Land. We're not in Lowell yet. *Allons!*

My great-grandfather, John O'Brian—my father's father's father—died of typhoid in 1890 at the age of thirty-six which means that he died oblivious to any notion of aeroplanes, radios, coup de villes, movies, Roosevelts,TV or cybernetics, leveraged buyouts, nukes, cold fusion, sit-down strikes, quantum free energy fields, quarks, bosons, or Elvis unless, as some believe, the dead sleep in our imagination, in the tachyon half-light, but when awakened by the living, have eyes and can see everything that transpires in the earthly realm, the flame of their being kept burning by the imagination and praise of the living, by the collective poetic memory at zero point; by an almost primitive desire that *that pale long-visaged company that airs in immortality* sees and hears the living with the same intensity and wonder with which the living speculate about them. (Make Yeats your poetry god and all else will be added unto you.) You can't extinguish the ego until you wrestle with the death angel.

Yes. *Unless*. But according to the mortal calculus, according to the facts, John Mortimer O'Brian was gone in 1890 and never saw nor heard of a flapper, a doughboy, a pierced labia (although we never really know, do we?), or of a New York Yankee, but he did leave behind a wife and three small boys. The middle one was Will, my father's father, and the other two, John Jr. and Tom, both became priests, Missionary Oblates of Mary Immaculate, whatever that means. (Oblate? WT*F*?) Uncle John, the eldest, was the "bad" priest.

"He was a bastard," my father said. More than once. "A real bastard. A son-of-a-bitch. He was in the house once for some party or celebration and I was running up and down the steps on Lafayette Avenue. I was no more than eight at the time. Running through the kitchen, running back and forth, and when I got to the vestibule, Uncle John swatted me with his umbrella. And it hurt. I can see him now, I can still see his roman collar. He got me up near my rib cage and he just whacked me. Mother marched up to the bastard from the kitchen and said 'John! Don't you *ever* touch *my* child in *my* house!' Said it in front of all the guests, too. And he never did again. Never did hit me again. But when he died, he left some money he'd saved with the church when he could have given it to Dad. The church gave it to Dad, anyway. He needed it more than they did."

The unfortunately nicknamed Uncle Tom, however, was the "good" priest. The nice one. Guess he'd have to be with that name.

"Uncle Tom was a great guy," my dad remarked with a subdued Gaelic enthusiasm. He's 90 now and never gives up. My father is the world. "A sweet guy, Tom was. A great sense of humor. Always smiling and joking. Would bring candy for the kids and he really listened to us, too, but he died young. In 1943, I'm pretty sure. I remember I was overseas at the time and he was the youngest of the three. *Jay-zus*, he was wonderful."

And they devoted their lives to Mary. Mary!

"How loony could they have been?" my cousin Bill said to me recently, "I mean, who can say 'no' to a blessed womb?"

Anyway, true or not, that was the narrative for many years: John was the bad one, the bad uncle, the bad priest; petty, authoritarian, irascible, violent, "a prick," as my dad finally put it while Tom, the baby, was benevolent, kind, attentive, generous and gone way too soon, like the sweet in chewing gum. But the story takes an interesting turn after my cousin, also named John O'Brian—the poet, John Pius O'Brian—puts together a genealogy of the family, which contains birth dates and birthplaces; death dates and death places and I'm cold-cocked past the compass of my wits when reading, just after moving out of New York City, back to my hometown upstate, that my great-uncle Tom, good Father Tom, died in 1943 while serving as a priest at St. Joseph's Parish in Lowell, Massachusetts.

"I think my great-uncle Tom might have heard Jack Kerouac's confession," I say over the phone to Joshua Moses, my friend and erstwhile editor, Gabby's son, who remembers everything and rarely curses except for the oath, 'goddamn' which he employs or sometimes *tries* to employ like some ancient bony-fingered New York patrician in a voice even higher and more adolescent-sounding than mine. Josh is known to our college friends and me as The Genius, more for his organization skills than for anything. (Today, you'd call it 'control freak.') Joshua and I met as college kids at the University of Buffalo when both of us wore long hair and beards and, to put it rather poetically, the reluctant sun thought its rarefied thoughts through us. Josh is earnest, learned, voluble and passionate about art and literature—far more learned than I—has more enthusiasm about life, music and death than it's hip to have or display—always greets you with a warm embrace—has read all of Dickens, all of Faulkner *twice;* has over a thousand CDs in his collection, thousands of songs on his iPod and smokes reefer like a Rastaman.

Listen here about Josh, you should know JoMo: Freshman year at Buffalo, Josh walked naked through the cafeteria at dinner time after his dorm mates bet him and each other a hat full of dollars that he wouldn't, and though Moses has been a citizen of stately, plump Mount Kisco for over a decade—his wings clipped somewhat, his Mosaic hirsuteness shorn and shrunken like a voodoo doll—looks more every day like Bob Balaban mixed in with the older Melvyn Douglas—the domestic life hasn't diminished one mite his enthusiasm for the winged life. He buys an exotic species of marijuana from a cartoonist in Manhattan, goes in for extreme sports with his kids—paint ball, bungee jumping, hang-gliding—and always manages to get season's tickets (the Mets) for the whole family. Has the metabolism of a hummingbird. His opinions are original.

"Updike is like Prince," The Genius once announced excitedly, standing up from an imitation Shaker chair. "Everything is sex and God, sex and God! Like Tolstoy! Like Prince!"

"Famous for fifteen minutes, how wrong was *that*?" he said one cold winter day. "Led Zeppelin's been on the radio for over thirty-five years. Everything's been stretched . . ."

Absolutely nothing PoMo about JoMo, except that he and I both have that distinctly male tendency to talk about big ideas, currents of history, biographical names, in other words, anything but feeling, the inner life. Blau talks easily about his feelings, but not Josh. Not easily.

"I don't want to talk about 'you and me,'" Moses once complained about a college girlfriend. "I want to talk about important things."

Of course, Mo's never said 'I love you' to his mother, either. Not important enough, apparently.

"What are you reading now?" I ask him.

"Eleanor Roosevelt's diaries."

"What the fuck for? Eleanor Roosevelt?"

"In a way, she was the best Roosevelt," Moses says at hummingbird New York City frequency. "Remember, she was Teddy's niece. Had an FBI file on her the size of Eliot Spitzer's black book. She had those buck teeth, then had 'em replaced with a bridge after she was slammed in the back of a cab. It's like the old joke: she got into a car accident and became beautiful."

"Just imagine yourself going down on her," my cousin Bill used to say. "Imagine her yelping in that shrill aristocratic voice: 'just a little to the left, Hick. Yes, that's it. Now, down just a little, Franklin. Oooohh, don't stop. Don't *stoppppp* . . .'"

"She reminds me of my *mothah*," says Moses, finally.

"She does not."

"Now, you're telling me what I think?"

"That's right. What do *you* know about your mother? You don't know anything about your mother."

Before I go on, let me say country simple that Josh Moses is my hero, my fucking *hero*, the son of a god, but sometimes we see different sides of the same moon. Moses used to have an ego like a lightning storm, all flash, thunder and repentance, until time and perhaps fate permanently chastened the skinny friend one can only describe as an honest crook, as a New Orleans politician who used to fantasize about doing the six o'clock perp walk, who could talk his way out of Auschwitz, but that was before the forces of Ahriman or Mephistopheles, the alien, not quite human cats who enslave pre-pubescent girls, rob retirement funds, loot charities, create massive debt, provoke countries into wars then finance and arm the opposition and peel the skin off of naked virgins without so much as blushing, who want you to think they're freaking God as they fuck with the weather and the ether and even the souls of the dead, control minds, and break the bones of old men and women, then ask for forgiveness when found out, who keep it all afloat with laundered drug money from the poppy fields of Afghanistan—you know, *those* people, the strange muses, the fallen gods, the human doubles that walk in the earth's shadows—finally got to Josh Moses and left him ragged and dirty, just this side of the promised land. In the wilderness. Even his sexual performance has been affected.

"There are recessions, then there are recessions," he says now.

The portion of you that hasn't been completely violated by the media—the national dream life, the ability of the country to imagine, has been almost completely usurped by television and "new media" hasn't it?—that which was once known as the soul, *alma*, Mother, moon, Mama Soul, has texture and color to it, like musical chords, and Joshua's soul is gold-yellow because while he still has plenty of sulphur in him, he burns slowly, that is, he isn't consumed easily, he doesn't burn, burn, burn like Dean Moriarty anymore. Moses isn't mad to live, exactly, not these days—often, one sees blue sparks popping out of the gold-yellow fire there—still he's generous and life-giving; passionate and opinionated but one kind of wishes he would start cursing more or do something out of the ordinary to relieve him of his 'I'm-just-another-upper-middle-class-working-man-who-found-out-what-it-is-to-be-ghettoized' frustration, say things like "you ignominious strand of asshole hair, you fucking unreconstructed cocksucker, why don't you jerk off to photos of the Forbes 400?!"—or something almost as eloquent—but, alas, Moses is burning slow and quiet like the eternal flame at Arlington when the two middle-aged men speak on a Saturday in late September, just before the days of awe.

"I always knew that Uncle Tom was the good priest, I mean, the good uncle," I tell Moses over the phone.

"He'd have to be with that goddamn name," Josh quips. You can hear the remnants of hay fever allergy in Josh's somewhat squeaky, cat-gut voice. He's sniffling and sneezing and sounds a little hazy from some antihistamine or other prescription. "Yessir, a real uncle Tom."

For decades, the great-uncle priest appeared in my mind with dark, almost black hair and eyebrows, like a younger, more slender Antonin Scalia. "I knew that he died young, during World War II, but I had no idea that he died in Lowell, Massachusetts. Now, that was 1943. I wonder . . ."

Moses has just signed a contract with a big British entertainment magazine, overseeing the design and launch of its new American web site, and he hates it, hates the work, still he dives right into the hypertexted morass, works like a serf amidst the fetish celebrity worship, even though he despises most things current and modern. Only the music and films of his youth will do. This scene, one might say, is the noisy, relentless and vulgar backdrop against which The Genius defines himself.

"You know the mass media, Slick," he likes to say, munching on a pretzel; getting into your face like Lyndon Johnson. "You didn't see what you saw. You don't know what you know . . . "

The big boss in London, to whom Moses refers alternately as "the British billionaire" and "the Jewish billionaire," told Josh not long ago that "if things work out, I will make you a wealthy man," so my old friend has his hand on the plow, his eyes on the prize in that midtown office near Grand Central, sleeping a little better now that he and Miriam and the kids have health insurance again and what's more, Moses is happy to chat about something or somebody other than Jennifer Aniston.

"I have to say, I don't love Kerouac the way I love Roth and Joyce Carol Oates and DeLillo, I just don't," says Josh over the phone. Try to imagine his eyes dilating. "He captured a moment, yes, he was something new and, I guess, exciting, but there are better American novelists and less bigoted ones, too, if I may say. For how many years did Uncle Tom live in Lowell?"

"I don't know, but by 1943, Kerouac had already left Lowell for New York."

"Yes, you're right and remember, they weren't walking around saying 'this is the Beat Generation,' you know, they were thinking about the end of the world, the apocalypse."

"They were pilgrims, really. Milleniallists."

"Yeh, yeh, but they didn't know it at the time. Like the 1960s; no one was saying 'this is the Sixties, this is an historic moment,' in fact, if I remember correctly, they called it the Now

Generation; it even got into the advertising, it was all about Right Now because we might not see tomorrow and that's what any sensitive soul, any desolate soul would have been thinking even back in the Forties when electricity had already burrowed its way into the skin, across the highways and abandoned fields, too, and then suddenly, you had atomic bombs and television and radar, but, you know, 'apocalypse' means 'revelation' so maybe something was revealed."

If you were listening, you'd notice that Joshua has stopped trying to lose his New York accent. For about two years, Moses had conscientiously pronounced his 'r's to "get ahead,"—you could hear it even in his voice-mail message ("leave your numberrr and I will call you laterrr")—but he's clearly given that up and is back to saying 'computah' and 'mothah' and 'how many *yeeeahhs*?' There are many ways to revise your life. Not all of them succeed.

As mentioned before, Jack Kerouac didn't believe in revising his work, didn't believe in revision ("it would be a sin to change even one line," he said) and I got my hands on my cousin John's genealogy at about the same time I began hearing about self-revision and had decided to make it my life's organizing principle, my life-saving shit—my good friend, Archie, introduced the idea to me—at the same time that that translucent thought had come to me like a sprite or a saint or like a girl with faraway eyes and a heart of gold who dresses slutty once in a while, and had whispered the words "it's finished" into my ear. Could say that Kerouac revised his life by traveling, by leaving town, but he didn't revise his writing and, after a while, he didn't even leave town. He was living as a drunk and a boor with *Memere*, his equally drunken and boorish mother, in fact, the man purposely drank himself to death and has, inscribed on his tombstone, ironically, the words, "he honored life." Ginsberg got to sanity, intimacy and completeness, but not Jack. Poor Naomi. Poor Jack.

"Listen to me, Slick," says Josh after some time. "Go check up on the Oblates of Mary, okay? Find out when Father Tom was assigned to that church and if Kerouac attended in the late Thirties."

"I don't even know what the hell an Oblate is. Isn't it a kind of verb?"

Moses responds with that playful antagonism appropriate to a world of duality, of light and shade, particularly appropriate to an oft-times contentious relationship. "That's *ablative*, you cretin. Ablative, stative, dative, transitive, remember all that?" Moses sniffles again. "The Missionary Oblates of Mary Immaculate is pretty much a Canadian order started by some Frenchman after the French Revolution."

"What . . . you're some kind of Vatican scholar now?" I say, rubbing my right eye.

We all know that numerousness is the hallmark of a curious intellect without a unifying concept—the suburbs of the mind—so, just imagine Moses, see The Genius, see his light brown coffee-with-cream eyes disappear behind those coal-black-framed specs as he grins, the contours of his face conforming to the dictates of an insane inner trickster the way soft clay conforms to the sculptor's hand and vision, the way, in sketch TV comedy, say, the mind wraps around the concept that a particular number can be funny: "thirty-*tooooo*" the gag writers finally settled upon, wasn't it? (Jews, Israel, Zionism, TV, Jews . . . aren't you *soooo* afraid?) Josh always presented himself as the hustler-trickster; Blau as the brooding but flip existentialist philosopher (and a master at cunnilingus; just ask him), but Blau can be funny, too, as funny as his grandpa Schlezo, who once joked about attending SUNY Buchenwald.

"*Vat* is *dis* SUNY Albany? SUNY Buffalo? I *vent* to ZUNY Buchen*v*ald!"

"Solomon had a thousand wives," Blau gravely remarked at still another Passover seder in his grandparents' home near the Bronx botanical garden. "A *thousand* wives," he repeated with quiet awe, just inches away from the lamb and gefilte fish. His hair was Eddie Munster slick and combed back.

"How do you think the prophets made out?"

Blau pinched his nostrils. "Too *intense*!" he squealed.

Couple years back, Blau won a Nieman fellowship to study at Harvard where he saw and heard John Kenneth Galbraith lecture.

"He was great," reported Blau who never misses an opportunity to drop a name. "He said 'you know that expression, when the shit hits the fan? I made that up.'"

Josh was not impressed.

"You know that expression 'go fuck yourself'?" responded JoMo in a rare moment of profane envy and schadenfreude. "*I* made that up."

Woo-hoo, the comics: dwelling in that nether region of sun-dried bones, the danger-fraught vale that lies between tragedy and music. One hot summer day, sun bright like a child, Josh came home in a tailored pin-striped suit and called his four kids out to their pool in the yard back of their

Mount Kisco home. Josh Moses then jumped into the water, tailored pin-striped suit and all, because, as he put it, his children "have to learn that in life, anything can happen." Taking a swipe at death with the sparks of life, that's Moses, and yet, Josh still acts as if he's my editor and that angers me somewhat because he never really employed me full-time, not even back in the Gnarly Nineties—no job with a salary, benefits, and vacation days—but to hear him tell it, he's custodian of mine art, my muse, my doppelgänger, I mean, we were like Damion and Pythias way back in the day, like Jack and Neal, but no more. We aren't completely estranged from each other as we were throughout much of the Eighties and Nineties, but it can still get tense with The Genius.

"Josh Moses is a lovely guy, actually," Blau once said. "Always throws his arms around you. He's the first to help out when you're in trouble. He'll make the phone call, he'll pick you up at the station, he'll set up the appointment for you, but he can get kind of self-involved, you know. *He* saw the towers fall on 911; *he* will never be the same after that day. That type of thing. *He* lost his shirt after the bubble popped. Like he was the only one. He's a genius, remember, not the Messiah."

(The problem with Moses? He never left town.)

"If memory serves, the Oblates came down into New England from Canada in the early 20th century," Josh says with a self-satisfied ring in his voice, not because he knows more about Catholicism than the lapsed Roman Catholic, but because, believe it or not, JM still wants to be . . . ahead of the curve. Debt, depression, anti-depression and more, and Moses is ever and onward, engineering his greatness, the hero of his own story. His mother's favorite . . .

"It's pretty much a French-Canadian thing," he says, finally.

"You're so full of shit," I say. "You're googling now as we speak. 'If memory serves.' You kill me."

"I am full of shit. You're right. I like to lie. I'm good at it. Sometimes, I just witness myself, you know, I just listen to myself lying and I'm amazed that anyone believes me. I get off on my lying and the work I put into it. I just weave falsehood with falsehood until I have one big beautiful mosaic of falsity and deceit. I'm an artist. It's the only way I can tell the truth."

Of course, St. Augustine had his confession; Rousseau, de Quincey . . . Tolstoy, bear on the side of the cliff . . . and for nearly a century, the world has suffered through the "true confessions" of people it doesn't even know, but the Roman Catholic sacrament of confession is for the purpose of reconciliation, is the water in which one is cleansed; is, in the words of one Catholic thinker, one of the greatest ways to overcome what they call 'sin.' Confession gives you "grace to avoid committing these sins, mortal and venial, in the future" but what the Catholic thinker doesn't take into account, aside from the fact that that kind of confession can't make anyone 'new again'—even if you want to mince endlessly or obsess over the word 'sin'—is this: who *really* wants to stop sinning?

(Horns aren't sin. Not exactly. And who even really wants to be *Sane????)*

"I'll research it all," I say. "I'll get the right years, the right dates and e-mail my cousin, John, who lives in England. I'll find out if Kerouac and his parents attended St. Joseph's Parish. I'll get back to you."

And I do. I discover that Jack Kerouac, *Ti Jean* as his family called him, did, in fact, attend the Oblate Fathers' School on Merrimack Street in Lowell. In *Doctor Sax*, Kerouac vividly describes the Oblates' Grotto, which was built to resemble Lourdes and is situated on the Merrimack River.

"*Mad, vast, religious,*" writes Jack, "*the Twelve Stations of the Cross . . . the roar of the river, mysteries of nature . . . fireflies in the night flickering to the waxy stare of statues . . .*" Epiphanic, beatific. Words like jewels, precious stones. Gives you the feeling that you're adorned. Decorated. Praised. Kerouac didn't write like many of today's bright lights, didn't use the language and sensibility of science—no restrained ecstasies or tempered revelations in his work—the italicized point had not yet replaced the exclamation point—very few spare sentences or passages delighted with their uncluttered economy (very few)—because Kerouac was an open nerve and furthermore, the spirits of the dead, trapped inside of plaster and waxen idols and in the mournful peel of church bells frightened and depressed young Jack as they do most young Catholics.

"*Everything there was to remind me of Death,*" he concluded. "*Nothing in* ***praise of Life****.*"

Except for Oblate Father Spike Morissette, who encouraged him to write and to excel at football, sounds as though *Ti Jean* encountered more Uncle Johns than Uncle Toms back at the Grotto and at school as he tells it in *Doctor Sax*. More of death than the life-giving waters our own Bernadette found in the south of France, in Lourdes.

(All hearts love the same way, but break in different ways, the heart of a Roman Catholic in its particularly dramatic, yet quiet and paralyzing way. Think Steve Dedalus. Agenbite of inwit. *Mortal* sin.) Kerouac's metaphor for death and insanity, for the death machine, in this retelling of Faust, *Doctor Sax*, is the Great World Snake, which is defeated, as it were, when he, the snake, is witnessed; seen for the impotent slug it is although a snake can be good thing, too, as everyone knows, if you can make it crawl up the staff of your wisdom. 'Word' is one letter away from 'sword.'

MENTAL HEALTH is all my argument—fair, kind and true—but about this time, I'm finding no evidence that the Kerouacs attended St. Joseph's Parish or that my great-uncle taught at the Oblate School on Merrimack Street and I'm insane with frustration. Jack left Oblate Fathers' after a year or two anyway, then graduated from Lowell High School in 1939. He was at Horace Mann Prep in New York by 1940, Columbia University right after, then the Merchant Marine for 1942 and '43. Probably was docked at Liverpool when Father Tom died, recollecting the facts of his young life like ancient Kronos or the Celtic Holly king with his magic scythe, his sword, his stylus, his pen. At a pretty young age, already a substantial writer. Think of this: Imagine *Ti Jean*, the little thoughtful Catholic boy, before he became sorrowful Buddha, listening to the river and to the ocean waves lapping up on the shore—the ocean is the mother, the river is the serpent—going to the matinee on Saturday, to Mass on Sunday, praying for the Lady to liberate Russia . . .

"Writing to me is like going to confession," Kerouac said. "You can't revise your confession once the father has closed the sliding panel. You can go back and confess again, as I did that second night: This in itself is a whole new theory of literature."

(Never went to Catholic school like my older brother and sisters, in fact, I can't even say a friggin' rosary, but I do remember this: no confession, no communion or state of grace. No justice, no peace. No penance or re-thinking, no horns. Just fragmentation & mental illness. Look it up . . .)

SIX

Have You Built Your Ship of Death?

"Death is for squares."—Robert Creeley

"I'm going to go to Lowell," I tell Joshua in the same phone call. "I'm being called by The Goddess. I want to know if it happened. I want to know if my great-uncle heard the greatest confession of all time. It's not an impossibility."

"Oh, anything can be impossible," says Josh. "If you follow my meaning."

"Actually, I don't."

"The Tav, the kreutzer, the moon and the winged life. The goddess. It's all a fantasy."

"You mean," I start, "that the Holocaust is sometimes right?"

"Oh, there's that crystalline logic again." The Genius sneers. No animal can quite sneer like that. "Always the Holocaust. Does everything come down to the Holocaust?"

"Yes."

"Why?"

"Because that's the human condition, bark off. Human aspiration in a sort of grotesque nutshell."

"Well, maybe," Josh allows, "but, what the hell would you know? You're Facebook friends with G. Gordon Liddy."

"So what? He's interesting . . ."

"You want to know what Hubert said about the truth?" Josh says. "He said step into a pile of dog shit. The truth is raped children. Poison gas. It's all commerce in the end. We have to invent these vile little concepts to escape boredom as we continue to inevitably and invariably plant the seeds of our own destruction. I'm just tired, Slick. Tired, tired, tired . . ."

If you listen through your receiver, even on the land line, you can hear Moses lighting his ceramic bowl, probably in his upstairs Mount Kisco bathroom, in the master bedroom, hiding his reefer session from the kids. Joints create too much smoke, he'll say, gotta use a bowl only, no joints. *I can't have smoke wafting down to the kids' bedrooms*. Carrying some trees, some chiba, around in your pocket is, like the subject of the Holocaust, another exquisite reminder of the human condition because you're always guilty of something when you do—something unlawful—the man is looking over your shoulder when you have some bud on your person even when you're using *Yerba Buena* to change you're state, to get a glimpse of the *real* world, lifted up, immune to gravity, the dream within the dream, the world Crazy Horse discovered when he was riding alone as a boy.

Pot's the proposition that you'll never have to be bored again. And never have to say you're sorry.

Just kidding.

"You know what, man?" says Josh. "All we hear about today is identity theft. I wish someone would steal *my* identity. With all my debts? Here's my identity. You can have it."

Josh is not a whiner. Only a devastating, outside-Plato's-cave **EXTERNAL**-type event like the most recent looting of the federal treasury could have forced a *teshuvah* on the likes of Joshua Moses, a mensch, a shirt-off-his-back kind of guy to be certain, but one ordained by Fucking God

Himself to be the center of attention at all times, doncha know. And there's Gabby, too. His mom.

"My debts are killing me," he says, "and I'm going to have three kids in college soon. I can't sleep. I barely eat. Everything makes me sick. Then, in the daytime, I can't stay awake. This is worse than the worst. And these fuckin' films they make me watch. Sorry, I didn't mean to curse. I can't bear to watch films anymore. The new films. What a waste of time. Read a book, instead. Or listen to the old rock 'n roll. When music had feeling, correct me if I'm wrong. A Celtic harp in a Baptist church. That's the only thing that brings me comfort now. The old songs and language, the written word. Delillo says it's the only way the dead can speak to the living."

"He stole that from Buckminster Fuller. Besides," I say more empathetically. "Films do that. Movies. The seventh art. Dead ghosts up there on the screen talking to you."

What can you do? You try to distract Josh with monkey mind stuff, because you don't want to be held hostage to his mood. That can happen.

"Yeh, but do they hear and see us? Can we be seen by *them*?"

"Who?"

"The dead."

"Well, Steiner says you have to read to the dead or ask them questions just before sleeping at night. In the morning, they answer."

"Really?"

"Yeh. It's kind of dreamy." I laugh. "Mo, have you ever heard of the forgotten song? The ancient melody?"

"Huh? Nah, man. Nothin' before the electric guitar . . ."

"I'm serious."

"You mean, can you make an idea manifest just with the sound of your own voice? Free energy? String theory? Quantum jumping? I've heard of that. We used to call it 'poetry.' Is that what you mean by forgotten song?"

"Sort of."

"I musta forgot."

"Well then, meditate," I suggest. "Smoke more pot. Pot is the steroids of poetry. Start doing all the stuff you used to be too cool for. Homilies on your refrigerator door. Shit like that. 'Mark my words,' Blau always says, index finger raised, 'the technologies of the 21st century are going to be psychic.' Imagination. Zero-point energy. You gotta take your mental health seriously, Mo. Awaken your inner gods. Of course, you never eat, so you'll never be near the fridge door . . ."

"Future? The world is going to hell, I'm telling you, and these films and the celebrity culture are destroying us. Sure, we all want to have a good name. A good reputation. But celebrity?" It's as if JoMo has crawled inside the last syllable. "I don't care about fame, but I want my children and grandchildren to think highly of me. I don't know . . . Do *you* think we've become a nation of cowards? What can you say about a country that displays its flag, the American flag, on command, then withdraws them, takes the flags down and stores them in the closet when they're told? On command? When it's no longer the popular thing to do? We're a nation of sheep. Sheep! I used to be happy. The Hare Krishna would approach me at Grand Central or at Penn Station and say 'this will change your life, this will make you happy' and I'd say 'I'm happy already. I don't need to change my life. It's life and life only. You just live it. Everything is fine, thank you.' But now I wonder if I can go on."

"I've been there."

"Yeh, but you don't have kids," says Moses, his voice high and low at the same time, like an Irish concertina. "You don't know what it's like. You're free as a bird. And my mother just gets worse. PSP. What a horrible disease. Like being buried alive. Trapped in her skull. How can you believe in a god that would do that to anyone? Meanwhile, my father's health is failing, too. High blood pressure. Has trouble walking. I guess time is the wind that tilts all the picture frames."

"*Whaat?* Have you lost your mind?"

"I'm just trying to make my speech more poetic. Metaphorical. Don't wanna carry my words around in my hands, ya know?"

"Well, try this," I say, "something I'm working on. 'Vaster than expected, secretly wise and incapable of being broken, the world is the heart of a stripper.' Whaddya think? You know how strippers are always getting their Ph.D or something . . ."

"Kind of Norman Mailer, don't you think?"

"Well . . ."

"I'm worried about the 'the's," Moses says. "*The* world, *the* heart. I would go with 'life,' myself. 'Forever panting, always evolving, life is the heart of a stripper.'"

"That's good. I like that."

"It's done," says Josh with a sniff. "Finished."

Moses sniffles again, then coughs as if he's giving up the ghost, *his* ghost, which has been burdened for about three years now with deep profound worry about his irretrievably bad investments, the god-awful *bubble*, don't you know, and by grief over his aging, ailing parents. Mad to live, he is not. Might have to file for bankruptcy. Then, he sneezes one of those thunderously loud sneezes, one designed, one can only believe, to drive away the dust of his evil thoughts and I wouldn't just say something like that. You'd never guess such a big sneeze could come from such a skinny guy.

"That was unnecessarily loud," I say. We're still on the phone. "When you sneeze . . . do you actually have to engage the vocal cords?"

"I say 'I am' now and I don't even know what it means," Josh continues, oblivious. "I actually get dizzy now. I have, like, three different prescriptions, three medications, but they're not doing anything. I don't know. I don't know . . ."

"Hey, what happened to therapy?" I ask with some tee-hee irony. "Going to your shrink? Used to be fashionable to say 'I have to see my analyst at two.' It's all meds, now, isn't it?"

"I guess you're right," Josh says weakly. His voice has become as thin as his silhouette and I'm more than a little startled.

"Hey . . . are you crying?"

"No, I don't cry."

"I thought you were sleeping well again. You're making good money, now, aren't you?"

"I can't sleep at night, then during the day, I can barely keep my eyes open. I'm in pain. All the time. It's good to be working again and to have benefits, but it's not enough. My mortgage is insane. I'm at the brink. We may have to sell the house and rent in town. I'm worth more dead than alive. Remember the ship of death? That's me."

Me 'n Moses used to sit in on Robert Creeley's poetry class at the University of Buffalo and listen and watch as he'd walk in, tall and thin, wearing his native-colored, woolen beatnik skull cap, shake the snow from his boots, sit down ("anybody got a cigarette?"), and read D.H. Lawrence with a low Yankee rhythm and in a somehow casual, yet earnest tone:

Have you built your ship of death
O, have you? O, build your ship of death
For you will need it . . . It is time to go, to bid farewell
To one's own self, and find an exit from the fallen self . . .

Swear to God, Creeley looked like Lawrence, too, with the neatly trimmed beard, the full head of straight black Puritan hair, looked like New Mexico even in the icy Northeastern winter. (Buffalo's a poet's town. There are records.) Occasionally, he'd even share some of his memories of Kerouac. Allen Ginsberg mentions Creeley in a poem about Jack's funeral, mentions Creeley's black eye-patch or one eye or something, and Kerouac himself raves about Creeley's subtle mind in *Big Sur*.

"The ship of death," repeats Moses. "I like the old colorful language. It's like you didn't have to take responsibility for anything. I prefer it when the fates conspire against you," he says. "I hate to think that I chose this. If I knew who my enemy was, I'd try and make the sun and moon stand still. If I drank, I would consciously drink myself to death like Jack. Jack Kerouac. He tried to leave the body, tried to leave the world through the whiskey but that doesn't work, does it?"

"No," says I. "You can get *gone* that way, as they used to say, real gone, but not totally gone. Not totally . . ."

No point in denying it.

The world hurts.

If you were a New Yorker about four or five years ago, post-911, you'd probably decide, as I did, that you'd had enough of Manhattan, enough of that promethean steel and glass, so, except for the occasional freelance assignment, you might turn your back on the slough of despond that is the world of New York publishing and editing and journalism and, like Parsifal and Zuckerman, go back home, upstate—leave town once again—for the revised life, for a *second* life, the atoning, penitent life—to write, start seeing Esmé again, and to maybe substitute teach. It wasn't post-911 cowardice or paranoia, Slick, it was exhaustion, I swear. I decided to revise everything.

Everything.

The Great Art, the great work. The dream of peace. The goddess, revision.

Mental Health.

Wouldn't be too difficult, either, to get yourself to believe that it was the Lady, praises to Lady Sanity, who impelled you to buy a Merchant Marine-blue 1999 Pontiac 6000 and drive it to city schools on the Youngmann, Kensington and Scajaquada Expressways in your hometown on the Niagara Frontier just four miles from the Canadas where the snow falls like tears off the face of a virgin Seneca girl; to get a New York State teaching certificate (social studies) and some story assignments; sub, save a little money, write some poetry, see a bit of the Virgin Esmé, the Diamond Esmé, pine wood and baby powder, then get to Lowell, Massachusetts in short order to get your horns or crown back and hear, in that language common to the living and the dead, the greatest confession of all time.

SEVEN

Sweet & Angelic
(My Father's Father's Father)

"Many have passed through the gate of death and when we grow conscious of the forces contained in what the dead leave behind, then a spiritual growth will be possible."—Rudolf Steiner

Online, I find St. Joseph's Cemetery located not in Lowell but in nearby Chelmsford. I call the office but the young lady can't find a Reverend Thomas O'Brian among their dead.

"When did he pass, sir?" she asks dispassionately, like hands on a clock.

"1943."

"I don't have anyone by that name," she says. You can hear her scrolling down on a computer. "Oh, wait. There's a Rose O'Brian."

"No, no. Are you affiliated with St. Joseph's Parish?"

"No, we're not affiliated with anyone."

"But you are St. Joseph's Cemetery. In Lowell."

"We're in Chelmsford, sir, not far from Lowell."

"Well, thank you. Have a great day."

I do find a St. Joseph's Parish online but they're in Salem, New Hampshire. Am going to have to get on the road to Lowell, Mass and sort through this myself. My cousin John, who put the family genealogy together and now teaches school in England, has no new information, either.

Superstitions are conceits. Superstitions are masturbatory. Still can't help thinking, though, about the first time I went to Holy Cross cemetery in Lackawanna, south of Buffalo (Tim Russert's old neighborhood), to visit the grave of my father's father's father. I'd paid off two bills, one of them for fifty-four dollars and the other for thirty-six.

"That adds up to ninety," I recall thinking as I drove to the cemetery. "An even 90."

At the cemetery, amid a palette of crosses and obelisks—the artwork of four centuries—I find, after some effort, John M. O'Brian's headstone and notice the dates: born 1854, died 1890. Age 36. Was this a message? A communication from the other side, from glad ghosts, from the grateful dead? A piece of the Ghost Dance in the virgin, untouched, key of C?

When you look at the two or three photos available of my father's father's father—formal, unsmiling, sepia-toned family portraits from a not-so gilded industrial age—you'll never fail to be struck by the look of kindness sort of woven into the man's face, stiffness notwithstanding, particularly as he gazes on his three little boys, dressed in those 19th century tarboosh-like caps and knee breeches. You can almost hear them breathing and see a smile in the face of my father's father's father. Almost but not quite. A softening in the eyes and mouth behind that handle-bar mustache describes a nurturing love for his sons and a Romanized Celtic sweetness that couldn't survive the century. Let's sing praises to a man, a tailor by trade, who couldn't even conceive of cheating his customers or of snorting a line of blow off of his wife's snow-white thigh, a soul too good and kind for the 20th century. Great-Uncle Tom must've got his sunny disposition from his father and great-Uncle John, perhaps, owed his petty, hermetic mean-spiritedness to his mother who lived for another sixty-two years after her husband was done in during Benjamin Harrison's administration by *salmonella enterica*. Shitty water.

"Nana was not my favorite person," my dad says over the phone. "You know, she won a car in the Irish sweepstakes. A 1936 Roadster and she sold it. My father sold insurance and had no car. He had to take streetcars all over the city to keep appointments and Nana sold the car she bought for a three-penny ticket. That's how much she paid for the ticket: three cents. And she lived with Mother and Dad for almost twenty years! Paid no rent. When she lived with us on Wellington, she'd spend the entire day up in her room, saying her rosary. She said that damned rosary so many times, she wore down the beads. Actually wore them down."

My sisters and older brother know from this Catholic school stuff, but I have to confess: I've never said a rosary in my goddamn life—rosary, lullaby for the soul—but I might need one now, good god, because I'm thinking of a proofreader I met in midtown Manhattan, a strange kind of actor cat, one foot on the pedal, one foot on the brake, who swooned over *Paradise Lost*—in fact, his pet name for Milton's epic was 'PL.'

"I went down to East Fourth Street to audition for the part of Jack Kerouac," says the proofreader, a dark-eyed good-looking kid. (Most every proofreader in NYC is 'really an actor.') "I forgot the name of the play but Allen Ginsberg was there, at the audition. So, I go up to read and the director won't even take me. Won't even let me read for the part. I ask him why and he won't even answer, he just kind of blows me off. So, I walk away saying 'fuck you, asshole. Faggot. Your play's gonna suck anyway' and who approaches me? Allen Ginsberg. He comes up to me and says 'you wouldn't have been right for the part, anyway. Jack was sweet and angelic and you've got all this hostility going on.' So, I say 'fuck you, Ginsberg! You don't know shit!' and I leave."

Can you imagine? Telling Allen Ginsberg to fuck off, telling him he doesn't know . . . shit? First met Ginsberg in Buffalo at the Nichols School on a very snowy January night. Ginsberg mentions Buffalo in one of his dream poems.

"Move in, please. Just be conscious . . ." he said that night as people filed into the auditorium. "Please move in."

Allen and Peter Orlovsky were giving a reading at the school and Peter brought along his banjo. Cold, snowy, January. Week night. Robert Creeley was in the audience. Leslie Fiedler, too.

"Move in, please," Ginsberg intones again into the microphone because the place is jammed. "Be more conscious."

The private school's wooden floor is becoming wet and slushy as more people trudge out from the snow and into the venue to see and hear the great man and his longtime companion but, mostly, to see and hear the great man. Ginsberg's a little impatient because much of the audience is stopping to gawk and that's holding things up. I'm one of those gawkers, hypnotized by the sight of the 20th century Whitman, the modern Moses, entranced by his deep authoritative voice. That voice! Kerouac was struck by the voice early on. The ancient prophetic voice of the bard. An actor who portrays Allen Ginsberg must have the right voice. The perfect voice. The voice of the world. I walk to Allen's right and sit on a window sill directly behind him. Ginsberg turns around, 180 degrees, and looks right at me. Here's my moment. He must think I'm special.

"Move *in*, please," he says impatiently, not smiling, his glassed wall eyes still looking almost directly into mine. "Be more conscious."

First encounter with the great American bard turns out to be a lesson in *shiflut.* Humility. Meekly, I stand up and walk, carrying a knit pullover sweater and the bard's heavy rebuke on my shoulders, toward the left side of the stage, then to a seat in the audience. Through the big auditorium windows, I can see only distant lights in the dark; snowflakes sticking to the street lamps like glittery little stars on wet paper. Like glitter make-up. Allen reads a poem called "Punk Rock." Peter plays the banjo and sings: *Sweet as summer tiiime* . . . then, reads his own poem.

"This was written when I decided to quit smoking," Peter says earnestly.

"Fat chance," says Allen from the side of the lectern.

I speak to Ginsberg after the reading. History streams around and is written into the architecture of his face. And those thick rubber car tire lips . . .

"So, what do *you* do, sport?" he asks with a smile. A cosmopolitan greeting. Suddenly, the man isn't the greatest of all beatniks anymore or Whitman or Moses or any of that, but Jay Gatsby or my dad. All is forgiven with Allen. I tell him that I love his poetry and that I've studied a little Mandarin Chinese. Ginsberg recommends that I read Gary Snyder. It's unfortunate that, as the years ran on, one more or less took Allen Ginsberg for granted primarily because in New York City, in the village, you could see him in his green down parka at the Ukrainian restaurants or in a necktie and corduroy jacket at a Second Avenue furniture store or at readings on Avenue B, at CBGB's—*Whom bomb? Saddam got a bomb*—and, of course, at Tompkins Square Park for demonstrations. He was just too available—he wasn't above running after you with lascivious intent—but, along with Ram Dass and George Harrison, he united East and West and never gave up the good fight—that's how I see it, anyway. How I choose to praise him . . .

Sweet and angelic: that's how ya might describe Father Tom who found his way to Lowell during the Great Depression.

"Will was the best of the three," my dad said the other day. He was speaking of his own father. "My father—his mother called him 'Will'—raised six kids during the Depression and never complained," Dad continues. "It was a very terrifying time. Desperate. Dad never complained but he did say that his brothers had chosen the easy life because, you know, they were freeloaders. No responsibilities. No bills. No kids. *(Celibacy's the easy life?)*

"It always amazed me that Uncle John would call up these old spinsters and ask to be taken here and there and they would do it. They would drive right over and take him on his errands. Take him shopping. Who knows what he did with those women? They thought a priest was right up there with Jesus Christ. The asshole. Your mother and I went to see John on the 50th anniversary of his ordination, went to Holy Angels, but we couldn't find him. You know where he was? Up in his room drinking a bottle of Old Overholt that he brought back from Pittsburgh. And Nana? She was smart and resourceful. She taught school and gave piano lessons and took in boarders when they lived over on Niagara Street by the Peace Bridge. She was a survivor but not a warm woman."

Survivors rarely are—openly warm, that is—especially if you're talking about a woman who was a widow for sixty-two years, although I do hope old Nana found some love and affection during the six decades of her widowhood, maybe once, on a snowy night while an innocent schoolgirl tapped out "I'll Take You Home Again, Kathleen" on the piano in some imaginary parlor downstairs, because if God = Sex, then guilt = perversion, thus, one can easily envision, in the interests of mental health and revision and making your joy complete, one can easily envision two lonely people redeeming all that insane Celtic-Roman spark-extinguishing peasant guilt by sculpting a humble offering for the ghost of love on a barren, forbidding night near the Niagara River; a night starless and habit black when the *sidhes* are invisible although they see you and they listen, too, from their earthly sub rosa mounds—they *listen*—sweet & angelic, impossible, right?

Right.

Impossible.

EIGHT

Esmé

"If men cease to believe that they will one day become gods, then they will surely become worms."—Henry Miller

The classrooms are always well heated, you have to grant them that. It's a cold October day, cold even for Buffalo, and snow's forecast. Had a little October snow back in high school, but it all disappeared in under two hours and that's what'll probably happen today, after I get done with this eighth grade class. Drawn forward. Ever forward . . . the naked goddess . . .

"When you rub your magic lamp, what comes out, kids?"

"A genie," they say.

"That's right. Your *genius* emerges," I say, stuffing a cheesy cracker in my mouth. "If you know how to rub the magic lamp, you will find your genius. How do you say 'people' in Spanish?"

"*Gente*," responds one Puerto Rican girl.

"Good. And what do you call the study of heredity? Chromosomes and . . ."

"Genes! Genetics!"

"Great! And when you buy something in the store without a brand name, it's . . ."

"Generic."

"Yes. Now, look at these words: gentle, generous, general, genteel, gender, genre, engineer, intelli*gent*. What's the first book of the Bible?" I'm still chewing.

"Genesis!"

"Wait, mister. We can't talk about this stuff in school," cautions a boy with wire-rimmed glasses.

"Who says? You really believe we can't even talk about something in school?" I wipe my mouth with a thin blue-colored napkin.

Up until 150 years ago, until the first industrial revolution, there was a spirit world. Now, it's gone. You had bloody decapitated heads on stakes from Vienna to Beijing, mass murder, slavery, pillage and rapine and torture, but there was a soul and it went somewhere after death if you built your ship. Electricity and other stuff changed all that. Steiner says in our time, you have to fight for the silent starry realm, else it'll get lost in the noise and neon and in the Bones of Her Face. When I was in eighth grade, though, I wasn't preoccupied with the silent starry realm, with the kingdom of silence, what I now call 'my inner Lowell, Massachusetts,' with making mental health my number one priority, nor with prayer in the public schools and such, although a third grade teacher made us stand quietly, then say 'amen' every morning, even after that Supreme Court decision—no, in eighth grade, I was far more concerned with concealing erections than with Hail Marys, so, visualize this: You're sitting in science class, dreaming about Cynthia Fasio, and you become erect, then, suddenly, the teacher asks you to turn off the lights for a film strip or something and you have to walk to the light switch and try to hide the blood-gorged boner you're certain everyone in the class can see swelling in your pants. *Jesus, if I can just make it to the light switch without incident, then it'll be dark and I'll be safe. Made it this time.* Then, there were the school dances. Slow dancing to slow ballads like "Color My World" meant an instant hardee. Does she feel it? I wondered. Years later, Christina, a college girlfriend, confirmed it.

"That always made me really nervous," I told her. "You knew the boy was hard?"

"You could feel it," she said, laughing.

"Very embarrassing," I'd said.

"I thought it was absolutely adorable," stated Christina who, I swear to God, looked just like Claudia Schiffer, the beautiful German model. "Adorable."

Even walking down the hallway with Lynette LaRue was problematic. A mere stroll with Lynette through the middle school or high school hallway brought on a big fat one as hard as knotted pine: the perfume, the fresh nubile body, the mystery, the breath, from the crown to the kingdom. Put the books over woody while walking. That'll have to do for now. How times change! How things change! Did some nude modeling for an art class a couple summers back—needed the money—and had no problem marching on to the platform in the buff but the pressing issue, as every man and *Seinfeld* watcher knows, was shrinkage and sure enough, the studio was heavily air-conditioned. It was summer and I walked out of the tiny dressing room there and my manhood shriveled almost to nothing in the man-made cold, the skin folding and contracting so that it looked like a Phillips screw, and during the break, I fairly ran back into the little dressing room and tried to give comfort to the most precious appendage Mister God can give to a man, blessed be His Name, and I said *Come on!* as I held it in my hand like a wounded bird, *let's warm up*, grow, grow, grow! There are women out there! But nothing happened. I was resigned to my fate. One of life's cruel ironies: You spend your early adolescence trying to get rid of persistent erections and your old age trying to get erect.

"I've seen the word 'love' trigger an erection," writes a knowing Naomi Wolf but sometimes, even 'like' will do the job. An opera singer I knew said she was with a man once who was having trouble making love to her.

"I don't understand this," her friend whispered, "because I like you."

"I like you, too," the prima donna whispered back and the rest of the evening, she says, was delirious and ecstatic. The genius of language, the genesis of meaning. *Rect*, to make straight or right. Correct. Rectitude.

Don't suffer from resurrectile dysfunction!

You can never hold back spring . . .

Here in the heated classroom, the kids're still debating about the Book of Genesis and public schools, and I tell them in various ways that they all have genius, every one of them, and that they're all able to access the genius genie without a great deal of effort, but then the inevitable: A kid raises his hand and says, "I don't mean to be disrespectful, mister, but what does this have to do with social studies?" and I have to respond almost sternly, saying, "Social studies is about citizenship, civic competence and you can't participate in a democracy if you think your opinions and thoughts don't matter. Rub your magic lamp and your genius will emerge. I promise."

"But, mister, how do we rub the magic lamp?"

"We'll talk about that some other time, okay?"

(That's the bright morning star, by the way. The genie, that is.)

Oh: did I mention that in some school districts, kids're being arrested, ARRESTED, for letting the genie out, for being kids? So-called adults working out their issues through children. I look out the window and see snow falling straight down like an unhappy face. The flakes are much larger than anticipated, but it'll melt in no time. It's only October 12. But it doesn't melt. Driving home on the expressway is actually kind of precarious, as the roads're like slippery elm and no one's prepared for the havoc. By 8 P.M. the power's starting to die in thousands of homes in the area. At 8:15 my electricity is out which means no heat. Snow's general and continues to fall effortlessly. Four days ago, we had an 80-degree Sunday. This is weird even for old weird Buffalo. Buffalonians never tire of whining about the snow. A monsoon could be approaching the Queen City and someone would say, all vowels flattened, "at least it's not snow," but even a prosaic person could wax poetic about this snow: in Spanish, it's *nieve*, like naïve, nubile, innocent and immaculate. How do you say 'girlfriend' in Spanish? *Novia*. Newness.

Don't whine about the snow, praise it! **Praise it!** A snow storm's one of the best ways to change your state, to reach a liminal state of awareness, if anyone wants my opinion. It's a trip; you want to paint it. Like summer in the French Quarter, it's a waking dream, the dream of an angel. And a genie. You're *gone* . . . and it does its thing in silence. The silent snow that humbles even the sun. Like being blinded. When the lake snow really starts to fall, the voices of children in the distance sound eerie and remote, like a secret language suggesting some kind of longing and, sometimes, it even rains snow—I don't mean sleet—when it's blowing in from Lake Ontario, from the north, the snow actually *rains* down, falls, like tears off the face of a virgin and, yet, a camaraderie, a companionship, is born in storms when strangers wave to each other because they feel secure. They wear the snow. Everyone else moved to Florida.

Seems that New York City has that man-made procession of varied intentions but a snow storm in Buffalo, western New York, in the Niagara region at the Canadian border, has all the fury of the gods and goddesses and beasts and of imagination, too—and since imagination is the free gift of the magi, beasts can be tamed with music and a sabre, and the gods have come down to us in the likeness of men and women (particularly women in low-riding jeans)—you can just close your eyes and let the snow take you into dreamland. The rest is commentary.

SILENCE
An Interlude

In the public schools, you have soft porn videos, sticky syrup soda, the moral superiority of the schoolmarm (the postmodern, p.c. version), and fatty fast food, but no intervals of silence, no unheard melodies, and, soon, no Christmas decorations—against the law—and, yes, there're a lotta 'liberal' teachers serving up their ambiguities and agendas to the kids, mostly in the suburbs—then, there are the in-the-trenches teachers, generally in the inner and outer city schools—but, like Dylan says "the naked truth is still taboo" because a teacher has to be kind of subversive to get some version of some kind of truth out to the kids—anyway, that's what I'm thinking as I drive on the expressway through the surprisingly and unseasonably forceful snow, thinking also about the greatest lesson of all time. Of ALL TIME. This one is for the brothers:

"Ya wanna know the biggest mistake you're going to make, boys? Getting busted? Joining a gang? Dropping out of school? No. The biggest mistake you're ever going to make in life is this: '*get the fuck outta my life, bitch!*' That's going to be your biggest mistake. You can do it at 18, 21, even 25, maybe even 30. But it may take you twenty years to find true love again. Even with Facebook."

All you women of the East Side and Jerusalem, help me to say this rightly: 'it may take you **twenty years** to find true love again.'"

The wind causes the trees to crack and break like toothpicks and because the snow's falling so early in the year, when big green leaves're still up in the air, the wet snow brings an especially heavy burden on to the branches, and poplars, maples and elms, start falling to the ground like the mob at Gethsemane, tearing telephone and electric wires down with them—no school tomorrow, for sure—so I steer my way over to see Esmé who lives in the village of Willoughby just off the Great Iroquois Trail, which is now Main Street where, already, power lines are down and blocking traffic in the unfathomable dark. The scene has changed, changed utterly, and another terrible beauty's born. The blades haven't even been put on the snow plows and none of the roads've been salted. **This is OCTOBER 12, people!** The four-mile drive to Esmé's takes me about half an hour. She has electricity and heat but her phone is dead. Al Gore'll make sure to mention the October storm when he comes to town half a year from now.

"Can you believe this, Beast?" Esmé says. When she calls me 'Beast,' that means she's feeling kind of lonely. A beast isn't an animal, but the shadow side of beauty. "Are you going to sleep here?"

"I was hoping I could."

Esmé's voice is feminine deep and aristocratic as I like to say but it also has the sound of someone who at some time in her life, witnessed a drowning. She draws and paints, is smarter than me, animated, and has a dancer's body, long, slender and graceful. Her shoulder-length hair is honey blonde and her eyes are ocean blue. She smells sweet, like pine after a rain shower, and sometimes, I can hear her thinking. ***Why doesn't my heart sing anymore? Men used to like me and I loved being embraced by their hungry and insistent masculinity. Now, the rhythm of love scares me. It's so foreign, another language. Where are the snows of yesteryear? Where has my sure purpose gone? Who will fill the empty amphora that is my heart?***

"The schools are closed," Esmé says as I hang up my jacket. "Your power is out?"

I tell her that I have neither electricity nor heat and that power lines are already severed and who would've thought, but the snow is relentless, wrapping the trees, streets, grass fields and the small red-brick driveway in a coating of vanilla frosting—ah, yes, there's nothing like a real storm—in Spanish, it's *tormenta*—excitement builds, it's in the air, a thick, sensual, paradoxically warm feeling of adventure, feels like the whole world is breathing in and out at exactly the same time. *Love, the crown of nature.* Fuck Florida. Very few cars are on the roads now. Street lamps are out and it's real dark outside now. Onyx black. Gonna have to rub a magic lamp.

"I don't think I'll have work tomorrow, either," says Esmé, the attorney. "The roads won't be ready. And the expressway. Forget it."

Esmé and I've grown apart and yet we need each other. We're family, like Jack and *Memere*, each of us is home for the other but we've grown apart in *that* way, thus, there's a feeling here of comfort coupled with desperation and paralysis. It only takes one *not* to tango. (I haven't jerked off this much since high school and I'm getting fat. And we were practically married. This isn't the virginity I'd envisioned . . .) Still, the woman is relentlessly charming—as relentless as the snow—consumed as she is by a delightful Annie Hall kind of insecurity.

"I'm way too skinny and angular," she always complains. "I might as well be invisible."

"You're lovely, you're beautiful," I always respond. "You can have any man you want."

Esmé's cultured and literate but emotionally raw, too. Emotions pour out of her like water down a gorge. Her heart's one long lament. As a child, Esmé hugged deer at the zoo; I've seen it in her home movies. She cries reading *Mexico City Blues* and Nijinsky's diary, cries when Nijinsky says he won't fly in "an aeroplane" because it'll "hurt the birds," weeps for the mad Russian dancer genius when he writes that he's God but still vulnerable; a lamb damaged by "those eagles" Diaghilev and Stravinsky. Esmé's heart is heavy reading Poe, too. *Ligeia* weighs her down with especial sorrow.

"Poor Edgar Allan Poe," she cries softly. "Poor Edgar . . ."

"So, which disease are you dying of today?" I ask her.

"Don't joke," she says, "I have to get blood work done."

"Well, in case you die, will you name me as a beneficiary?"

"When I'm terminally ill, you won't think it's so funny."

When I was still living in New York City, in Queens, Esmé read *The Catcher in the Rye* to me over the phone—the entire novel in about six days. It was just after September 11 and most everyone was as raw and as quietly desperate as Holden Caufield, tight in the jaws, and like Holden, Esmé was freaked about the ducks in the pond by Central Park South and the Plaza Hotel. Esmé's house, built in the 1830's and refurbished with maple syrup stain and with a starburst pattern in the wood, sits on a corner in the village of Willoughby at the intersection of two alleys. It's not the suburbs, not the city, nor is it the country. It's the village. The Glen Park waterfall and the old red mill, built in 1811, are down the road. A trifle faded, the red in the mill is still as bright as the drops of menstrual blood you sometimes see on Esmé's snow-white bathroom floor. You'd want to paint it: The red mill in winter, nestled in the mountains of ice and snow by the frozen falls. Dog, deer and rabbit tracks in the virgin white. Paint exactly what you see, not your interpretation. *Speak to your lady of* things . . .

Three days after the storm, electric power's still out for half a million people. The National Guard has been called in and literally sleeps by the door. In the city, beautiful old maples at Soldier's Place by the Buffalo Seminary are bent and split. Fresh white-yellow-pink wood exposed like Caucasian baby flesh in the middle of the traffic circle. **This is funny. Ironic**: the previous summer, in July, I went to my high school reunion and talked with Billy Mulroney, a tough Irish kid who's now kind of thick-set, mustachioed, bespectacled and foggy-eyed from too much drink. Freshman year, we played soccer together and during one practice, got into a fight.

"Who won that fight?" Billy asked with a laugh as we inhaled beer and pretzels at Island Park in the village. It was hot and muggy.

"You," I answered, wiping sweat from my brow with a napkin. "You, definitely."

"Well, I'm really sorry," he said as his smiled waned. He wasn't kidding. "No, seriously. I hope you weren't too hurt. I feel bad about that."

We laughed again and he slapped me on the back like a lodge brother (that's right: like a lodge brother) and we downed more beers near the rock band that played old songs under the huge tent and Billy said that his divorce had hurt him a lot and that he missed his kids. A great story of redemption and forgiveness. Bittersweet but the heart had softened. Forgiveness, mercy, revision, the keys to happiness, the Face of the Fucking Savior.

The first Sunday after the October storm, snow still covers the ground and the branches like white shadows, but the roads are clear and dry and I drive to the post office by the airport, which is usually open every day but not this day. No electricity or heat. Banks still closed, too. On the way back to Esmé's, I have to make a quick, change-of-mind turn into another lane and I cut off a BMW, which then speeds up and follows my tail. When we both stop at the traffic light, the BMW driver, at my right, opens his window and sticks his head out into the prematurely icy air.

"Hey asshole!" he shouts at me, "what are you doinggggg???"

I squint. The salt-and-pepper mustache. The big wire-rimmed glasses. The foggy eyes. It's Billy Mulroney and I don't think he recognized me in my knit winter cap and glasses, but before I can say anything, he throws his deluxe-size plastic cup of cola at my car, splashing the suds and syrup all over my windshield and right fender. Mulroney hits the accelerator and is off. I never did get along with other Irish Catholics. Father was a butcher. Cut meat.

"Did I meet him?" Esmé asks when I tell her the story later. "At the reunion?"

She had. Briefly. Mulroney was three sheets to the wind and drowning in blood sorrow. Esmé and I drive around my old neighborhood and survey the damage: street lamps pulled out of the concrete, completely trapping a car in its driveway; Ellicott Creek flooded over, water rising to the first floor of matchbox houses by the high school. The storm's no longer a wondrous, charming adventure but that lawless, aggressive, war-like demi-god, a clawed crone: think of a pissed-off goddess. Where are the snows of yesteryear? Gone. In the car, Esmé's insecurities reappear like a mangled corpse on the shore.

"I've got to get out of this town, I have to," she insists as we continue to follow Tonawanda

Creek as it winds northward toward the Erie Canal. "I'm a pariah. I'm not cut out for this place. People think I'm a freak because I'm skinny and live alone. I'm ugly."

"You're *not* ugly," I say, "and you don't live alone."

"No, I am."

"No. You're beautiful."

"No."

"Yes, you're beautiful."

"Do you really think so?" Esmé asks, brightening a bit, her ocean blue eyes vivid against a backdrop of white. "Do you really think I'm beautiful or is it, like, everybody's beautiful inside?"

NINE

A Dangerous Place

For years, he struggled to find the right words
The old cedarwood house
On the corner, the
Village alleyways near the red
Mill and the waterfall
The apple blossoms and lilacs
In the front yard, pansies in
The garden.

Inside, antique Kittenger chairs and tables, a
man and a woman who
No longer make love.

In the spring, one of
Them left the gas stove on
Ever so slightly.

"Didn't you notice it?"
She asked, the anger rising
In her voice, "why didn't you
Make sure the gas was off?
That's deadly. You could have
Burned down the house."

She was right. And
So were the words.

A house without
Love is a dangerous
Place.

TEN

I Offer Myself as a Victim of Holocaust to Thy Merciful Love

"That which is our eternal nature remains in the world that we share with the dead."—Rudolf Steiner

The whole thing about Jack Kerouac's favorite saint, Thérèse de Lisieux, the little French girl who now rivals Joan of Arc and Bernadette as the hippest saint around—Edith Piaf hip—is that she's real, I mean, she's an illusion, of course, just a dream, but she holds a key to this story, to this confession. A key . . .

The bitch.

Here's what happened: you're in a conference room at Morgan Stanley on Sixth Avenue in New York, Avenue of the Americas, doing temporary proofing work and the man next to you is on the phone talking to someone about summary judgment, the well-pleaded complaint and so on. The dead, blood-chilling drone of legalese.

"Excuse me," you start, "but, are you an attorney?"

"Yes," he answers. "Part-time."

"I have a law degree," you say. "Where did you go to law school?"

"Rutgers."

"Really? I went to the University at Buffalo."

"I'm from North Tonawanda," the man replies.

"I was born there. The Erie Canal!"

The man's name is Tom, he's one of twelve children, and you both have Rudolf Steiner books on your persons. What are the odds? After talking for less than ten minutes, you ask Tom about one particular saint because you feel the eternal feminine somewhere in your chest, enjoining you to ask, sounds dopey, but it's true, I mean, why would I lie?

"Theresa," you say, "not Mother Theresa, not Theresa of Avila, but the other one. She died at twenty-four."

"You mean Thérèse of Lisieux," Tom says. "Yeh. It's pronounced 'Tur-ez.'"

"What about her?" you ask him. "I keep hearing things about this woman."

"Well, I hope you won't think I'm weird," Tom begins, "but she's living in my apartment in Brooklyn."

Tom tells you about Thérèse and "the little way," the way of humility and meekness, tells you that Billie Holiday felt a connection with her as did Edith Piaf who, reportedly, was cured of near-blindness after praying to the saint as a kid.

"Jack Kerouac writes about Thérèse," Tom says cheerfully. "His mother had a shrine, a statue of her in their home in Lowell. Kerouac's older brother, Gerard, who died young, was especially connected to Thérèse, in fact, they both died of tuberculosis."

She was born Thérèse Martin in 1873. At age eleven, she petitioned the pope in hopes of joining the Carmelites but was told to wait and, now, it seems, the saint's simplicity and humility have inspired the world. Kerouac was taught to pray to Thérèse; in fact, his first novel, *The Town and the City*, features the Martin family, a reference, an homage, to the baby-faced saint. Tom goes on to say that his birthday is March 13, the day after Kerouac's, and that Thérèse's saint day is October 1.

"That's my birthday," you say with some wonder. "October 1."

"Oh, then, you have a connection, too," Tom says with a smile. He wears wire-rimmed glasses and is very thin. Tom is delicate. "Watch it, though. If you invoke her and I think you have, she'll play tricks. She'll mess with you . . ."

"Well, what do you mean that she's living in your apartment?"

"Let's just say that if I came home one day and found her sitting in my kitchen, I wouldn't be surprised. She's a bitch. She'll test you. She'll knock you down, knock you on your ass. She'll puncture your pride and arrogance."

You never get any specifics from Tom and you never see him again after that day. Then, the synchronicities start happening: you're in your brother's apartment in Asheville, North Carolina, on your birthday, on October 1—you're fasting because this Yom Kippur has fallen on your 40th birthday—and notice Thérèse's memoir, *The Story of a Soul*, in your brother's bookcase.

"I offer myself as a victim of holocaust to Thy merciful love," writes the saint, "asking you to consume me incessantly . . . I want to seek out a means of going to heaven by a little way, a way that is very straight, very short, and totally **new**. God cannot inspire unrealizable desires."

It's passionate, even sexy. Something Yeats might have written. *I offer myself . . .* You become more curious about this woman, become smitten with her. You admire her faith, envy it; her desire to be God's fiery lover and you love looking at her child-like, welcoming face. You call into your phone machine and there are two messages, the first from a schoolmate, a convert to Catholicism, who tells you that his wife's given birth to their third son, born on this day, October 1; and the second, from Tom, who says in his earnest, delicate voice, "I just wanted to call you because it's your birthday and, as you know, this day means a lot to me, too."

But there's more.

Less than a week after meeting Tom, you get some freelance writing work, from the Heritage people, writing sketches of New York businesses, one of which, oddly enough, is Saint Patrick's Cathedral. You have an appointment to speak with one of their spokesmen and after meeting with him in his East 50th Street office, you walk to the Cathedral, enter, and are overwhelmed with portraits and icons of and literature about Saint Thérèse. A rock star. The church is celebrating the centennial of her death, "held over" for one year because of her popularity. You buy some photos of Sœur Thérèse, which you tack on to your kitchen and bedroom walls in Queens.

Two years later: It's a hot day in July, hot for New York, and there's an unusually warm and dry wind blowing as you walk to the subway that'll take you from your Astoria neighborhood to the law firm on the East Side where you work the evening shift, obsequiously editing memos of law and stipulated purchase agreements. You're perspiring and irritable. Feels like the body of the earth has been turned inside out. Suddenly, a piece of grit hits you in your right eye. You place your right hand over the eye, sure that it'll come out soon. It doesn't. You sit on the subway for the whole ride, your hand over your right eye, sweat on your brow, thick summer air in your lungs. You take an elevator to the 50th floor with a hand over your eye. You sit at the computer, hand over eye. Superstitions are conceits, but you want to know: Is this a cosmic joke? Is this a lesson or something, like, take the log out of your own eye before you go to take the speck out of your brother's eye? A warning against judgment? A call to atonement? To stop being so damn insolent?

***The choice to judge rather than to know is the cause of the loss of peace.* (A Course in Miracles.)**

The piece of grit won't come out. Office mates offer advice. Try a wet cloth, turn the eyelid inside out, just like that pivotal early scene in *Brief Encounter*. Finally, the grit does come out after two hours or so and there's a scratch on your cornea, which leaves your vision somewhat foggy for an hour or so afterward. A car takes you home and when you walk into your kitchen in Astoria, you notice that the picture of Thérèse tacked up near one of the kitchen windows is gone. The window'd been left open because of the heat and the wind had, obviously, been strong enough to knock the portrait off the wall. It was a picture of the older more earnest Thérèse in her Carmelite habit, not the sweet little eight-year-old.

"It must have gone out the window," you say, and go to bed.

In the morning, you're sitting at your kitchen table. At your feet, on the kitchen floor, is a piece of paper. It's the picture of Thérèse face down.

"There it is," you say to yourself. "It didn't fly out the window, it's right here."

You reach for the photo. You pick it up, turn it around, and there's the photo of Saint Thérèse de Lisieux with a black smudge over her right eye, swear to motherfucking God.

So, this is your 'Little Way,' huh?

Bitch.

O, Thérèse, Queen of the Atonement, I know you didn't really die at the convent; you're asleep in my imagination, waiting for me to wake you up, to love you as you've never been loved . . . you are the great soul in a black dress, your excellence is your combination of passion and compassion . . .

Passion and compassion***: what life's all about . . .***

I long to kiss your beautiful mouth, your divine face, your heaving breasts, the treasure and heat between your legs. O, saint de Lisieux, you were made for love, made to be fucked . . . your beauty inspires me, inspires the world . . . That melody emanating from your hair. You're the treasure of the world. October 1 saint day, my birthday. The days of awe. I offer myself to your all-consuming love . . .

You will answer me directly some day, won't you? No need for a sign . . . you'll speak to me some day, won't you, little lady of the child Jesus face?

Won't you?

ELEVEN

Archie

"Rivers, Mountains, Cities, Villages, All are ***Human*** *& when you enter into their Bosoms you walk . . . in your imagination of which this World of Mortality is but a Shadow."—Blake*

After a tiring day subbing in one of the schools, I sometimes find myself at Archie's house on Elmwood Avenue—that's Archie, a tall, white-haired, white-bearded 75-year-old Scotsman, an American of Scottish ancestry, who smokes El Presidente cigars and speaks in a deep sonorous voice about the astral and etheric planes, about Waldorf education, anthroposophy, Rudolf Steiner; he's unique, Archie is, for one, because he's a man of New Age sensibilities but unreconstructed at the same time, that is, he's not delicate, not at all fey in his bearing or countenance, but a regular guy, proudly macho, basically unrevised ironically enough, and he adores his cigars. It's like he makes love to them. Combining passion with workmanlike accuracy, he rams an ice pick through the stogie after biting off the foreskin, then licks the end thoroughly, like he's giving head, before placing it between his teeth and lighting it. Once the cigar is lit, Archie leans back satisfied and you know he wouldn't trade all the diamonds in King Solomon's mines for his cigar and cup of roasted coffee.

"In my drinking days, I'd have a snifter of brandy with my cigar," he says from behind his desk which is cluttered with letters, bills, ash trays, old tape reels, and coffee-stained magazines. "The brandy calms you down and the tobacco gets into your saliva, so that after a while, you've got a nice hazy feeling, like you're deep in the etheric, you know what I mean, pal?"

Archie has the walk and talk of a tribal leader. If there were a North American Book of the Dead, he'd be in it. He has greatness. He's like one of the mighty men of old in the Bible, like Nimrod, the ones that predated the patriarchs. He's elemental as well as intellectual: Falstaffian in a way, but not quite as innocent. A lascivious Santa Claus. Actually, Archie's a dead ringer now for the older Lucien Carr, the man who introduced Kerouac to Ginsberg. Reminiscent of Dave Van Ronk, too. Looks like the North Sea. Archie purchased the three-storey Depression-era house with his son and lives on the second floor, renting out rooms on the first and third floors. His walls are lined with books by Steiner on speech and drama and homeopathic medicine, on the Mexican mysteries, the Inquisition, string theory, education, the secrets of metals, occult practices, cold fusion, "new" energy, the three-fold social order, the Gospels, biodynamic farming, the cabala, man as symphony of the creative word; he has the Urantia book, the keys of Enoch, books on Tesla and the secret rites of the Masonic orders and more, but none of Kerouac's works. He has his mother's ancient roll-top desk in one corner and, at the window overlooking Elmwood Avenue, a little shrine featuring a Celtic cross that can be seen from the street. I always look for it when driving by. Even in the dead of winter, Archie keeps a fan in his window, which he leaves open to drive the cigar smoke out of the room. In his living room with all the books, Archie presides over meetings and discussions, so his home is a kind of salon, an old and musty salon but clean somehow and he rents a room at the Unitarian church, where he gives talks on the Fibonacci number series, the golden mean and the nature of evil, which are always attended by about two dozen people who pay ten dollars a head admission. Archie asked me to give a talk, but I didn't see a penny after my lecture on *A Course in Miracles*—the honor of being asked, apparently, was its own reward. These damn Highlanders. Archie reminds me of a deceased friend, Hubert—more about Hubert later, Allons! Allons!—because he's domineering, egotistical, loud, opinionated, extremely bright and physically imposing—about 6'4"—but you never knew if Hubert was going to strike you down dead where you stood while Archie isn't given to physical violence except, he recalled, for the time he once seriously considered pushing his ex-wife down their cellar steps.

"She was literally killing me," Archie explained. "I was at the end of my rope, drinking a fifth of Scotch a day. I just wanted to get rid of her."

Unlike many new thought or health food types, Archie isn't a racist nor an elitist wearing the garment of free-spirited tolerance. For example, you'll never hear the word 'multicultural' coming from Archie. I used to barbecue lamb shoulder chops on Archie's front porch, on his gas grill, and the *demi-monde*, one-by-one, made its way from the sidewalk up the steps, to the porch to talk with Archie as he sat on the gliding chair, smoking his cigar, waiting for his meal like Henry the Fucking Eighth, I mean, there was Freddie, who worked at the church kitchen on the other side of Elmwood; he always dropped by as did Rick James's half-brother who lives across the street, and there was Mama Rose, an 82-year-old former stripper who ran a sporting house for sailors docked at the Buffalo harbor on Lake Erie during World War II. Johnny Hill, "Half-Breed" Johnny, was and is a regular, too, rolling his own cigarettes, chatting everyone up about secret Iroquois rituals about which he is forbidden to speak, and Johnny is from Hiawatha's tribe, an Onondaga, right?

"*Barefoot* Onondaga," he always says while standing close to Archie whom he sometimes calls 'Dad.' "You guys stole our form of government, our culture, the eagle, the whole thing. Look at your names: Chicago, Omaha, Tennessee, Ontario, Canada, Ohio, Iowa, Lackawanna, all native names. I could go on and on. Niagara. Oklahoma. The home of the brave, that means us. Now, you're cursed with a scary world. Your kids don't respect you and your technology is going to kill you. I know *I* couldn't teach in the schools today. My ex-wife is up in Canada at the Six-Nation rez and even up there it's different. The kids haven't become completely unhinged like here. We gotta go back to tradition, like the way it is in Korea. Teacher say it, you do it. In Korea, a student can't even stand in his teacher's shadow. I'm serious. But, you know, it's hitting the natives, too. You've got all these damn gambling casinos and the kids joke now and say 'I was on a vision quest and fasted for four days. You know what I envisioned after four days of fasting? A snickers bar.'" Johnny laughs heartily, a laugh just perfect for a nearly destroyed people, and pulls out from his pocket a pouch of tobacco and papers and begins rolling up a cigarette like Sam Spade. "A snickers bar," he says again, laughing. (BTW, natives don't refer to themselves as 'native American;' it's 'native' or 'Indian.')

Archie looks at Half-Breed Johnny. "It's good to be old," he says with a harrumph. "I grew up at just the right time, so I've been blessed," he says. Archie's face breaks out into a big ass grin as Mama Rose massages his shoulders beneath the sky's baby-blue veil. "So fortunate, so blessed."

One Good Friday evening, Archie decided to read, to a few of us, something he'd written about his days in Toronto when he ran a health food store and book shop. After taking a vow of celibacy, the women "came out of the woodwork," he said, one of whom was a long-legged Danish girl who shed her clothes and climbed into bed with the big guy every morning only to be turned away by his virtue. Archie kept reading his elegantly written memoir of sorts and the pages dropped like autumn leaves on to the coffee table in front of him. After reading, Archie pulled out a string of dental floss and flossed his teeth, leaning back in his easy chair. Moreover, he often pulls out his dentures and cleans them right in front of you, sometimes with his tongue, but I love him anyway, I praise the big bastard and I'm in awe of his knowledge and wisdom and his experience, so here, at Archie's, is where I find myself now on autumn afternoons after playing teacher for the Somali, Yemeni, Sudanese, Puerto Rican, Italian, native and African-American kids from the east and west sides of the Queen City.

"Everything okay, pal?" he asks as I sit on the other side of his cluttered desk. "You want a cigar?" I refuse and tell Archie that I can't shake an anxious feeling that keeps gnawing at me, usually in the mornings, a feeling of both nausea and sorrow, of complete and manifest failure—a feeling that I'm a pitiful shadow of my former New York halcyon self, when I was a one-man revolution. Archie strokes at his white beard, which, near his mouth, is stained with yellow-amber waves of cigar resin. He stares up at the ceiling as I pour my bitter, tormented heart out into the smoky air, then looks at me. He's like a Viking. Still got his horns, but he wouldn't put it that way.

"New York was a sweet time," I whine to him, conveniently forgetting the awful, stifling 3 AM walks through the Lower East Side. "I shook hands with Buckminster Fuller and Bob Dylan and Paul Simon. Talked to B.F. Skinner on the phone. Bill Moyers. I was a one-man revolution defying entropy. Bucky Fuller called it 'syntropy.' Now, I'm nothing. An insurgent. Strap a bomb to me and I'm good to go."

"Let me ask you something," he begins sympathetically. "What is wisdom?"

"Uhm, wisdom is vision," I start, faltering, my thoughts like small snowflakes evaporating as they touch the window. "It has to come from another source. It's revealed truth either directly from the source or from scriptural writings."

"Okay, that's part of it." Archie's voice is deep and accented slightly from his days in Toronto and at Findhorn in Scotland. His 'a's, for example, are long and rounded, unlike the flat Buffalo and Chicago 'a': *Hey, Baaaab!* Archie's words are precise. "Wisdom comes from suffering," he says. "You have to be thankful for your troubles because you learn from them. Suffering exists so that we can wrest power away from the gods and establish ourselves as individuals. I'm serious."

"Yes, but . . . you know, Joyce Carol Oates said that suffering is not necessary. What you get from suffering can be accomplished with an act of imagination. That's my homegirl! We can overcome pain by accepting the fact that we're really beasts. Or maybe she's saying just the opposite." I laugh as if drunk. "*Any day now* . . . I shall be a beast . . ."

(Am thinking of Josh Moses now, imagining him happy, prosperous, confident—I'm trying to revise him—it's make-believe but imagining's more real than real if you know what I mean—but he has a touch of the martyr complex, JoMo, that is.

"I have to admit," he once said, "I kind of fantasize about doing a perp walk. Straddled by agents on the six o'clock news . . .")

"I like to put it this way," says Archie. "The wise man learns from the mistakes of others but the fool not even from his own." Archie's pleased with himself, pleased he's successfully ripped off this maxim from Benjamin Franklin, and his big eyes narrow like the Straits of Hormuz as his face breaks out into another big smoky grin. Like Falstaff, but even more reminiscent of Orson Welles himself in his later years. The stories, the cigars, the beard, the girth. That voice. Miles Davis named Orson as one of his primary influences because of that voice.

"There's a great sound, my friend, a great song," Archie continues, "that's where wisdom lives. You can hear the song but it's not tuned to concert pitch, to A=440, but to A=444. I used to play the viola, I know. Have to tune up. You can hear the great sound any time. You already have the power. It's like hearing a hit song for the first time on the hit parade and it already sounds familiar. "Hey Jude" was like that. It was in the blood. But most of us are going to have to suffer first. Sorry. That's just how it is. It's like falling in love. Love is everywhere, but we're too busy with our dramas to feel it. The etheric realm is not extinct, it's just obscured. It's kept secret. You tap into the ether and you have man-made volcanoes and tsunamis and UFO's. Underground cities we don't even hear about. That's the power of the mind, pal. But suffering comes first."

Falling in love. Hit radio. *Gone . . .* Archie pauses for a moment like a train putting on its brakes, then starts rebuilding momentum, speaking very carefully and deliberately.

"Remember when Martin Luther King died and Bobby Kennedy gave that speech off the cuff? In Indiana, I think. He said 'my favorite poet was Aeschylus . . .' Remember how high his voice was?" Archie laughs, a deep baritone laugh, then lends a nasal, adenoidal touch to his voice to make it sound like Kennedy's. JoMo's. Like mine. "'My favorite poet was Aeschylus who said *even in our sleep, pain which can not forget falls drop by drop upon the heart. Until out of our deepest despair, against our* wheeel, *comes wisdom through the awful grace of God.*' You don't have to live through all this crap, not really, but be thankful for it anyway. The world is finite, it's going to end, we're going to be gone eventually and we won't even remember most of it but love it anyway. Wrest power from the gods. Just love it. Love it. Lift it up, pal. Revise it. Lift it up."

TWELVE

The Beast and The Genius

"Melody has power a whole world to transform."—The Urantia Book

The October snow's long gone, but the trees still bear the marks of trauma and violation, which is to say they've been chastened, emasculated, traduced, and cut down and I need to take a trip before Thanksgiving or I'm going to fade like red on a cotton shirt.

"I'm going down to the city after I finish this letter to the Oblates in Tewskbury," I say to Esmé. "Tewksbury, Massachusetts."

"As soon you get some time off, you leave town," Esmé frets. "You leave me here. Why do you always leave?"

"Because you're cute."

"No, really. Why? Are you the prodigal son or something?"

(Actually, I feel more like Odysseus. The *Iliad* is leaving town, golden Friday sunset; hope, tremor of excitement. The *Odyssey* is going home, Monday morning, heart torn to shreds . . .)

Josh and Miriam Moses and their kids live in Mount Kisco in Westchester County, thirty or forty miles north of New York City. Financially, things are still very sluggish, but recently, Mo got a surprise call on a Thursday and was off to Tokyo on Friday to launch a new website there. (Glad to be of help.) You can revise the lives of others, don't you know. When Neville Goddard said that 'ideas enveloped in feeling are creative actions,' he was bringing together the bird, the lion and the bull—thinking, feeling, and willing—in one statement: ideas (bird), enveloped in feeling (the lion heart) are creative actions (bull, will impulse). Word becomes flesh. But, what about the serpents? The beasts? A beast isn't an animal, but the shadow side of beauty. Animals are innocent.

I decide to take the New York State thruway, I-90, to see Josh and Mimi who've raised four kids in a Tudor style home just off the Taconic Parkway, a house filled with a thousand or more books, CD's, videos, DVD's, teenage bric-a-brac, sneakers, three cats, a tagu and an iguana. Mo's a bit of a control freak, but he and Mimi have a real marriage, not just a legal partnership based on the 'I promise not to fuck anyone else' prohibition. How would George Carlin put it?

"Marriage today is based on one absurd, unrealizable condition," he might say. "'I promise not to be tempted by anyone else.' Right? 'I'm under no obligation to encourage you, praise you, forgive you or help make your dreams come true. There's one premise to this holy arrangement and only one: I promise not to fuck anyone else. Ever. Doesn't matter if you're religious, irreligious, hold tradition dear or not; doesn't matter if one of us has gained 75 pounds, doesn't matter if we hardly ever fuck anymore or don't fuck at all. You just can't do it with anyone else. Ever.' You may now kiss the bride . . . "

Okay, but there's one more thing—Josh Mo doesn't know this and you can't ever tell him—it's kind of no big deal, but you can't ever tell him: I made out with Mimi. Only once. And it was a long,

long, time ago. But they were already married. He probably wouldn't make a big deal even out of a big deal but Josh can't ever know and I'll leave it at that. I do feel guilty, though, guilty enough to not give many details, but I'll reveal one thing: Mimi liked it when a man said to her 'I'm going to mash your clit, you bitch. I love your cunt.' That was how she liked to be praised. Not trying to sound worldly, but there's the kind of woman who says 'I love you' easily and there's a kind of woman who says 'I love your cock' even more easily and Miriam, though I have no first-hand knowledge, always struck me as the kind who could say *both* quite easily. Nuf sed. No more. What do *I* know?

She's a Jewish woman . . . she likes cerebral men, right?

Driving on the thruway's a good way to get 'gone,' to clear your mind, because leaving town is about leaving the stupid self behind and yet, as I drive east, past Fort Stanwix and the ghosts of war and revolution that sometimes howl in the icy wind, I feel the inner beast emerge, my double, a beast with red eyes, not because I made out with Mo's wife over twenty years ago at their 4th of July party, not because I called her a hot cunt after telling her that I love her long Semitic nose and her liquid eyes (I understand why John McCain yelled out, 'you cunt,' to his wife: he loves her), no, the Beast emerges for reasons I can't explain and anyway, how can there be a beast without horns—how did I get like this?—your horns being two thin beams of white light, radiating from the forehead, which means that upon attainment, you can or might revise the past and accomplish fate?

Moses is standing now—he's about the Beast's height—and while his yellow-gold aura begins to fill his living room like golden magic ink being poured into one of those old-fashioned ink wells, even the Beast is a little uncomfortable because The Genius is tall enough to get up in his face when he's making a point, right up into his face like Lyndon Johnson, high squeaky voice notwithstanding, although, of course, the Beast often does the same even as he feels for a bump, a sign of activity on the skin of his forehead. The tagu stirs a bit, the iguana is motionless. Conversations between the Beast and the Genius often go like this:

> **BEAST:** Journalism sucks. It's bullshit. I'm very grateful to you for sending me to London years ago, but, except for Blau, Breslin, Doctor Thompson and Murray Kempton, journalists are not expansive; they're not big picture people. They get caught up in the myriad distractions. And journalists fawn over power and the powerful. They have to ask the right questions and they don't, but, listen, we should be sending good thoughts to each other. Like, when I come here, I try to bring a blessing, an Iroqouis power circle blessing, and give it out.
>
> **GENIUS**: And buy pot from my kids.
>
> **BEAST**: That, too. Love the chronic, that sticky green hydroponic stuff. Oh. And Moyers. Love Bill Moyers . . .
>
> Or, they go like this—you know, more monkey-mind talk, man talk, outside-

the-cup, cerebral, angel-of-things-gone-nuts talk:

BEAST: Mo, crediting Reagan with ending the Cold War is like believing that Eisenhower invented rock 'n roll. It makes just as much sense. What was Reagan's plan? What was his vision? What specific steps did he take to bring peace to Europe? Ask Tatiana about rock 'n roll behind the Iron Curtain. Ask Vaclav Havel. He'll tell you that Ginsberg getting thrown out of Czechoslovakia had more impact on the freedom movement in Eastern Europe than any B actor. Joan Baez singing in Prague. Bowie singing "Heroes" . . . You want to know who ended the Cold War? Jack Kerouac. Ginsberg. Elvis. Martin Luther King and the civil rights marchers. Odetta. Pete Seeger and the beatniks. My brother was a waiter at DaSilvano's on Sixth Avenue. Who came into the place all the time? Vaclav Havel with Lou Reed. Not with Reagan. He comes in with Laurie Anderson and Lou Reed! Two hundred thousand Russians jammed into Red Square, singing "The Long and Winding Road" with McCartney—each guitar string, a vibrating planet—is where it's at, not Mister 666 and the false peace.

GENIUS: What are you babbling about? I'd rather listen to the sound of my own piss. You think I don't know that you're bitter and resentful, that you're still angry with me for not putting you on staff? That is, when I had a staff. It's because you come on too strong. You're too much and you're all over the place. *Beaucoup trop*. You're impossible to deal with. And you're unfocused.

BEAST: I thought it was because I'm a gentile.

GENIUS: No, I'm serious. Moderate yourself. Revise yourself. It's no wonder you're not married. You're too difficult. You should put an ad in the paper or post on Craigslist: *over-the-hill, financially insecure writer-substitute teacher seeks rich, submissive heiress or dowager to sponge off of for long-term 'commitment.' Big tits a plus. I like beer, getting high and watching you do my laundry. Will send most recent mug shot*. Goddamn, you think I'm an ignoramus? I've been an editor or a publisher for over a quarter-century. I've motorcycled up the Nile with Malcolm Forbes. I'm a great project manager. I'm a brilliant editor. I've worked closely with Jann Wenner and I've given you lots of work. A lot of work. And a lot of pot. You know, I gave Christopher Hitchens work, too. Back in the Eighties.

BEAST: Another waste of time and flesh. Sells his soul to drink champagne with Tony Blair. Hey, speaking of Wenner, you never showed him my story on the Navajo and the Hopi, did you? The Big Mountain story? You said he didn't like it, but he never saw it, did he?

GENIUS: Are you calling me a liar?

BEAST: No, I'm calling you an asshole.

GENIUS: You still owe me for traveling expenses.

BEAST: And you still owe me a kill-fee. You know, you act like you're my editor, that you can revise what I write, and then you're inconsistent. You're arbitrary.

GENIUS: Like what? What are you talking about?

BEAST: Well, that thing I sent to *The New Yorker*.

GENIUS: What? You mean, the Joyce Carol Oates parody? The story about the young reporter from Niagara Falls who's sexually assaulted by the Arkansas governor?

BEAST: Yes. That.

GENIUS: Ugh. What can I say? If you don't want honest criticism, what can I say? But, I liked your description of the governor's cigars-and-brandy breath and of his 'porcine pink flesh'. What did you want me to say? I loved it? What would you have done?

BEAST: You do the only honorable thing: you lie. You say 'it was great. Great literature is . . .' Now, what would you say? How would *you* put it? 'Great literature is the . . .'

GENIUS: . . . is the breast our infant nation cries for . . . (laughs)

BEAST: Yeh, perfect (laughs) . . . The breast . . . cries for . . .

Then, there's the interminable chain of e-mails, like this one, from the Genius to the Beast:

B:

There's one conspiracy and only one, the conspiracy aimed at preventing you from being free. You think the Bill of Rights means something and that Lincoln was a great man, that the goddess and free energy and gyroscopes and string theory will save us and all that, then you say that I have a tentative relationship with the truth.

Who's lying now?

We are slaves. The goddess doesn't exist. There are no great men and acting 'as if,' pretending that there are great men and goddesses is nothing more than lying to yourself. You call it 'revision,' but I call it lying. And silly. You think you're going to find a pot of gold or something in Lowell; you're going to make this pilgrimage, find the virgin and be healed. Start your life anew. Let me tell you something: you're a slave. We're all slaves. Look at you: you seek to be validated and honored by the very mass media you constantly malign. You can't wait to get your books published and appear on TV and on the covers of magazines, showing off your sacred heart. That's your definition of being seen. Get a life.

You used to tell Hubert what he wanted to hear because you were afraid of him, but I told him the way it was. I told him he was selfish and hypocritical. You never did. And I'm supposed to be the most dishonest person in the world! The New Orleans pol.

You want to know what I believe in? Fiction. The truth is in fiction, except I don't believe it's literally true and you believe your self-serving affirmations are something other than fairy stories you tell yourself to feel better. You believe they're literally true. At least I know these stories are lies. Actually, I believe in something else, what Kenneth Patchen called 'passionate mercy.' I have passionate mercy for Mimi and the kids, for the kids in my community. I used to give money every month to my little girl in the Dominican Republic because it's the right thing to do. It's life. You just live it. I'm not the man I was. I don't have a big budget or a big staff anymore but I'm not going to be imprisoned by these myths,

Slick. Get out of the wilderness. Stop being a slave.

Publius

P.S. No seasons' tickets this year. First time in over twenty years. Fuck Citi Field. Citi of the dead . . .

THIRTEEN

Bless Me, Father . . .

"Happiness? That isn't what attracts me to heaven. O, it's love! To be loved."—Saint Thérèse of Lisieux

You know, it's hurtful to think of vital, ebullient Gabrielle Moses flat on her eighty-year-old back, unable to see or speak, no longer able to reorder, with husky-voiced diatribes, the world she oft-times detested, no longer capable of raising her fist in anger at her son and two daughters while speaking on the phone.

"Settle down or you're going to get it . . ."

Gabby could be coarse and critical but never unattractive, in fact, Gabby's pulchritude only increased with time and age—you see it in their photographs, you see clearly that Gabby and Harry were a perfect fit: she, the feisty copper-haired Brooklyn girl who wrote letters to Adlai Stevenson and George McGovern and he, the post-war free spirit, the proto-Beatnik, the would-be Artie Shaw with his clarinet and full-head of black hair; a true individual, trapped eventually inside the body and the psyche of an accountant. Although Gabby often complained to Mimi Moses that Harry was "too flirty" with the other women at the old-folks' place (especially with Phil Rizzuto's widow, Cora), too willing to talk about the big bands with the ladies and show off his talent, you could see in their embrace, in their authentic, unforced smiles as the couple posed for the cameras throughout the

American decades that they were crazy about each other and that Harry was proud of his somewhat belligerent wife, proud of the marriage, an unlikely fusion of excitable copper-red *chutzpah* and thoughtful ebony-black plangency. Harry even had his New York license plates engraved with this configuration: **T42U4ME**.

"Dear Senator McGovern," began one of Gabby's all-caps letters; copies went out to Ted Kennedy, Jacob Javits and to two dozen or more United States senators. Dated November 30, 1974. Jericho , New York , 11516 . "I am deeply disturbed by the unfortunate remarks of General George S. Brown, the Chairman of the Joint Chiefs of Staff."

General Brown had enjoined a crowd at Duke University to "look where the Jewish money is" for clarity regarding many of the foreign policy decisions of the day.

"Notwithstanding the explanations and excuses offered," wrote Gabby, "the statements he made were blatantly anti-Semitic and cannot be ignored or glossed over. They are highly reminiscent of remarks made in Germany in the 1930's.

"One wonders," she continued, "whether important decisions affecting the nation's security would be determined by good judgment or by his obviously biased point of view."

In the last paragraph, Gabby "strongly" urged "that General Brown be dismissed. Only then can the American people be assured that the day of the cover-up is at an end, and that Congress is truly safeguarding the principles of democracy and freedom laid down by the Founding Fathers."

McGovern wrote back as did Kennedy, Javits, Fritz Hollings and about seventeen other senators, highly sensitized by a seemingly contagious, post-Watergate populism—all of them "deeply regretful" of the general's "insensitive" and "prejudiced comments."

"My grandfather was very religious," Gabby once said with sandy Brooklyn languor in her voice as her hair was changing from red to white, like a moon rising. "During the high holy days, my father put a cigarette in his mouth and began to light it. *Zeyda*, my grandpa, knocked it out of his mouth. Just like that. I screamed at him. 'Don't you dare treat my father that way!' I yelled at the top of my lungs. My father tried to keep me quiet but I wouldn't shut up. This was during the war. I think my grandfather was a little scared of me, may he rest in peace." Gabby laughed again, a laugh from her throat, not her diaphragm. "That's why I have no use for religion. It does nothing but *destroo-oy*. What good is religion if it causes a man to hit his son like that? I think my upbringing made me distrustful of all authority. If what the Jews and Christians say is true, that the world is ruled by Satan and Satan doesn't really exist, because, truth is, he doesn't really exist, isn't it fair to say, therefore, that the world is in the grip of a fantastic but fairly stupid illusion? I used to march in all the anti-nuclear demonstrations in the Fifties. I marched to integrate the schools. Went to many many rallies. That makes a lot more sense to me than religion."

"I don't understand religion," kitten-like Ilona Klein said recently, "I mean, the ones that exclude an entire gender, which is to say all of them. You'll never get the whole picture with one sex. I used to go out with a guy who traded bonds and I'm convinced that if more women were on Wall Street, we wouldn't have had this meltdown. Men go from A to B. Or A to Z. They don't see the whole picture. Women think about consequences. Their children. Men have to be told exactly what to do but women are more imaginative."

"How so?"

"God had to tell Abraham and Moses every single thing, but He told Rebekah to get the birthright away from Esau and just make it happen. God left it up to Rebekah's imagination. And she made it happen. What's the best CEO training you can get? An MBA program? No. Become a mother. They have to manage three, four, five different personalities and get them singing the same tune. The floor at the exchange is all men. All of 'em. If more women were on Wall Street, we could have avoided this recession."

FOURTEEN

The Morning Star
(Pixie)

"It is not man and the earth at their loveliest, but you practicing the art of revision that makes paradise." — Neville Goddard

Before we get to Lowell and to mental health, you need to hear the story of Pixie Morningstar not only because it's, for all intents and purposes, a true story about someone who no longer exists (by virtue of revision: the Catholics would call it an Act of Reparation), but also because you might want to know that Life is not a Bitch and Then You Die. You might want to know.

The morning is the toughest time of all; that's the time the inner demons, the *rakshasas*, the flesh-eaters, have their way with you, isn't that right? The uncolored lance of despair tears at the heart, carves it up like a Thanksgiving turkey and the whisperings come into your ear: *You're a failure, you're nothing. Don't even try . . .* Some friends say that their crises come later in the day, but most agree that the morning's the most difficult; the morning's devastating, actually, the morning's the time when a thousand-pound weight sits on your chest, when fortune isn't smiling that smug ass smile, so why do you hear that if you hold fast to your principles and convictions, you'll be given the morning star? Kerouac and legend have it that the first star seen in the morning is Lucifer, the light-giver, the devil, the one that puffs you up with pride, greed and unquenchable ambition, while others say that the morning star is Venus. Ishtar. The Morning Star: sounds like a newspaper, like a New England daily, so why's the morning star the pearl of great price?

Because Everybody's Beat.

The world hurts.

Like a fallen god trembling at the approach of fiery red dawn.

Eli eli lamma sabachthani ?????????????

(Erica Jong said in so many words that it's verboten for writers to be happy. "We are supposed to be miserable," she wrote, but I'm not buying it and, neither, apparently, is Ms. Jong. Although Aldous Huxley would find it all very tedious ["there is something curiously boring about somebody else's happiness," he maintained], I'm a T.B., a **True Believer**, while all around reel shadows of indignant desert birds with their icky vocabulary—noumena, autarky, *modalities*: how does the poet construct a world out of this jargon, this loveless language of the new puritans, addled by the haunting fear that someone, somewhere might be happy? Sylvia said that after *The Bell Jar*, a chronicle of misery and madness *and* of genius, she was going to write one from the perspective of health, so, I've resolved to never surrender, but alas, alack: Lincoln, a superb writer, said 'when I do good, I feel good,' but some say he was turbo-melancholic. Gurdjieff was hyper-stressed, couldn't get any sleep, and notice Doctor King, the prophet of peace, never found inner peace while preparing the love feast—he said as much in his writings. And Sylvia never did write that second book.)

On the expressway, even in the 21st century when hunger and all manner of oppression were supposed to have been abolished, I can barely keep my eyes open. Try to see it through my eyes: The weight of the world. Sub-prime what? Throwing children in jail for being children. *(Tell a new story! The New Story!)* It's not loneliness, but, rather, the fear of loneliness, that gets you piqued—you're afraid you'll miss out on the party, the big barbecue, the summer banquet that "everyone else" knows and laughs knowingly about; the love feast where the goddess appears from behind moss and leaves wearing a garland of stars and a shirt just a little too small on her. Love feast. You can even smell the tofu cooking on the grill as the smoke rises above the lawns of heaven . . . The sky's mirage gray again. *Pebble* gray. It'll probably rain. Or snow. You never know in this town. Sometimes you love Buffalo. Other times, you wish the British would burn it to the ground again as they did during the War of 1812. The trees are still bent and damaged from the freakish October storm a month ago. They look human or animal in some way, aware that they'd been violated by the elements.

Hurt.

ALL RIGHT, FUCK YOU, I'll stop whining, but let me just finish by saying that I love the snow, but it really does contain a gelid virginity or something like it for me; hometown paralysis, like I've never left town, never left my childhood home and still the suitors've come calling. I'm an unlit candle. Ask Lady Day. *So you stare, call it despair. Big Stuff* . . . I make a half-assed attempt to cast my dark mood on to the Niagara River, which I can see from the expressway, but that doesn't help, and I envy the rapids, that Seneca warrior tachyon energy that Tesla harnessed, furiously rushing north like a gang of runaway slaves to the thunderous falls, across the border into Canada, nation of fire, then, suddenly, I start thinking about Pixie Morningstar.

First met her in Tompkins Square Park, in New York City, during the unsettled days following the squatters' riots there, when Billy Boy and Asher and the others, some People of the Hill, brothers from the Six-Nation Reservation in Ontario, Ricky and Billy Hill, held court and stopped time, conversed freely with the dead, in fact, Billy Hill even did some of the Ghost Dance near the fountain in the park where the rioters and protestors first convened, just picture it: a lanky, clay-red skinned, crow-black haired Tompkins Square Park drunk, thin stringy mustache and hair like Jean Lafitte, shuckles right down to the tar and concrete ground and makes like a bird, legs and arms flailing, like I know you've seen in an old old newsreel but this is right in front of your eyes. He just falls. The ghost dance. Pixie and I sang old pop songs on the green park benches near the band shell before it was brought down Berlin Wall-style, before I would go to work obsequious second shifts like Bartleby the Scrivener for the leviathan-like law firms in midtown Manhattan, down at 14 Wall Street, too, and even for some firm on the 57th floor of World Trade Center One for a time; revising stock purchase agreements and indentured agreements instead of revising my life. Pixie is what I called drunk-crazy; virtually incapable of completing a sentence. Not too tall but skinny; beautiful smile, beautiful coffee-colored skin—coffee, maybe caramel—short-cut afro with a pink and purple head band.

"I used to shoot up," she tells me one summer, late morning in the park, "but I said 'get thee behind me, devil.'" Pixie motions with her right arm, casting out Satan with one easy gesture. Her face never contorts in anger, though; it's always buoyant, defined by her high cheekbones and her eyes, which are bright, child-like and innocent. She's seen it all, however: Saint Thérèse of Lisieux with a right hook but absolutely no meanness. Extraordinary. None at all. I'd seen Pixie before—as I was getting on the subway for work, in the park, just around—but one evening in late May, she's in my neighborhood, walking on Avenue B with a wine cooler in her hand, straw sticking out of the bottle.

"Daddy, could you lend me a dollar?" she asks with a guttural laugh, a laugh appropriate for a woman who's been raped and rent asunder. It's like her skinny body has contorted into a question mark. "I wanna get some wine, I mean, a bottle of red wine."

At the liquor store on Houston and Clinton, I buy us something cheap and red and Pixie follows me to my place at Stanton Street. We walk up the stairs to my apartment as if it were the most natural thing in the world and sit on my dilapidated couch drinking the wine.

"When you get to those gates," Pixie begins, "you're gonna see all those beautiful pearls. Onyx, jasper, agate . . ." Pixie laughs again, one of her eerie guttural laughs, like some wild beast from the Book of Revelation, then, she gives me a deep look, gazes right into me and says, "Let me look into your eyes" and there's silence for a moment.

"How much do you pay for this place?" the woman asks.

"Five hundred."

"You can get a real cheap apartment in Harlem," she says. "Much cheaper than Manhattan."

"Honey, Harlem *is* Manhattan."

"Everything from 100th Street up to 155th is Harlem. Below 100, everything changes."

Suddenly, the effulgent gold-dawn face becomes sad; time and gravity are catching up with Pixie Morningstar, and she begins to cry a little. "Thank you for taking care of me," she says. "Thank you, Daddy." She closes her soul-of-a-child eyes and puts her head down on a pillow, and from my bedroom, I retrieve an afghan my grandmother'd made, a nice old afghan with bright yellow, green and red patterns on it, and I spread it across Pixie's skinny body. Good night, my little child, my sweet little drunk-crazy friend.

Next morning, I climb down from my bunk bed and espy Pixie on the couch crying again.

"What's the matter, Pixie?"

"I need something to drink." She sobs pathetically. If mornings are tough for me, imagine what they're like for poor little Pixie Morningstar.

"It's gonna rain later," the woman says, looking out the window. "I know because I'm part Cherokee." Pixie asks if she can take a shower because, innocent as she is, the unwashed woman does smell like a funky chicken soup. I say 'sure' and walk to the bathroom to get her a towel, and when I come back to the living room, Pixie's standing up without a stitch on. She's beautiful. Innocent. A redbone. Her skin is lovely, copper and golden brown like the Ethiopian sun, and her breasts are, too, although they hang like empty paper sacks.

"My breasts have no milk," she says as she examines them. (As brown as *grapes!*) "It's from shooting up." We walk toward each other and kiss tenderly. We don't embrace at first. Just kiss. Then the embrace: sweet and desperate. We're both needy like two cats, maybe, meeting in some back alley, in a meeting place that only a human mind could have conceived of.

"I love you," she whispers. "I love you, Daddy."

I run a hand along her shiny gold brown little baby ass.

"Go in and get washed up," says I.

For about three or four years after that, I'd see Pixie in Tompkins Square Park and we'd talk a little, sometimes sing. Once, I saw her in one of the East Village clubs and we slow-danced but she was too drunk-crazy to bring anything to completion; too damaged for human-spiritual intimacy, her genius, her essence having vanished, leaving behind just an empty bottle, a drained cup smelling of liquor and old soup. How long will she be alive? You'd have had to wonder not only because she was drinking herself to death but because she was, in some way, too good for this world, I mean, what did Pixie know about corporate law firms or tax havens in the Cayman Islands or bilking old people out of their life savings or nasty art gallery and art world arrogance? She was broken, yes, but the corrupt world couldn't really touch the shards, couldn't overtake her completely, so I begin to envision good things for Pixie—as if in a dream, eyes closed—imagine her in a nice home surrounded by nice things, see her sober and happy. Lift it up! Revise this scene. Spiral it Up. Even get down on my knees and pray for her, not every night, but many nights; praying to The Goddess to intervene for Pixie. *Take care of Pixie, Divine Lady. See that she's safe. Please . . .*

(Don't you still love Jennifer Jones in *The Song of Bernadette?*

"I saw a lady . . . the most beautiful *lady* . . .")

Then, one autumn day, I see Pixie in the park in a wheelchair! Hanging with some of the other denizens. Oh, merciful lady-chick, this is it! It's only a matter of time until Pixie crosses the threshold, leaving the vale of tears for sure, soon to be another Tompkins Square ghost, and I'm too embarrassed or whatever to approach her, but then, about a year after the wheelchair thing, early evening, am walking with some friends on First Avenue at 10th Street, friends from out-of-town, and the four of us pass the mosque at 11th Street, a mosque called Madina Masjid, and in front of us, appearing suddenly, is a woman in what appears to be black Islamic garb. I can see only her back. She's talking with two other women, then walks away from them.

"I love you," she calls out to the women as they separate. I know that voice, so, I walk quickly to get ahead of her so that I can turn around and get a better look at her face. Could it be? Yes. It's she. It's Pixie Morningstar! Clean, sober and seemingly at peace. Still with that child-like smile. Led by her heart. And she's beautiful—not drunk, not crazy—looking as pure and as innocent in her Nation of

Islam habit as Thérèse or as Jennifer Jones in *The Song of Bernadette.* Queen Esther. Pure as the key of C. Her face is confident and so is her stride but she's humble, too—submissive to Allah and to the crescent and even to Venus, the star of the dawn—and I wonder if she recognizes me. Pixie's eyes are still starlit, they light up the sidewalk— *Did I not say 'ye are gods'? And goddesses?*—although her head is pointed down slightly with beatified humility and she's probably no longer known as Pixie Morningstar. The beast had been let out, *goddamn look what the goddess and the prophet laid down . . .* I don't say anything. She turns the corner at 12th Street and is gone. I never see her again.

I didn't imagine this, did *not*, that is, I didn't just imagine seeing Pixie Morningstar in the flesh, in that black garment walking on First Avenue, although I did imagine her sane and sober for years before that—this is real, real as mud—it was imagined but it's real, too, and anyone would want to take credit for this miracle; you'd want to think that you helped make this happen, and I heard her say 'I love you' to those women that night just as she'd said it to me on that morning at least seven years ago. Over dinner, I manage to chat with my old friends from out of town but I'm fixated on Pixie. This must be what old Archie is talking about. Revision of the past. Take a sad song and make it better. Engage the snake, make it spiral up out of the wheel of recurrence, out of time, into Tesla's free energy field, but how? **1.** Know that it's finished: you don't create, you just groove on creation and dig infinity's aesthetic sense; and **2.** speak well and think well of everyone at all times—even those who've passed on, as impossibly hokified as that sounds—tell a new story—because your tongue-snake is a sword, one letter from 'word,' but don't scream it from the rooftops until you've taken the Xanax®.

Just kidding.

Walk into the dream.

Archie would've said "don't doubt. It was your imagination that saved that woman's life. See what one person can do? It's a jubilee." Early next morning, looking out my window from that old couch, the couch where Pixie once lay, I can see Venus, that solitary red-orange light, blinking naked in the morning sky.

True story.

Sweardafucking*ahd*.

FIFTEEN

Speak to the Living

From Tewksbury, Massachusetts . . .

Dear Mr. O'Brian:

In response to your e-mail of last Wednesday, your great uncle, Fr Thomas F. O'Brian, OMI, died while serving as Superior and Master of Novices here at the Immaculate Heart of Mary Novitiate in Tewksbury, MA. He is buried in the Oblate cemetery here on the grounds.

An obituary was published in the June 1943 issue of the Oblate World and I will be happy to make a copy of it and mail it to you if you wish. You would need to e-mail me your address.

If there is anything else we can help you with, we will certainly be happy to try.

Sincerely,
Clarissa J. Saunders

And from somewhere in Brazil . . .

Hi, Robert,

Without much doubt I feel secure in saying that Fr. Tom died in Lowell. He was probably treated at Saint John´s Hospital in Lowell and could have resided either at the Immaculate Conception or Sacred Heart parish in Lowell. In the Forties Tewksbury was just a little village and the IHM house was mostly a residence for the members of the mission band who preached missions in the parishes which requested them- back in the pre-tv and no fear to be out at night days. Have a blessed season.

Love and prayers, Pastor Dan

PART II: THE RELATIVE MINOR

One-Man Revolution

ONE

In Praise of City Lights
(Nazz Never Did Nuthin Simple)

It's mathematical, really, how I lost the Lady and my horns and went from being a one-man revolution to a desperate and frightened mercenary; fell from a place of sanity and grace to one of isolation and near-perdition, i.e., descended from the tonic C chord to the relative A minor down to the subdominant. It was cause and effect, actually. Raw entropy.

The Beast scared the Goddess away.

I forgot to praise.

Without praise, your inner gods remain asleep and it's a bad dream.

Listen.

Living in New York City in those days really was about the horns, about defying time, about "true" sanity, but with a lot of sweaty randomness mixed in.

"It's in the embrace," Blau used to say. "*Abbraccio.*"

If you were to think of it poetically, multidimensionally, and let your thoughts become winged for a second, you'd be thinking of it as the ghost dance, as the eternal song's backbeat with a lot of smoke and bravado: dreaming while awake during the day and being conscious while dreaming at night—the land of metaphor—but, then, something happened, something important was forgotten: no gratitude, no praise, taking everything for granted—it's not a sentimental notion, it's FUCKING TRUE, you have to PRAISE, if not, the Beast'll take over completely, at least, that's what happened to me, just before the yuppies and the gentrifiers took over the city . . .

Would be almost cliché, certainly expected, to compare living down on the Lower East Side, on Clinton Street in the 1980s, compare it to one of Chagall's paintings or stain-glass windows, but that's kind of the case, because when I lived on Clinton Street, near Delancey Street, Rivington, Ludlow, Pitt, Ridge, Attorney, Cherry Street, George Washington's old place, the Henry Street Settlement, Essex Street shops selling Judaica, it did seem as though the language was BREATHING, you could see it, hear it, Hebrew letters cascading across ancient storefront signs, rocking slowly in the wind, then the old guys walk up ancient rusted stairs and ingest, inside, Torahs, Gamaras, mezuzahs, yarmulkes, Maimomedes, phylacteries, murals depicting *Olam Haba*, the World to Come, everyone in black and white, in *paes* and yarmulkes reading Torah, singing Psalms, women in shawls and lacey head coverings, lit candles; you *could* feel as if you'd grown a second body, a twin, married to your shadow, it was that intense; was as if angels of fire and quicksilver were dreaming you into the new life. Like the Beats, you kind of felt ready for the apocalypse. A one-person revolution.

A one-man revolution means telling your boss to fuck off and putting black musicians on the magazine cover despite the boss's racism and racist injunctions; means showing up for work when you want, dressed as you want to be dressed and Blau is the man, an accomplice, a man for this revolution. Josh Moses is already married to Miriam—in fact, he and I have become estranged (I'm coming into my own, JoMo's a control freak)—but Blau is the scene-maker; always finds the right restaurants, the right parties with the right people.

"Hee-hee, that's our Blau," I used to say to the Brown-Eyed Belle of St. Mark, "burning blue at the fire's center, the way Hubert used to burn, his finger ever on the pulse of society and fashion."

Like when Blau called the man who invented cloud seeding, Bernard Vonnegut, when Dr. Vonnegut was a professor at U Albany, and asked, "are you Kurt Vonnegut's brother?" ("Yes," replied the poor beleaguered man); like when suddenly, everything was Bill Kennedy this and Bill Kennedy that—William Kennedy, the novelist, who sang of Albany just as Joyce had sung of Dublin. Blau had been an almost wide-eyed kid in Kennedy's journalism class when we were grad students at Albany and now he's subletting Kennedy's tiny writing garret on West 14th Street for the summer, padlock on the door, toilet in the hallway; he's meeting Kennedy for drinks at Pete's Tavern and at the Old Town Bar where they'll discuss Hemingway and Bill's good friends, Hunter Thompson and Gabriel Garcia Marquez. *Ironweed* has just been published and even Saul Bellow's taken notice; the film version will be out soon starring Jack Nicholson and Tom Waits and I'm kind of jealous and even scornful until reading *Ironweed*, a masterpiece of Celtic magical realism, a perfect novel, so with a few fluid sentences on some fancy letterheaded paper, Kennedy'll get Blau into Columbia University's Graduate School of Journalism, then, later, on to the staff of the *Tribune* in Chicago.

"Become an expert at something," Kennedy advised Blau.

(Actually, Blau already claimed to be an expert at cunnilingus, by way of his ABC method.

"You can't stay in one place, even on the clitoris," he said with no smugness over Hungarian pastries. "She'll get bored because the area becomes desensitized with too much attention. Do the alphabet on her pussy. Do an 'A' with your tongue, then a 'B,' then 'C,' then, do the entire alphabet. That'll do it. Every time. It's classy, man. She'll be screaming *help, police* by the time you get to 'J'.")

"I'm going to write about the Orthodox," I tell Blau. "I'm going to pitch a story to the *Daily News* about the Hasidim. Maybe even to the *Times*. Did you see that book out by Ari Goldman? Something about the search for God at Harvard?"

"Fuck that," Blau says with cosmopolitan self-assurance and tenacity: strong and swift but smooth in his delivery like—it's the Eighties, right?—like, one of Ron Guidry's fastballs. "What about the search for God on the streets of New *Yawk*? Don't write about the good Hasidic Jew and his saintliness and wisdom and prayerful devotion. None of that *hava nagilah* shit. Write about the Hasid and his secret Ukrainian hooker. Write about the guy from Crown Heights who smokes crack with the Dominican kids in East New York. Write about the rabbi on the Day of Atonement and his bad breath from twenty-four hours of fasting and no toothpaste. Write about that."

If you were me, you'd have felt weightless in those Manhattan-drunk days, the hero of your own story because manna and petty cash pretty much rained down from the fluorescent light ceilings and Manhattan was just like the mustard seed and the big deal about the mustard seed is that it acts just as a mustard seed should, symbolizing nothing more than its own creation and fecundity and this alone, without striving, is the *Deee-eal*: hey, you don't have to die to watch a tree grow. You don't have to make a big deal over a big deal. Don't have to break the fuckin furniture. NYC enlarges you.

Get gone.

Say 'I am' and the cops and yuppies fall to the ground . . .

Imagine yourself putting lots of mustard on your pastrami sandwich at Katz's Deli and paying at the door, walking past the kosher *Chinese* restaurant and past crack hookers, roosters strutting in the back lot gardens—roosters crow every morning on Clinton Street at Stanton, every morning—past heroin dealers—*White lightning, white lightning* is their carnival bark—and dope, dope, dope, doesn't mean 'pot' anymore; hasn't since the Eighties, 'dope' is always heroin, bless-ED heroin, hip like the Mob, past Santeria shops and tiny stores selling nylon-string guitars and maracas. All gone now . . . Way way back, this neighborhood was Dutch, then Irish, then Russian and Polish Jewish, now Clinton Street is solidly Spanish-speaking, Dominican, with a few remaining Jewish shopkeepers, a storefront at every single door from East Houston to Delancey Street—even the apartment buildings have a store attached. Kossar's Bialys is on the south side of Delancey, just a stone's throw from the Seward Park apartments and the library and what remains of Hester Street. I always loved this sarabande, this flamenco world of the troubadours: the roosters crowing, the salsa and meringue trumpets and piano, the Jamaican pies, the furtive poetry haunts—*Loisaida*—the furious Spanish conversations on the crowded sidewalks, the danger, life and life only, you don't have to die to watch a tree grow. Courtly love, a new renaissance, and I still don't know what the hell a sarabande is.

The 1980s: watch the US of America choose Barabbas over the Bard; choose the Reagan illusion over Truth, goddamn capital "T." (Lennon and Marley are dead already and Josh Moses says, during one of our periodic rapprochements, that Jann Wenner voted for Reagan. Shit. Told Mo himself while the two were burning a joint in the front seat of Wenner's car out in Southampton.)

"No, we want *him*!" the mob shouts. "We don't want the truth, we want that man, **Barabbas**!"

And you got 'im.

"But not on the Lower East Side. Not now," you'd say if you were me, "I'm a one-man renaissance . . ."

Walk now to the Essex Street Market, take the stairs down to get an F train to the magazine office, midtown, where Ira Bloom, one of the ad execs, is rolling joints, preparing for his second or third reefer-smoking session of the morning. I've gravitated away from The Genius, from Josh M, and have become friendly with Ira. No melodrama, no yelling. Just a withdrawal. *Don't need your Big Easy politics, Mo . . . You're not going to edit or revise me, anymore . . .* Midtown Manhattan office: near the Museum of Modern Art, the library, Carnegie Deli, Broadway. Not at 30 Rock anymore. Ira Bloom doesn't waste time. Walk into the office and see that, already, he's off and running, but, like Moses, Ira sometimes carries his words around in his hands.

"Hey, man," he says, "what do you think of this? Jesus is on the cross and what does he say? What does he cry out? '*Abba*!' Okay? That's '*Daddy*.' Then he says *to his mother*, 'woman behold your son' and basically tells John to take his mother and make a home with her. As what? As her lover? Her husband? Sounds incestuous to me. And where was Joseph while all this was going on? The guy's going to die and maybe rise again, so he tells his brother to take care of his mother? Who was taking care of her before all that shit happened? I'm tellin' you, man, you gotta get away from all that ancient history and all those ancient records. You're too influenced by them," Ira warns as he exhales smoke through his nose. He has salt-and-pepper hair and beard and wire-rimmed glasses. His accent is LA. "Freud was right. It's all that Oedipal shit, that incestuous, Judaeo-Christian dysfunctional weirdness. Look at Aeschylus, the House of Atreus, the Greeks, the Egyptians. Sons fucking their mothers, fathers eating their children and for what? Power. Greed. More power. Why do you hold to that Biblical stuff, man? Do you think it's any different than the ancient Egyptian internecine fighting and war stuff?" Ira barely takes the time to inhale before sucking another hit off of his oily joint. I look at him and wonder if, apart from the herb smoking, he has many peaceful moments. How many lifetimes are stored behind those bloodshot brown shoe-leather eyes? I miss Ira. A one-man heresy . . .

"Who raised Moses? The Egyptians, right? It all began in Egypt with Tutankhamen and monotheism. Or Akhnaten. You know, 'Moses' is not far from 'messiah.' The name means 'son.' And 'messiah' is 'moschiach' in Hebrew and 'meshugenah' in Yiddish. Crazy. But what do I care about that shit? Just another myth. You wanna know what heaven means to a billion Muslims? Fucking and sucking for an eternity, that's what. You wanna know what Jesus was? Just another dead Jew hanging from a tree, that's what. Another dead Jew on a tree. What do you think, my friend?" Ira has no New York accent. Grew up in LA. His voice is deep, not nasal, and smooth; dark and smooth like Guinness. His eyes are little meat pies in red applesauce.

"Wait till he gets his horns," I'm thinking. "His horns."

"Got a call from one of the veterans' organizations today," says Ira whose smooth voice is reaching an almost menacing pitch, kind of like a baby's cry becoming a feverish or even threatening wail. "I told that guy the only Vietnam vets I'll work with are the ones who admit that the war was wrong. So you lost a leg over there, big fucking deal. You shouldn't have gone, motherfucker."

"Some of those guys were 17 and 18 when they went over," the other man, me, says. "You're being really unfair."

"*I* was 17 and 18, too, and *I* didn't go," is Ira's response. He rests his right hand on his desk, which is covered with memos, envelopes and some mementoes with corporate logos. "We spent all that money and killed all those people so that they could have their freedom? What a crock! Then we deny freedom at home like Murrow said about McCarthy. But you know, I'll say one thing for Nixon. He got us out of that war. The Kennedys are killed, King is killed, all the while they're talking about peace and who ends the war? The little Quaker boy from California. 'Peace with honor,' 'peace is at hand,' hah! But he did it, man. He got us out of Vietnam finally, but not until we walked on the moon, thanks to Nazi science. The moon, the silver moon, your gonads, the holy grail. Kerouac died right after the first walk on the moon if you believe in that shit. You'll never get through the Van Allen belts . . .

"Then we get rid of him, whaddya know? I mean Nixon. Nixon ends up running home to San Clemente talking about his mother and the Quakers. Says he's going to find *peace at the center*. Well, maybe he did. The son-of-a-bitch. Did you know that 'Clemente' means peace? Actually, it's forgiveness. Mercy. Here, this is just about done," says Ira, holding up the little roach. "You want some of this?" I take one little hit, then, with a show of defiance, like a robin plucking worms out of the earth with his beak, Ira grabs the roach and extracts one last toke from it as if to say, 'I don't take my reefer for granted.' There's silence briefly, then Ira speaks again.

"I used to think that enlightenment was a place, you know? That you arrived at peace and freedom and you were, you know, *there* at the top of the mountain," he says softly with a faraway look, but not too soft nor too far away. He's calmer now but intent on making his point. "That's what I thought when I went out on the road with my hair down to my ass and my thumb out saying 'Jesus will protect me, I'm safe.' Thought I'd find Olympus. But it's not like that. You struggle and move forward and you look back at what you've done and you say 'this is what I've learned. This is what I've become.' Then you struggle and go forward again and look back again." Ira takes a few steps forward and jiggles like an earthworm burrowing through the ground, illustrating the search for enlightenment with his whole body. "You never *really* arrive. It never *really* ends. The road goes on forever. If you go through life looking for perfection, you will definitely lose your mind. All you can do is look back at your journey and learn from it. But you'll always be on the quest in some way. You don't have to strive, really, you don't have to . . . you know what it is, man? You know what it's all about?" Ira walks close up, gets virtually into my face, almost like a German shepherd waiting to be pet. Not like Lyndon B. Johnson. "All you need is love," he says with a smile.

"That's it, Rasta. All you need is *love.*"

TWO

One-Man Resurrection

E-mail from Blau

Slick,

I found this on an old yellow pad. It has to be Allen, it's his language, but I swear: you won't find this anywhere online . . .

"The parts that embarrass you the most are usually the most interesting poetically, are usually the most naked of all, the rawest, the goofiest, the strangest and most eccentric and at the same time, most representative, most universal—that was something I learned from Kerouac, which was that spontaneous writing could be embarrassing—the cure for that is to write things down which you will not publish and which you won't show people. To write secretly—so you can actually be free to say anything you want—means abandoning being a poet, abandoning your careerism, abandoning even the idea of writing any poetry, really giving up as hopeless, abandoning the possibility, of really expressing yourself to the nations of the world. Abandoning the idea of being a prophet with honor and dignity, and abandoning the glory of poetry and just settling down in the muck of your own mind.

You really have to make a resolution just to write for yourself—in the sense of not writing to impress yourself but just WRITING WHAT YOUR SELF IS SAYING."—*Allen Ginsberg*

THREE

God of the Hebrews

"I write ghost stories."—Isaac Bashevis Singer

We buried Hubert on the first day of spring more than a dozen years ago. It was a Jewish service, according to his wishes, and I delivered the eulogy to about sixty mourners. To my knowledge, Hubert hadn't requested the cold, miserable and incessant rain which that day made soft and sensual mud of the soil we all meant to throw over his coffin, but it was somehow fitting that the big man would be laid to rest in stormy and inconvenient weather.

The two great milestones of my youth: reading *On the Road* senior year of high school and meeting Hubert in Albany. This, verily, was a one-man revolution and by that, I mean, or I'm referring to, rather, a *honi soit qui mal y pense* change of mind that gives you and your sword enough power over the unknown to establish your own kingdom, to really sprout your horns like those damn Vikings—it's like the great art of revision is your sword, which is your oath and humility is your shield—Evil to him who thinks it—and Hubert had the sword, the staff, in his big, bad hand. I once said to him, "had I not met you, I might have become a typical grad school liberal" or something like that and I now laugh when recalling the rebellious, freewheeling Hubert cautioning me about hitchhiking on I-87, almost always down to Manhattan.

"It's dangerous, man. You're not an eighteen-year-old beatnik anymore."

Now, this is the thing: Hubert definitely contacted me after he passed on; after his death. Hubert's passing, as much as anything, convinced me finally that the dead and the living must learn to speak a common language and help build the ship of death, no hyperbole or posturing about it.

"This is what the dead can do," lectured Rudolf Steiner. "He paints every thought he sees; he himself creates the thoughts anew, as it were, and experiences his own activity. A large portion of the life between death and a new birth consists in this—in a creative copying of what exists in the spiritual world as thought-formations. We must learn to create these anew, with the dead."

People, listen: I didn't cover the one mirror in my cramped Lower East Side apartment after Hubert succumbed to heart failure brought on by decades of fried food, a lack of exercise, about a thousand quarts of sticky, syrupy soda and a bad temper, as I am a gentile not required by Jewish law or custom to sit *Shiva* for a week; to cover all the mirrors in my house, rend my garments and weep and reflect on the life that had just shuffled off its mortal and, in this case, massive coil. Now I'm thinking that maybe I should have. Covered my mirror, that is.

There was no wake, of course, with the open casket, as in the Catholic services I'd witnessed since I was about seven and a half, no, at the Parkside Memorial Chapel in Forest Hills, Queens, New York City, Hubert's mortal remains were almost incidental to this gathering of friends as he had no family that we knew of and no one, aside from Miriam Moses and I, had any desire to take a last look at the bulky and lifeless dark brown husk that for thirty-seven years had housed a most troubled and truculent soul.

"I'm more than ready to go," Hubert had said about a month before his passing. "In heaven, I can chill, visit friends and who knows? Maybe there'll be some nice ladies up there. Ain't nothin' in the Bible says you can't fuck . . ."

Cynthia arrives late, clutching an umbrella, and from Rabbi Hoch's chambers I watch her pace back and forth, alone in the chapel lobby, a modest mournful cloth covering her crown, and I'm thinking that I haven't seen Cynthia in nearly seven years and neither had Hubert who, for all of his obsessive sexism, had loved this somewhat complicated woman more than he'd ever loved anything else. At the time of his death, Hubert was living with Deirdre who'd essentially supported him for close to a decade.

"I went and did something stupid," Hubert said that summer day in Albany just after he'd moved in with Deirdre, "I went and got me a girlfriend."

The big man had been homeless for about a year when Deirdre took him in and had somehow managed, within another year, to convince his old flame, Cynthia, to move in with them. Perfect! Perfect! Built on the insecurity of two women, this was just the sort of *ménage à trois* that only a manipulative autocrat like Hubert could have orchestrated. (The cat's been dead for twenty years and I *still* get pissed off at him.)

"Cynthia," I call to the round-faced woman with the sparrow-brown hair after the head-to-head with Rabbi Hoch. "Do you want to have a look at Hubert?"

Cynthia hesitates, then gestures indefinitely that she's willing to view the body of her former lover. She drops her umbrella in a silver-colored aluminum umbrella bin used on rainy days and walks with me toward the quiet oak box. As mourners clamor in the other room, I lift the top half of the coffin's cover, split into two like Dutch doors, and Cynthia lets out a scream.

"I wasn't ready for that," she exclaims breathlessly. "He's aged. I'm not used to this."

Cynthia and I sit down on one of the chapel's rust-brown bus station-type sofas nearby and she lights a cigarette. Reminiscent of Ilona Klein.

"I had a dream he died," she says, almost frenetically exhaling smoke. "And I don't even believe in that stuff. Normally, I have dumb dreams like I'm waiting on line at the bank or something. But after you called Mike and he told me that Hubert died, I said 'I know.'"

I don't know: do *you* agree with people who say 'when it's your time it's your time'? Old Hubert had been living on borrowed time for years. His heart'd grown to the size of a pumpkin—literally, if not figuratively—and even climbing stairs had become a problem. He was like a portable monument. As Hubert had scrupulously avoided gainful employment for years, his weight soared, shot up like mercury, because all he did was stay home, watch cable TV, smoke weed, read, and eat. A Buddha for our times. He wrote a little, too. Yellow pad.

"Don't go judgin' me sweetheart," Hubert once lashed out at Cynthia, "if you were black like me, you'd be out on the street, too. Shit, you lazier than I am."

Years before, someone'd written a little poem that appeared in the school paper and it ended like this: 'Hubert's the way my sister likes her coffee: black and bitter.' Hubert liked that line and repeated it to me often but, take it from me, there was much more to the man than bitterness. Hubert was brilliant. He'd been president of his class at college and chairman of the concert board and other organizations; was listed in the *Who's Who of American College Students* and was well-versed in Marx, Galbraith, Freud, Henry George, the economist, and the Bible. Hubert read Chinese stories of intrigue ("cloak-and-dagger to the max," he called them), the sacred texts of all the world's religions and had a passion for politics and conspiracy theories. He talked at length about the Trilateral Commission, the Illuminati and the so-called Invisible College. The banks, too.

"Before the goth kids, the hippies and before even the beatniks were the Wobblies," Hubert said on the campus podium late one autumn afternoon, dusk almost a warm hand on the forehead. "And the Wobblies were hip. Hubert Harrison, man. They knew that a system that allows banks to lend out money they don't have and to charge interest on it, is unjust and will not be sustained. All wars, famines and economic recessions are man-made. I'm tellin' you. You gotta straighten out the squares . . ."

Hubert once said that the Second World War should have been fought in the Middle East with the Allied and Axis powers meeting in India in order to stave off a *third* world war. We spent hours together, probably too many, discussing everything from medieval heresies to MTV. It's like it never stopped . . .

“The intellectual will always sell out to the fascist,” Hubert once said, taking a hit off his clay pipe. “Always. They believe in their facts and figures and do what their corporate masters tell them to do. Corporations aren’t bad, they’re just not God. The corporation was modeled on the Church. The Pope is the CEO, the cardinals are the executive vice-presidents. But even the Church isn’t all bad. It’s just not God.”

Hubert was older than me and distinct from my other friends at that time because he was passionate about his convictions: he kept the Sabbath every week, observed the Passover and the High Holy Days, and had little use for the moral relativism of his time, in fact, in one of our last conversations, he swore at Frederich Nietzsche, as he had for as long as I knew him, for his notion that one can transcend morality or go ‘beyond good and evil.’

“All dis talk about conspiracy; ya wanna know the real conspiracy? You’re a god. Better than the angels, and you’re not supposed to know that, you supposed to be afraid, cowed, a nigger. If you don’t know you’re a god, you’ll go and buy all da underarm spray and sacrifice your kids in a white man’s war. In the end, the Beatniks was about just that: don’t be a nigger.”

Being a religious man, Hubert had a keen sense of justice. Being a black American, Hubert experienced injustice nearly every day of his life.

“The truth is too big,” he once said, “to be the exclusive property of any one people.”

This contention, that the varied peoples of the earth have only “pieces of the truth” is the root cause of all the world’s conflicts, Hubert believed, so it was like hand-in-glove that the man was vexed by those who wouldn't accept him as a Jew because of his African heritage. ("Who says a Jew has to be a Caucasian from Europe?" he asked.) For the entire dozen years of our friendship, Hubert extolled the virtues of his adopted Jewishness proudly and without any irony; he would play the role, he'd be heir to the big-time covenants made with Abraham and Joseph and Moses.

"The only way to be fulfilled in life," he said on his last Thanksgiving Day, "is to live according to the Torah. But people mess up—Christians and Jews—if they think the truth lounges peacefully in some well-scrubbed, nicely appointed place. Nah, nah, man, you gotta look in the prisons and the asylums and in the hospitals and on the Bowery. Look where people are suffering."

Hubert wouldn't allow the word 'goddamn' to be uttered in his presence and he absolutely hated it when people wrote 'god' for 'God' because, as he explained, "for Christ's sake, you capitalize 'Milwaukee,' but not the name of the Supreme Fucking Being?" Hubert kept a copy of the Torah beside his *siddur,* his *Hagaddah,* his economics texts, Ellery Queen mysteries, pedagogies of the oppressed, histories and many other books. Hubert wasn't drawn to novels—he said, more than once, that he didn't "believe in fiction"—and although he admired the Impressionists and some modern art, he didn't bandy or carry on about aesthetics and style. He was a sports fanatic and was avid about music, too—in the end, very cerebral, like Josh, like Blau—would've thrived in the Internet Age—but his anima or feminine side would be this: his greatest interest was in people. To this day, I've never met anyone who watched and analyzed people the way he did. As Deirdre once said of

Hubert, "he denied no one his complexity." One time, I casually asked Hubert something or other about a young woman with whom he was enraptured.

"I got to go lightly," he said. "She's the cultured type, ya know? Gonna have to learn about sailing and boats and rap about key things like antiques, horses, French poetry and a little bit o' history, ya see? Keep on top o' current events, too, but know my way around some *Louis Quatorze* drawers. Talk about the grain and the finish on the wood. If she asks about horses and ridin', I'm gonna say that I can ride English style. That's better than country style. I'll talk about thoroughbreds and all the stables I been to, then quote some French poet like Bawdylair or something. No kidding! I'll talk about, I don't know, the dark night of the soul and how I can't wait to get back to Paris, but not in the summertime, of course! This is a woman I'm gonna have to keep constantly stimulated, bro. Unless I keep her constantly stimulated, I won't get over."

One thing's certain: the ladies loved on Hubert. That's how he presented himself, anyway.

"Her lips were talkin' to him, but her legs were talkin' to *me*," he once asserted after the two of us left one of Blau's Upper East Side parties. This is what the man had to say about Josh Moses:

"Moses, he's into that pure thought shit," Hubert said one afternoon when JoMo had his office door locked. Captive to his mood. We had started walking toward Central Park West. "Kierkegaard, Schopenhauer. He doesn't seem to be able to open himself up, so he seeks refuge in an arena where his real beliefs and his character don't have to be tested, ya know what I mean? In the end, it may be a man's ability to interact with other people that really counts. For example, why has he never given you a staff job? You know why? He's afraid of your talent and your intensity. He's certainly afraid of me. I know that. You got to be real, man, and sometimes my man isn't real. He doesn't even write anymore; all he does is manipulate images." We stopped because Hubert was short of breath. His heart. Steel spike in his knee. "Josh will have his time in the wilderness, though," he continued, his words and form like a jackhammer on the Manhattan pavement. "Look at the Hebrew children in the desert. They wandered in the desert for forty years but God loved His children so much, He gave them manna to eat the whole time. He must've loved His motherfuckin' children to give them that manna after they sinned. Yup. He must have *loved* His motherfuckin' children."

We were in Central Park, near the Plaza Hotel, in early spring. Hubert looked rather suave with his vanilla beret, green shades, green as the pond in the Park, silver zip-up jacket, and white scarf with Islamic calligraphy printed on it. The well-dressed commando, black oaks, brown ducks and big yellow checker cabs in the background.

"But he is a man of genius," Hubert went on. "I can't deny Moses that. He'll wrestle with his genie. He neither craves nor seeks fame and he loves his friends. This is not a petty man. He's got a big heart. He'll jump up to help ya, no matter what, and he's a crazy motherfucker. If it's outrageous, he likes it. If it's different, he'll go for it. He's not afraid of being thought 'weird,' the word that now has absolutely no meaning which is why my boy will never become one of those ice-cold intellectuals, trapped inside his skull. Still, he tries to be all things to all people when he's in his manic phases, which means that he runs the risk of being nothing authentic to anybody. He's a contradiction. Josh Moses should take a vow of silence and withdraw for a time. Well, anyway, you tell that Jew bastard I love him and to call me, okay?"

"Cynthia," a voice calls from the other room. Deirdre, an exquisite graphic artist who specializes in erotica, joins us.

"We're going to have a party Friday night in Rego Park," she says, keeping her composure and I say 'composure' because ever since Cynthia quit the *ménage à trois* one spring day seven years before, Hubert had made it clear to Deirdre that any contact with her was an act of betrayal.

"Instead of sitting *Shiva,* we're going to have a little party and remember Hubert, okay?"

Cynthia nods and lights up another cigarette. Sitting *Shiva* involves tearing one's clothes, sitting on uncomfortable crates and covering the mirrors in one's house with cloth to be reminded, one supposes, of the intrinsic vanity of our short lives, like Ash Wednesday. Deirdre decided to bury Hubert in his favorite pinstriped suit and with the camel-colored beret and dark pond-green sunglasses he was never without and, look, the man just barely fits into the casket—in fact, he looks uncomfortable, as Hubert stood about 6'5" and, at his peak, weighed close to 350 pounds. Cynthia, Deirdre and I peer once again at Hubert and notice that his lower lip is curled down and that just over the dark shades, his raven-black eyebrows are knit together like two furry caterpillars below the two atrophied bumps on his forehead, his horns, so that, even in death, his face looks angry, as only the living, to be sure, can do something about their anger, right?

"I'm over 30 years old," Hubert once said as the two of us trudged together through dirty snow in mid-February. "I'm not in jail, I ain't done no military service and I ain't dead! For a black man in this country, that's damn near a miracle!"

The viewing of Hubert is a kind of re-enactment of an earlier scene. Years before, I came to call on Cynthia and Deirdre when we all lived in Albany and Hubert was away in New York for a few days. It's a hot night in July and the three of us have found refuge in their air-conditioned apartment across the street from Albany Academy where Learned Hand went to school. (Learned Hand?) Hubert's gone, but his presence looms large like the ghost of Big Brother. One thing leads to another and the three of us somehow end up dancing naked to Patti Smith, Bill Withers and the B-52s in the cool indoors—Cynthia with the larger build shaking it and Deirdre reveling in the incarnation of one of her erotic drawings while the big boss man is 150 miles away in Manhattan.

It was a stupid thing to do. Unimpeachably stupid and Hubert must never know, we agree. You'd lie about this, wouldn't you, Slick? *Wouldn't you*? Nothing very terrible had happened. Nobody was compromised, really; but Hubert can never know that I danced and carried on naked in what, ostensibly, is his home. Cynthia and Deirdre both agree never to say anything, yet the next time that I come to call on the triad—almost a week later—I can tell that Hubert senses something. It's another hot night and the air-conditioner's particularly loud, offset as it is by the pregnant silences and awkward comings and goings.

"Deirdre, will you please get a cold drink for our guest?" Hubert asks by way of command. Neither of Deirdre's dark artist eyes look at me, eyes tiny and black like punctuation that nevertheless imagine and conjure purple dragon-women in serpentine embraces; neither look my way as she obediently gets out of her chair, mixes a gin-and-tonic with a twist of lime and hands it to me like a teller at a cash-checking place. Deirdre is pissed. I hadn't treated her right, she believes. Cynthia sits quietly smoking as Hubert labors over a card table, pouring a small amount of marijuana through a screen and cleaning it of seeds and stalks.

"How was New York?" I ask him.

"Same old thing," answers the big man. "People runnin' around like they ain't got a conscience. I can see it all up to a point, but . . . my soul? Sure, I'll hustle a little bit; do what I got ta do, maybe something unscrupulous, but my soul? I don't care if you're Charles Manson. You got a conscience and it's gonna tell on you."

Hubert's being remarkably perceptive, much to my discomfort. Supersensible. His words are drops of icy water on my head.

"I can't let it get to me," the big man continues over the drone of the air-conditioner. "At school, my professors, even my advisor, were all black nationalists. I alienated them because I told 'em that I refuse to hate white people. They just couldn't get with that. It ain't about black and white, it's about right and wrong."

"But who decides what's right or wrong?" I ask, sipping on my gin-and-tonic.

"God decides," answers Hubert who stops cleaning the pot. "And what He says in His law will not be changed."

"But is there really right or wrong if I don't acknowledge them?" I say without humility, considering what I'd done less than a week before in that same living room. "And the Bible," I continue, "that's just a book a bunch of men put together in the 16th century. We don't know if it goes back any further than that."

Hubert casts an angry ominous look my way, the gaze of fate.

"There's no historical proof that any of the Bible's characters actually existed. It's a fiction," I continue further, pushing past the man's ironclad boundaries. "And another thing: you keep calling God 'He.' How can God have any gender?"

"The God of the Hebrews was a man!" Hubert thunders.

"How do you know?"

"The God of the Hebrews was a man!" he bellows again. No room for the goddess woman, apparently.

"You don't know!" I exclaim.

"The God of the Hebrews was a man!" he intones once more and then gets up out of his chair, knocking over the card table. The weed, stalks and seeds spill on to the shag rug and, before you know it, the big bastard is on top of me, his hands around my throat.

"You fucked my woman!" he shouts.

"I did not!" I manage to say while pinned beneath this gargantuan figure, the avenging angelfucker, this massive Moor defending the honor of his two Desdemonas. So, this is how Jonah and Ahab felt in the belly of the whale. Deirdre runs in from the bedroom screaming and Cynthia stands up, silent.

"Stop it, Hubert! Stop!" cries Deirdre.

"Ever since I came back from New York, you two have been dropping hints and acting weird. Now, what happened?"

"Don't make fun of God in this house!" yells Deirdre, more out of deference to Hubert than to her Creator. Cynthia remains silent, because, clearly, she feels I've received my comeuppance for being so cavalier as to dance naked with her and then leave as if nothing had happened. On the stairs, as I make my way out, I fire out another provocation.

"And you talk about being real!" I shout, because the most abject insult Hubert could levy was 'he ain't real.'

Swifter than the Light Brigade and more terrifying than Ceteyano, the great Zulu warrior, Hubert runs after me, despite a steel spike in his knee, down the steps into the stairwell—barefoot!—and puts his hands around my throat again.

"Well, right now, you're about as real as shit!" he says as he forces my head into the cement wall. Stone on stone. "You wanna die tonight, asshole? Huh? You wanna die?? I'll *kill* you, motherfucker!"

With blood coursing furiously like hot river rapids through my arms and legs, I leave, hearing Hubert's bearish barefooted steps trudging back up the stairs, then, less than an hour later, I call the three of them up from a phone booth across the street. Pre-cell phone.

"I want to speak with Hubert," I say to Deirdre.

"I don't think that's a good idea," she says. Hubert grabs the phone from her.

"Sure, man. I'll come out," he says nonchalantly. Hubert "shushes" Deirdre, telling her, I can hear: "Ain't nothin' hurtin' that boy but his pride." Before long, Hubert appears in the hot humid night like a big ocean liner emerging from dense fog. He's become my conscience.

"What do you want?" I ask him. He shrugs and raises his eyebrows, implying that there's nothing that he really wants.

"What do you think I want?" I ask and he sort of shrugs again.

"All I know is that somebody said that you tried to fuck Cynthia. You never cared particularly about Cynthia any damn way."

"That's not true," I say. I'm lying just a bit. Revising the story. "Are you offended at something I said? Did I insult your religion?"

"Priests and rabbis and ministers don't know nothin'," replies Hubert. "This is something the three of you are going to have to work out." He pauses and looks me up and down with faint concern. "How's your head?"

"It's okay," I say. "It's just my neck . . ." Hubert's grip has left purple marks on my jugular that look like streaks in the sky before an evening storm.

"Well, I'm sorry for that. I'm sorry. That's a part of myself I don't like. See, my mother died when I was very young. I was raised by my grandmother and my aunt. They wanted me to be straight and upright, you know? They wouldn't let me play with black kids. In school, the teachers took to me because I was so precocious. I was the nigger they wanted to succeed, so they had me in calculus class and leadership groups and so on."

We continue walking through the hot and balmy night, shadows in a summer dream.

"I was able to play the game for a while, you know, but after Pops died in '76 and Katherine, my fiancee, left me, I became a live wire. I was rootless. I know I'm a loud, cantankerous son-of-a-bitch and I don't know why anyone would want to spend time with me. I told you they had me in Catholic school for a while there, when I was growing up in the Catskills during the 60s, had me sayin' the rosary, crossing myself, going to confession, and praying for the Virgin Mary to bring capitalism to Russia. I was a prize for all the little white girls who were too old for sleepaway camp and wanted to do something rebellious. They had me runnin' in every damn direction for years, but I know what I believe and I won't change. I have a particularly hard road but let me tell you, just growing up the way I did brings with it a rage all its own."

I close the lid on the coffin.

"Well," says Cynthia, finally, "we'd better go meet with the others."

As we deliver our eulogies, praising Hubert for his brilliance—hymns to his intellectual beauty—I recall a line from the big man's diary, which Deirdre has given me: *no one says the healing word until the man is dead.* After the service, the cars form a procession that drives through the rain to Mount Lebanon Cemetery in Queens where Hebrew letter-characters dance like the righteous on dead stone. The letters breathe. About forty of us stand in the pouring rain and cry.

The rabbi speaks briefly, then Hubert's lowered into the mud.

"Keep your friendships," Rabbi Hoch says to all of us from under an umbrella, "stay friends."

We all go back to the house in Rego Park where Deirdre had discovered Hubert's body and we eat, drink and laugh, rain tapping on the windows like gossip. Three days later, on the Sabbath, about twenty of us assemble at Deirdre's where we tell stories about Hubert, like the time he spat in the street and almost picked a fight with a fat, gooey kid who was wearing a T-shirt that read: "Be a man among men: Rhodesian Army." There was the outdoor music festival where Hubert, blasted by a hit of window-pane, and a local bar slut, consummated the act of sexual love before everyone's eyes—in broad daylight—and dared anybody who watched to pass judgment.

"If they stood by and watched and they did," Hubert surmised loudly, "they couldn't have been too offended."

At the magazine, one of the ad executives, a sweet golden-haired women who wore a silk blouse under a pearl collar necklace, asked Hubert as he helped her put on her pink chinchilla winter coat, "so, how come you smoke so much pot?"

"Because I can't deal with life," he answered immediately. End of discussion. Things got dicey, though, when Hubert said to another ad exec:

"I'm sorry I have balls, lady. But I was born with 'em and I intend to keep 'em."

Then Josh Moses steps forward.

"I can see Hubert standing in our Battery Park City living room," he says softly, only the rain and the sound of footsteps in the kitchen competing with his voice. “We had a view of the World Trade Center and the Statue of Liberty and we had a party for the Statue of Liberty’s centennial on that Fourth of July. Our place was jammed—you needed tickets to get into the building—and some of you were even there!”

Shit, yes. That’s the night everyone was doing ecstasy, the night I traded spit with Mimi, when no one was looking.

“Having finished a tirade about foreign policy or something,” Josh continues, “Hubert says ‘you know, we don’t really care about politics, news, issues and policy as much as we’d like to think. We care a little but for the most part, we’re preoccupied with worries about money, getting the laundry done, shopping for food, getting the rent paid, are my friends loyal and will I ever find true love? That’s what we really care about, not news.’”

Seems like there’s an aura of gold around him. His voice is high but bears authority, and you’re wondering if he knows, if Miriam ever told him . . .

“We all sort of drew a blank,” Mo continues, “We were bewildered, intimidated and uncomfortable. Bob was there. Deirdre. The Brown-Eyed Belle of Saint Mark. Blau. We all wanted to escape the man’s gaze because Hubert really did wear at his heart the fire’s center and he could be exhausting. Then day turned to night and when the fireworks and rockets red glare lit up the harbor below, with the aircraft carriers and the tall ships and the Statue of Liberty, Hubert cried out, pretty much to everyone’s surprise, ‘look at that lady! Will you look at that *lady*!’”

I remember that and was among the surprised; surprised when Hubert repeated, "Will you look at that *lay-dee*?!"

Amos, the pasty-faced Irish raconteur from Albany can't attend this gathering in Queens—some ten subway stops from Ozone Park where Kerouac began writing *On the Road*—but Clyde is here, trying to borrow money. Howard, a semi-orthodox Jew, takes offense at the celebrating.

"I don't think this is right," he says with avuncular displeasure, sounding more like a bugle sounding taps than the *shofar* at the new year. "We should be mourning and lamenting," he's wheezing, "but instead, we're just having another party. It's not right."

Again, someone invoked right and wrong. None of the assembled sit on crates. Deirdre does cover one of her mirrors with cloth, the only *memento mori* at this party, but no one tears his garments this night or says *kaddish* for a man who wrestled with his angel every day; who cried one night that he was a hollow man and incapable of love; who would not be denied the right to call himself a Jew, to light candles on the Sabbath and celebrate his freedom, his release from Pharaoh every *pesach*—it's true, this was a man who probably never fasted on the Day of Atonement, but whose toenails once fell out from malnutrition; a man who intimidated most everyone he knew with his presence and unshakable convictions—with his horns—a one-man revolution hungering for justice in a world that really had no place for him.

I'll be honest and say that no one left that party with the humility and gravity required of adults when a loved one has passed on. None of us, I don't believe, ruminated on or atoned for the vanitas of our temporal lives, but when I got home that Friday night after the rain had stopped, I swear, as the God of the Hebrews is my eyewitness, even though I'm not supposed to swear, I swear that the one mirror in my apartment, the medicine-chest mirror in my Lower East Side bathroom which I'd left uncovered, was shattered and creased, looking like a spider web suspended between two thin branches of a willow tree.

FOUR

Grace

"I hope it is true that a man can die and yet not only live in others but give them life, and not only life, but that great consciousness of life."—Jack Kerouac

When you were a high school and college kid, didn't you dream about living a thousand and one nights in New York City, and if that dream were to come true—say, after years of hitchhiking down there from Albany—don't you think you'd have felt some self expand, because New York's magnitude doesn't dwarf but, rather, enlarges you, dignifies you, like the Excalibur placed on your velvet epaulette? I'm not too jaded or sophisticated to admit that it was thrilling to meet many of the big *stars,* the music stars (pentagrams?) and some of the film luminaries while living in Manhattan and working for the magazine, and here's how it went: the publicist would call the editor, you'd read the bio they'd messengered over and then you'd meet the artist at the record label office or at the studio; maybe, at the hotel or at a coffee shop with a tape recorder, and you felt like an East Coast Studs Terkel or like Alan Lomax or like Parcifal asking the right questions; it's like living down on the Lower East Side was the minor key and working and writing at the midtown magazine offices (before we moved down to Little Italy), and flying around the world, was major key stuff. Outside the cup.

"The key of C is the key of virginity," a skinny musician told me in London. "But sometimes you have to modulate."

In addition to flying to London, I flew to LA and Chicago, to Martha's Vineyard, to Sydney, to Cartagena, Colombia for interviews—George Clinton in snowy Detroit—and, in town, there was Paul Simon's office in the Brill Building on Broadway: he had a tuna fish sandwich on rye, a Magritte on the wall. Roger Waters was in the Berkshire Regent hotel up in the East 60s or 70s, Johnny Rotten, too. Leonard Cohen, Joan Baez, Philip Glass, Al Green backstage at the Apollo, all great interviews: they weren't petty or small, had nothing to prove. Called you by your name. They knew, of course, that real art, the new art, is about sanity, the Temple, the Ship of You Know What, not about a spoiled child's cacophony—one afternoon, in fact, I finally spoke directly to the dead, to the Grateful Dead lyricist, poet Robert Hunter.

"I told Allen Ginsberg, 'you've got a great way with words, but you have alot of cockroaches running around in your poems,'" Hunter said from San Francisco. "And Ginsberg replied, '*cockroach* is a *beautiful* word.'" Hunter laughed. "I guess it's a matter of taste. I wouldn't use the word 'cockroach' in a poem because, uhm, I don't find it beautiful."

Beautiful words???

"Music is the cup that holds the wine of silence," posited guitar great Robert Fripp in an 8th street falafel place.

"I have decided to seek beauty the way other men return to the religion of their fathers," said Leonard Cohen over the phone from LA. "Make love like the gods . . ."

Louis Armstrong once said "when you leave New York City, you ain't goin' nowhere." Long-haired, bearded, manic and almost always stoned Josh Moses was flush with money in those days—big freelance budget, lotsa petty cash in the early days, too—thus, there was no need to even leave goddam town except to fly to Sydney or LA or to London, so let me just say that yuppie times, I've got to admit, were good times for me. Was very confident in those days, much more confident than I should've been, like a one-man militia, like Martin Luther calling out the devil: ***Hey, asshole, I've got shit in my drawers. Would you like some?*** Very assertive I was—convinced that rock 'n roll was bringing down the Berlin Wall—and impatient with JoMo's attempts to control every situation, and there's something else about this 'sweet time unafflicted,' this grace period: you could get into a building in Manhattan without doing your patriot act—no security check, no laminated ID, no corporate paranoia—it was another world: you could take the fire escape up to the tar-shingled roof at lunchtime and dream the dreams of the neon angels, the sullen but illuminated gods of Times Square, but those doors are locked now. Had passes to a million rock and jazz shows—Little Richard at Tramps downtown was the greatest rock 'n roll show ever—free admission, and passes, as well, to movie premiers and to press conferences—James Brown at the Cat Club, Joseph Campbell at Lincoln Center. Miles Davis on Dick Cavett's show at 30 Rock and all over the Lower East Side, too, of course, was the quintessentially rootless cosmopolitan, Allen Ginsberg.

"Allen, I just saw you in that film, the Kerouac film . . ." I say to Ginsberg who's walking south on Avenue A in his green down parka, circa 1987.

"The one at the Bleecker Street cinema?" he says.

"Yeh. You and Burroughs."

"Do you know of any restaurants near here?" Allen asks. We're both still walking. He doesn't smile, but there's his voice. That voice!

"Well, there's the Kiev," I say.

"No, that's too far." He points east on Sixth Street. "What's down there?"

"I don't know. Maybe Leshko's." Another Ukrainian café. Good. Reasonable.

"Are you a musician?" he asks, those round rubber lips finally breaking into a smile like tires inflating, then deflating.

"Yeh," I say. He offers his hand and we shake.

"I have to stop and breathe," Allen says.

The out-of-the-way places in Manhattan were fine, as well—the Waterfall Café on West 107th Street, a walk-down basement bistro with Nordic rune blocks at each table; Chumley's and Arthur's in the West Village; the Kiev in the East Village; the West End Café near Columbia University where the beats first met, nothing but hills, heights, winged morningside, marble, and divine and never-finished Saint John, its back turned to Harlem—and I was in love: first with Margo, then with the Brown-Eyed Belle of Saint Mark who once stated in a whisper: "I can control when I'm going to come. Mind. It's all in the mind."

"Thanks."

"No, seriously," she said, sitting up in bed, "the orgasm is much stronger than the climax." The Belle's eyebrows rose like black smoke.

"Wait," I said, "you're making a distinction? What's the difference between a climax and an orgasm?"

"The climax is a great warm feeling below, but the orgasm is . . . well, it's like my head is going to explode. The crown of my head. It's like being blinded temporarily. Like some mysterious music. My body is ripped in half and I climb out of my skull." The Belle is dark, Jackie O beautiful; has snow-white hands and the fragrance of honeysuckle, ginger and fresh sweat and you'd feel like a one-man revolution, too, if your GF said to you: "Do you know what's it like to fake it? It's like being an actress in a soap opera, saying the same things over and over again. A part in a Broadway play. He thinks he's a stud and you're thinking about where you're parked and the best route home. I never came with a man before you. That's my confession. But, we have to be kissing at the same time. My tongue has to be in your mouth. With you, I don't have multiple orgasms. I have exponential orgasms. Like when you kiss me or touch me or do something that sets me off. Kiss my nipples. Bite my nipples. Then, I'm just coming and coming. Like a fountain. I can't stop. You're pussy candy, dearest. Sometimes, even words . . . like when you say 'I'm going to mash your clit with my cock,' I start coming. Just the idea sets me off. Or when . . . someone says 'I love you.' That's what I mean by coming with my mind . . . "

It was a time of raised awareness and sensations and I don't mean the alpha state of television: One evening, I swear I saw gold light surrounding everything in my apartment, the plants, the picture frames, the gas oven and stove, everything bathed in golden liquid light—like gold blood—an aura surrounding all material things, and this was when I was alone, in that unchartered country, somewhere between sleep and insanity; between the living and the dead, then, on another night, I saw white light coming out of the Brown-Eyed Belle's navel, a thin column of white light shooting right out of her belly–button and I devoured it, devoured her, ate and drank the Belle from head and tongue to painted toe nail. We'd fallen asleep and my subtle body or something rose up, like the Shekinah, to her ceiling on St. Mark's Place and saw the two of us lying on the bed—I remember it distinctly—on the night Reagan bombed Libya and killed Qaddafi's daughter, the only time this happened: my astral body, my soul, lifted out of the physical, as it does every night, but this time, it stopped at the ceiling and the eyes of my soul saw the two bodies lying motionless, entwined, naked and raw in the realm of the senses, in the kingdom of time below. Espying life through the eyes of the dead.

O, Brown-Eyed Belle, I think of you oftener now. Resting on the antique wooden chairs yesterday, I realized that I never said "I love you" to you. Not even once. Remember the six-floor walk up on St. Mark's Place not far from W.H. Auden's? The tears of seven saints' sorrow? The commotion on First Avenue below? Remember your sacred doubt? Riding around Staten Island on a bus as a kid, wondering what

the Big City would be like? I remember your cobalt blue robe, your raven black hair and black Irish eyes; your wit, the old movie house, your snow-white hands, your honeysuckle perfume, your perfect face, your smile like the Left Bank. These fragments are all I have left of you.

You once said, "I think you like the idea of me more than me," but that wasn't so. The whole of you was just too smart, too elegant, too refined, too lovely for me to try and contain and so these fragments are all I have now, they are the you I still cherish and have always loved.

PART III: THE SUBDOMINANT CHORD

Any Day Now

ONE

The Body

*"You don't have to make a big deal out of a big deal."—
R. O'Brian*

This is it, country simple, this is how I got to Lowell, Mass and heard Jack Kerouac's confession; how I reunited with the Lady, got my horns, which is to say, my life and soul and sanity, back and how I learned to shape the world into a perfectly atuned and proportioned work of art, just as Cain and Tubal the magician built the house of the holy at Jerusalem.

Build your ship of death, for you will need it . . .

Am exaggerating a bit, but the story's worth telling, worth hearing. You have to take your mental health seriously . . .

We're in the present again, not the eternal indivisible one, but the fragmented one, the Hubert is dead, Berlin Wall torn down, shouting on TV, fallen-from-grace, fear-gripped, refusal-to-praise, insolent, present: horns cut off, Tompkins Square evacuated, love pretty much outlawed, chagrined and reproached, an Ugly Time in America, don't you think? This is the subdominant chord, F. For 'fuck you.'

"In a sense, everyone's beat," says Allen Ginsberg at this time, which means that now even Mom and Dad and Buddy and Sis are starving, hysterical, naked, dragging themselves through the negro streets at dawn looking for an angry fix because, well, look at it: the terrorism of mental illness and depression. No more therapy, just prescription medication; ever more so since the Gnarly Nineties, when insolence began to drown out the praise.

Sex and the city? The Goddess is gone, now, but my friend Tatiana's willing to stand in for the eternal feminine. She can play the part. It's important to meet and know Tatiana, or 'Gopi,' as her sidha-yoga friends call her, because this is what a messenger from the beyond looks like; this is how the divine maid-servant talks; here's a ministering angel for troubled times.

Kidding.

She's a pain in the ass. But you'd have some love for her, too, if you knew her. Look at this: It's warm for November and Tatiana wants to see and hear this white-haired minister who speaks every Sunday on AM radio and at Avery Fisher Hall at Lincoln Center in New York. I'm in the city for some freelance copy-editing work. The titanic Chagall murals—two of them, *The Sources of Music* and *The Triumph of Music*—flank the top of the entrances at Avery Fisher or Alice Tully Hall, I always forget. Chagall painted the real world, a sane world. The tones of life. Almost no gravity. Everyone and everything is alive in his work. Like the Lower East Side. Chagall didn't paint a dying world.

"After the service," Tatiana says, "we can go up and shake hands with Eric and Olga. Dat would be good for you."

"Why are you always telling me what would be good for me?" I protest to the Czech-born Tatiana. "I never asked you to be my teacher. I appreciate your wisdom, but there's no need to hover over my head. Good for me? Like what? Who? That condescending preacher?"

"Who? Eric?" Tatiana is taken aback.

"No, the first one that came out and talked about the writing class on Wednesdays. The tall guy."

"Oh, Peter," she says. "He was an actor for many years."

"Yeh, right. What's with the condescension and contempt? That guy was downright contemptuous. I've seen this before. It must be a thing with preachers. They really want to be rock stars. Or think they should be actors. Contemptuous. 'They're really hanging on to *my* every word? *Suckers*.'"

"You always invalidate anything new," Tatiana says earnestly, wiping strands of her shoulder-length ebony-black air from her face and forehead. "Dat is not what he thinks. You don't know him for what he is."

"What? A condescending prick?"

"Oh, sssshhhh," says Tatiana turning to face the lectern. "Eric and Olga are going to speak."

The elderly man and woman, husband and wife, are great: enlightening, soft-spoken but strong, focused, humble, helpful, they're all about the infinite power of the mind, the world is your canvass, change your thought, change your life but without any self-aggrandizing oratory, kind of like Beatnik-Zen-Dhammapada Buddhist right thinking. Revision. They're even in their tone and expression like winter wind on the bare leafless trees; the branches shake but the trunk is secure and life will return in the spring, you can count on it.

"Let's go up and meet dem," says Tatiana, eager as a kid on Christmas morning.

"Wait," I say sternly. "When we go up there, please don't say 'this is my friend, Robert,' or anything like that. Please do not introduce me, you know what I mean? I just want to go up to the podium, shake their hands, say one or two words and that's it. No 'and this is my friend. This is his first time here.' Got it?"

"What are you worried about? You're so self-absorbed. You sink it's all about you. What am I going to say?"

"Well, every time I've gone up to the Catskills with you, it's been 'oh hi, *hiiiiiiiiiiiiiii*' and this circle of friends. I thought you went up to the ashram for quiet and meditation. And I am *not* self-absorbed."

"You are."

"Self-absorbed means you can't even talk about politics or ideas or about anyone else. I'm self-centered, maybe, sometimes selfish, but not self-absorbed. Josh Moses is self-absorbed, well, pretty close to it. I mean, he's one of the few people who neither craves nor seeks fame, but the more his fortunes wane, the more self-obsessed he becomes. The market tanks and it's all about him. A new Springsteen record comes out and it's about Josh. How it affected *him*. Mr. Passionate Mercy. It's madness. Like a fire alarm ringing from a gray suit. And he lies. He just fucking lies . . ."

"Josh? He puts you up in his home. He gives you assignments. What are you talkink about? Maybe it's you who is self-obsessed. What is dee matter wiz you? Josh loves you. And he's a truthful liar, you know dat."

"You know, he's never said 'I love you' to his Mom? He told me. How can you not be depressed and in bondage if you refuse to praise your mother?" I soften a bit. "She's still alive, but she's gone now. Gabby loved it when Harry used to sing to her: *I'm confessin' that I love you . . . tell me that you love me, too . . .*"

Tatiana and I get out of our seats and make for the stage where a line has formed, a line of people waiting to meet and speak briefly with the white-haired minister and his bottle-brown-haired wife. The hall's still dense and difficult to negotiate, so we head for the lobby, through the big glass doors, and who's standing by one of the stairways that lead to the balcony but Maya Angelou, standing all alone like the solitary oak in a forest clearing.

"I didn't know you came to this church," I say to the bard who towers over me like a rocket over its launch pad. "It's an honor to meet you."

"Thank you," Dr. Angelou replies with Old World elegance. "I've always been a seeker of truth."

"Well, it shows in all your books," Tatiana says somewhat unctuously. Angelou's regal in her bearing, tall, erect, head like an eagle's, turning to each of us as she listens with purpose and penetrating insight. You feel exposed in her presence, like she can see your veins, like, you're not going to get away with lying, duplicity nor even with frivolity, although Angelou has those sympathetic Aztec eyes. Her inflection is aristocratic but lyrical, genuine. Calming. We spend only a quick moment with the poet laureate from Stamps, Arkansas and San Francisco and Egypt, Ghana, and Wake Forest, then go to wait on line for a good five or six minutes until we approach Eric,

Olga and Peter, and when Tatiana meets Peter, the under-assistant preacher and erstwhile actor, she says to him: "I want to ask you about your writing class," then turning to me, she continues, "because he is a writer and he might be interested. I think it would do him a lot of good."

I'm livid. The younger minister takes my hand and makes perhaps the most horridly disingenuous utterance I've ever heard directed at me. The most horridly patronizing tone is in his preacher voice—the god of insincerity visited this man's bed at night and left an imprint on his forehead and on his subtle goddam body, weasels ripped his flesh—and he says, without looking me in the eyes, "That's great. I know from experience that, no matter what, you *can do it*." He's looking at something over the top of my head, apparently, and, even though your depression comes from your insolence and your refusal to praise, I want to kill someone right now, but I wait until Tatiana and I are walking uptown on Central Park West before I start to vent and spill venom into the autumn air.

"I fucking told you, I asked you not to introduce me in any way." I'm fuming, volcanic, something out of a nightmare. "I specifically asked you not to do that."

"What did I do?"

"You know what you did! Stop playing games. I can't stand this. And what is this 'it shows in all your books'? You've never read anything by Maya Angelou in your life. Do you think you fooled her?" The two of us are walking at a quick pace up Central Park West, past the Center for Ethical Culture and the Dakota. It's fall and we have coats on but no scarves or hats. "I'm glad," I go on, "I'm glad you have no problem with the fact that nothing you say has any validity. Let's get a cab." *Judge the* state, *not the person who inhabits that state*, a rabbi from Crown Heights used to tell me. *Lift it up, lift it up.* Even a beast can lift it up.

"No, let's walk," Tatiana says and we walk in stony silence up to 100th Street.

Tatiana's place is rent-controlled, 18th floor, with a picture window overlooking most of Central Park. You take in the Sheep Meadow, the Great Lawn and the Plaza Hotel with one gulp, one glance, the immensity, the green, red, orange, yellow etheric life—like those Chagall murals during the colorful days of awe: the pulse and the electricity, the fallen autumn light, earth-bound light, fills you up after one or two looks out on to the park, and when you watch the shadows fall on the lawns and trees and on those sculptures and the lake, of course, as you stand on Tatiana's little terrace up on the 18th floor, it's as if, well, if you just let yourself dream for a moment, it's as if a dark angel is fanning out its gown to block out the garish yet indifferent sun—furtively, though, the shadows fall, furtively, like an angel's gown unfurling, like strands of black hair is the approaching night: strands of black hair accumulating on the bathroom floor.

"Tania, I'm sorry I snapped at you," I say as the woman prepares Japanese tea in the kitchen. "But I asked you specifically . . ."

"You know what I sink? I sink you eat too many spicy foods and get all riled up and you insist on wrestling wiz your angel, I'm saying?" Tatiana's English is excellent, but her accent is thick, like Zoltan Blau's Hungarian English, and she often tags 'I'm saying?' onto the end of her sentences when she means to say, 'You know what I'm saying?'

She brings the pot of Japanese tea from the kitchen to her coffee table and pours into two cups. "You are driven too much by your passions," she continues. "You want to force your will on to sings. You can't change the world, but you can change how you sink about the world. You make peace wiz your imperfections and when you notice somesing that your ego mind is doing, what your body is doing, stand back and witness it."

"That's easy to say," is my Yossarian-like response. "But how do you witness your lower self when it's insane with fear or in pain?"

"You don't act on dee fear," says Tatiana. "Don't you know zat zis is all a dream? Zis is not reality, zis world, it is our projection. It is fantasy, I'm saying? The body is nozink. What is the body? Chust an illusion."

Tatiana's dream was that she was born in Bratslava, Czechoslovakia just after World War II, and that her father was a brilliant chemist and a devout Communist, and when he was six years old he heard his friend's mother tell her little boy not to play with Ludwig, Tatiana's dad, because he was "common." From then on, it was the dictatorship of the proletariat or nothing. Tatiana's mother, on the other hand, had come from a well-to-do family that lost everything after the Revolution. She hated the Party but loved her husband and together they survived Hitler and Stalin. Tatiana was a gymnast, a dancer and a writer when she was younger. Her favorite novel, growing up, was *Sister Carrie.* From the time she was about five, Tatiana dreamed of leaving Bratslava and coming to America. Tatiana defected on a strawberry-picking trip to Britain and, after two years in "Swinging London," came to the States, became a citizen right away and embraced everything American, refusing to associate with the Slovaks who emigrated here.

"Slovaks don't like anybody but Slovaks," said Tatiana. "But I came here to forget dee past."

Tatiana, it seems, had successfully revised herself. Once in America, she became a student of *siddha* yoga, which, to some extent, estranged her from the North American mainstream. She stopped watching television and began meditating, sometimes for hours at a time. Great stuff, but her newfound zeal fostered a kind of hypocrisy or, at the very least, a blindness as to her natural urges.

"You're very inspiring, Tanichka," I say as I blow on the hot tea. "But, as usual, you're ignoring a few things."

"Like what?" she says with a look of sincere surprise. "You mean sex? I am celibate. I am nun. You sink I'm so crazy about you, but I'm not. I'm not attached. All right, so sometimes I can't resist you because you are like Sicilian bull. I mean, I never had a man throw me down and fuck me before. Most men are so dysfunctional. You come on wiz sweet innocent voice, 'hello, Tania, how are you?' but zen it becomes hard and deep, 'what's your phone number? Write it on dee post-it . . .'" She laughs a deep throaty lusty laugh that sounds like a car engine without a muffler. "I used to be so drawn to you, but it brought me nozink but pain. Now I am nun. I am like the guru. You cannot understand zis because for men, sex is like a meal. You chust finish it and you're done. We women get all emotional and gooey but you don't care. You can chust throw me down or dat poor roommate of yours. What was her name? Ramona? You could just throw her down and have her on the living room rug and dat is dee end of it. Women are different. We get attached."

"So do we . . ."

I sip some tea and look at Tatiana. She has that sapphire-blue-black hair that falls to her shoulders. She keeps her taut and voluptuous figure by swimming and occasionally working out. In her chair across the sofa from where I'm sitting, I'm reminded of the middle-aged Kate Hepburn as Tatiana imparts her views and listens to mine so intently, her head resting on her open right hand. Thinking through her fingers. Then, she speaks.

"I'm just like dee guru now," she says. "I have mastered my passions."

"You're like the guru?" I snort bestially. "Just because someone teaches you something—even if it's the truth—that's still no reason to have twenty pictures of her in your house." Tatiana has likenesses of her guru in her kitchen, in her living room atop a little shrine over her CD player and books. She has photos of the guru in her bedroom and even her bathroom. "Do you think it's healthy," I say, "to have all these pictures of her in your house? You don't have to make a big deal out of a big deal, ya know."

"Leave her alone," Tatiana says. "I want nozink but to imbibe dee teachings and dee guru is my example, I'm saying?"

There's a lull in our conversation for a full ten seconds. Tatiana: another friend with Hubert-sized *shakti* or presence and, shit, the two never met and I remember, can hear, Tatiana saying to Josh and Miriam Moses:

"Bob even tells me I remind him of this Hubert."

Like a stone dropping into a backyard pond, I break the silence.

"So, guess who's coming to New York," I say.

"Who?"

"Lyla."

"You're kiddink. Lyla?" Tatiana sits upright, stunned like a kid who just stuck her finger into a wall socket. "What is she coming here for?"

"Well, she likes to come up to New York to shop, apparently, so she'll bring her daughter and they'll go to Macy's or whatever but we're supposed to meet."

"Where's she staying?"

"At the Roosevelt Hotel."

"Near Grand Central? Yes, I know what will happen. You will be having dinner at the hotel, in the restaurant, and Lyla will have all these shopping bags and boxes and she's going to throw on dee charm and say 'you're such a big strong man, can you help me wiz dee boxes?' and she's going to get you to go up to her room and zen she will have you like spider has fly."

"No, no, she's coming with her daughter."

"You wait and see."

Tatiana's such a trip and she's seen it all. Not three weeks after coming to New York for the first time, a would-be paramour took her to the Concert for Bangla Desh at Madison Square Garden.

"I was always drawn to George, even as child," Tatiana once said. "I thought he was the cutest one. We used to hear dee Beatles from radio station in Vienna. The Communists wanted to block out dee station but the big officials liked the music too much. And they liked dee TV shows, too, so they didn't bother. But I loved the Beatles and dee Stones. That was when music had feeling. Now, the feeling is gone, I'm saying?"

As a child, Tatiana could see, from her apartment complex in Bratslava, the huge ferris wheel in Vienna, the one immortalized in *The Third Man*, reisenraudt. She attended a party where the kids were dancing the Twist but the party was broken up by a "Young Pioneer" who found the dance to be decadent and western. Later, it was discovered that the Young Pioneer was a child molester. Imagine it: forcing your way into someone's home to stop the Twist from being danced.

"When I saw George at Bangla Desh concert, he looked right at me," Tatiana went on. "It was like getting *shaktipad* from dee guru. He passed some of his power on to me. I could feel it. Zis was way before I went to India. Before I even met dee guru." But now, Tatiana is upset that I have plans to see Lyla.

"You know, I was very hurt when you didn't call me all those months," she says as she crosses her legs and pushes the jet-black hair away from her forehead. She's always fixing her hair. "I needed you. And, look, I got dis scar when I fell on my face. Look."

"What scar?" I say as I swallow more tea. Ever since she'd drunk too much wine one night and had fallen down and cut herself on a doorstop, she'd been going on endlessly about an imaginary scar. "You do *not* have a scar on your face, Tania. I swear it. What is with this scar? There *is* no scar!"

"I didn't leave my house for week!" she exclaims as she reaches over to pour more tea into my cup. "Not dat I really care about a ridiculous scar. I mean, dee body is nozink. What's dee body? But you chust forgot all about me because of zis Lyla. So, you found a woman who really turns you on and you forget about Tanichka. Who cares about Tania anymore? Not you."

I stand up from the couch to look out on what's becoming a brilliant orange late autumn sunset. Tatiana, always so full of sage advice, is coming apart. For some time now, she'd been talking about plots on her life: the landlord wants her dead because her apartment's rent-controlled; the upstairs neighbor's intent on destroying her. Intense paranoia.

"I'm all alone in dee world," she was saying with increasing frequency. "Who cares for me? You? You have a great life. You come and go as you please. You have great home wiz Esmé upstate and you come down and get freelance work in dee city. I have no family and I'm close to fifty. I'm afraid dat I'm going to grow old alone and die alone. And my face has fallen. Look."

Tatiana then gestures with both hands, with both of her forefingers, exactly as the Brown-Eyed Belle and Ilona gesture—with a downward motion of her fingers that describes two equal sides of an isosceles triangle—gestures to indicate that her face has fallen and that she's no longer 'fresh,' as women love to say. Not a spring chicken anymore.

"How can you say all this?" I protest sympathetically. "You're a student of the Vedas. You're almost a yogi . . ."

"Not yet."

"Well, almost. Why don't you use that technique you were telling me about? Say 'remember when I was depressed and afraid? Remember way back when, I was unable to sleep at night?' Put the present into the past and it's done. Complete. The ancient, forgotten, eternal, orgasm. And I don't mean jerking off. Archie says that, too. You can revise the present as well as the past. Or you can refer to the future like it's the present. 'Don't you just love my new country home up in the Catskills?' That's what you want, right?"

"Yes," she says dreamily, "you're right. I've been whining too much. Me, of all people. Why do I get dese morbid soughts about death? Dee mind always creates. It can't stop creating, so if you imagine somesing is true, you can make it true. We had big bonfire funeral when Baba died. People came to Ganeshpuri from all oafer dee world. Big huge bonfire to celebrate life although he gave up his body. *Mahasamadhi* it is called. You chust give up dee body. And dee body is nozink, it just falls away, I'm saying? Dee soul, dee essence of dee person remains."

Then, she becomes playful. "So, what are you going to do now, my American man? Hmmm? You have any words for me?"

I look down for a moment at Tatiana's thick gray carpet and then stand up. Ever feel like there's something gnawing at you, like a rat in a garbage pail? My scheduled rendez-vous with Lyla has put a restless feeling inside me that literally makes my feet tingle in a way that's almost unpleasant, like hot needles, like when you're overly sentimental and drowning in memories and exotic sensations at your keyboard on windswept country days or alone at night in the city. ***Take this life, my story, take this cruel heart. I don't want it anymore. Just take it. My gift to you. My gift to the dead.*** I need to get away from the smell of incense and tamari. I want to be in my own space.

“Well,” I say abruptly, “I’ve got to get going. I’m catching a train up to Mount Kisco.”

“You’re goink?” says Tatiana. “We chust got here.”

“I have to,” I say as I head for the door.

“It’s because of zis Lyla, isn’t it? Don’t be so attached. Come on. Can’t you stay for chust a little while? I’ll give you nice rub.” Tatiana reaches over and puts her hands on my neck. “You don’t haf to sleep wiz me. I’m not attached. I chust want to give you rub. It will be a spiritual experience, I’m saying?”

“No, no. Look, I’m sorry. I’m going to jump out of my skin,” I say. “I’ll call you real soon. Tomorrow night, maybe. Okay?”

“You are a pain,” Tatiana says.

LET’S BREAK THE FOURTH WALL: don’t you hate those pop movies that are all about, usually, some private detective hero who, while he’s stalking the bad guys, has his hands full fending off clinging, adoring women? I *hate* those films. Yes, there are clingy, obsessive women, there was Calypso with Odysseus, but there are in the world, if anyone wants my opinion, just as many clinging obsessive men and this is never portrayed on the screen except as some kind of anomaly. One day, it hit me: these films are the result, the manifestations of, the young screenwriter’s fantasies. Nothing but fantasy. This kid screenwriter from Ohio or Nebraska or New York City doesn’t seem to understand that even Brad Pitt has had his heart broken. John F. Kennedy, Jr. had his heart broken. It’s his fantasy, the screenwriter’s fantasy, apparently, to portray and thereby

glorify male heroes who can never be hurt, not even by gunfire or ruptured love.

We all love *The Maltese Falcon* and *Casablanca*, but it all really began—this screenwriter fantasy bullshit—with Bogart in these very films, or maybe it really began with Tiresias being blinded for saying women enjoy sex more than men . . . . in any case, by *The Big Sleep*, Bogart or Philip Marlowe, is literally besieged in nearly every scene by ravenous, demanding women who won't take 'no' and the human interest, as a result, is seriously compromised if not depleted altogether. The heroine, if she even rises to that level, throws herself at the hero because maybe *she* will be able to finally understand him and calm the raging tempest in his soul but, alas, poor Slick, he's usually too distracted, too messed up, too busy solving crimes, apprehending enemies of the state and fending off the advances of a dozen other women—his streetwise soliloquies and lamentations punctuated by an endless stream of obscenities and imprecations—to really love the girl the ways she wants to be loved, I mean, if I were from another planet and I had to form an impression of the mating habits of humans based on what I saw in movies and TV, I would think that women are the super-aggressive gender when it comes to reproduction and romance and that men are nothing but passive and irresistible Ken dolls: discreet, well-dressed and heartless. Adolescent nonsense. The music of masturbation. 007. Stories not for men or women, but for boys. That's what these films are: stories for *boys*. Not like the Beatniks. At the same time, Tatiana really was and is as

portrayed here. She really does talk this way and act this way, so, let's get back to "the present" . . .

"Hit and run—dat is all you ever do," she says with some anger, trailing behind me. "Don't you want nice rub? Dat would be good, hmm?"

I refuse.

"You are pain in dee neck," she says as she unfastens the three locks on her apartment door. "Well, call me, tomorrow or next night, okay? Maybe we can get togezer in evening. I'm patient," she says, opening the door. "I'm not attached, really. Everysing is all right wiz me. I rely on my inner resources; on dee teachings I imbibe from dee guru. This is all a dream and I'm just going to witness zis latest affront to my dignity. Go ahead. Leave. Leave me here alone. I don't need zis drama. I'll stay here and meditate or go upstate to ashram. I can be by myself. I don't need ozer people. I don't need some *man* to make my life miserable. You sink I am attached to you just because you used to be hot macho lover? Hear dat? *Used* to be. You'll see. I just need to adjust my sinking and everysing in dee manifest world will take care of itself—I'm saying? This is fine. I am absolutely at peace wiz myself. Only an unenlightened person needs someone else to be fulfilled—I'm saying? After all," she says, forcing a smile as I get ready to exit, "what is dee body?"

TWO

What Would Blau Do?

"Mutual Forgiveness of each Vice
Such are the Gates of Paradise."
—Blake, For the Sexes

The lobby of the Roosevelt Hotel isn't especially cold but my palms are like ice as I sit on the ottoman, waiting for Lyla in my black suit jacket and gold silk tie over my only white dress cotton shirt. I want to look good. Walked from my freelance gig at West 52nd Street and Sixth Avenue, crossed town to that Grand Central nexus, noisy and crowded Madison Avenue, Vanderbilt Place and Park Avenue where yellow cabs still line up to transport suits and brief cases uptown, east and west, and downtown. As indicated by the portraits in the lobby and bar, the hotel was named for Theodore Roosevelt, not for Eleanor or Franklin or their relationship, so it's kind of ironic that this monument to the Rough Rider and Trust Buster is known as the Grand Dame of Madison Avenue. And it is grand. Lyla isn't about to stay at a Holiday Inn, don't you know. The chandeliers are shiny, effulgent, godawesome; the wood is varnished oak, the carpets are plush and deep like the wine dark sea.

I'm nervous, having not seen the Lady of Leesburg for nearly five years and I'm getting colder by the minute. What would Blau do? He always has the right word, the right gift. His good friends, Les Harris, Charlie Adler and Steve Lang, also sons of the Holocaust, are like that, too. Suave. *Raffine.* Impeccably dressed. Chocolates, white lilies, a book of poems. I'm kind of in awe of them and their sense of style. Blau reminds me of Robert DeNiro as the young Vito Corleone in *Godfather II*, even looks like him a little. Still a poor working man in Little Italy, DeNiro comes home with just an apple for his wife. You all know the scene. Takes the apple out from a folded newspaper, rubs it of black print, and places it on the tiny tenement dining room table for her. That's Blau. He proposed to his wife in Paris for heaven's sake.

What would Blau do now? It's just after 6 P.M. What would he say? ***If ya did her good, she'll be back,*** he'd say. ***Your worst times are your best. That's when the flame burns the brightest. It's the*** **desire** ***for completeness that makes for completeness***, he'd say. Something like that. And Blau always brought a gift. ***The key is generosity. Gallantry. Like Dante said. Just be generous with a lady and you'll affect her on a cellular, essential, interdimensional, subatomic, level. Makes the wings of her heart flutter. Like she's being protected,*** he'd say in his Flushing, Queens patois. Still, if you were me, a strange, subterranean mixture of fear and desire lives inside you now. You're not nervous in anticipation of any quarrel or great confrontation. Not afraid that you won't be able to perform, or that you're too fat, nothing like that, even if you have gained a paunch in the intervening nears, no, you're near to trembling because Lyla messed you up so profoundly five and six years ago that you sought help from a hypnotherapist. You wanted to be deprogrammed, de-Lyla'd as the Lady put it herself, hypnotized back to sanity. You're vulnerable to say the least.

One of our last arguments went like this:

"Wait, are you saying that God *approves* of slavery? Are you nuts?"

"It says in the Bible. In the Epistles: 'slaves be obedient to your masters.'"

"So, it was immoral for slaves to run away to freedom?"

"*Ah* don't know. Maybe."

"Even if the slaves are white and the slave owners are black?" She was silent because she knew that I had her. (I like to win arguments.) "If you became a slave and I came to free you, you'd say 'no sir. I'm a slave and it's immoral for me to be disobedient to my master. My black master.' That's what you'd say, right?"

So long ago. And Tatiana's virtually forgotten now. Gone. Like a withered plant next to the full blush of Lyla's blood-red lips. Paint it with magic . . . see it. Like an angelic figure from a Depression era film, harp strings in the background, Lyla appears on the plush Persian carpet in a black business suit, flamenco brown hair resting on her shoulders. We embrace, a quick kiss on the cheek.

"Oooh, your hands are *cold*," she says, taking them in hers.

"It's this lobby," I say. "They must still have the air-conditioning on or something. Where's Stephanie?"

"She didn't come. I'm here on business but I'll tell you all about it. Where do you want to go for dinner?"

I steer the two of us toward Restaurant Row—West 46th Street between Eighth and Ninth Avenues—remarkable for its lack of parking ramps and anything modern—that's old Restaurant Row, a procession of brownstones and townhouses, a lovely and charming anachronism near Hell's Kitchen. Like sunbonnets on display at Victoria's Secret.

"Would you *mond* very much if *ah* took your arm?" Lyla says not looking at me, rhythm of her voice in sync with our steps. The deep-set eyes, the naturally black hair. The subdued smile. Shiny white skin and self-assured stride. Feels like I *know* this woman, not just I used to be her lover five years ago, but she's family. I *know* her. "*Ah* just need you to steady me," she says. I take her hand instead and we walk across Broadway, then on mythic sidewalks, passing the French restaurant, the Italian one, the Irish pub, the Dixieland place and, strolling hand-in-hand in our finery, I'm thinking that we might make an attractive couple if that's not too immodest, then, suddenly, I stop walking, turn, and kiss Lyla on her crimson red lips.

"I had to do that," I say.

"Well, *ah* didn't expect anything less," she says with a laugh. "You don't waste any *tom*."

I take her to an outdoor café and order white wine. It's becoming cool, but there's no wind.

"So, you're here on business?"

"Yes, I'm with Central Florida Legal Services."

"Legal services? You mean . . ."

"Uh-hunh. Poor and indigent. Most of *mah* clients are African-American but not all. You'd be surprised at the stories they have to tell. The burden that some of *mah* clients carry around is so great. So great. The system is entirely corrupt and racist. There are so many innocent men and women in prison and I just felt that I had to do something."

You could have knocked me over with a sprig of baby's breath. No, really. Lyla fighting the good fight? And in Central Florida?

"What brings you to New York, then?" I ask Lyla as the waitress brings over the wine.

"Well, one of *mah* clients is a New Yorker who skipped down to Orlando. You know about Florida, the place to escape your debts. I got tired of faxing and e-mailing back and forth with Scheck, Barry Scheck, so I thought I'd come up to see him. And to see you, too. How are yooooo?"

"Barry Scheck?" I repeat the name with surprise and near-reverence. Mister Defend-the-Innocent. "Lyla, this is some kind of miracle. Really. You've come all the way up to New York for *habeas corpus* claims?"

"Let me tell you, I went through some terrible terrible years. Terrible pain. Like a bad dream. I was dead, really. But then, I asked myself, 'do you want to live or die?' You either kill yourself or decide you're not going to be depressed anymore. And you have to decide moment by moment. And what was I doing anyway? Living this fantasy life dreamed up by men who wear navy blue jackets and penny loafers with no socks. Drinking champagne for breakfast, Thanksgiving dinner at the country club. It's like I woke up suddenly." Lyla's radiant. Her deep brown Spanish, Scots-Irish eyes are larger than her head; they extend out to Ninth Avenue. She takes a sip of wine. "You have to make that decision over and over. Every second, every moment, you make the decision. Life or death. Yes or no. Happiness or despair." The waitress comes to take our order and, afterward, Lyla resumes talking. "You really have to come out of yourself and start focusing on others.

So, I decided to start giving back. You know how I love Stephanie and *ah* ache to see her happy, but I will admit to you, I had no idea how pervasive injustice is. It's not enough just to care about your family. Well, we're all family, really. Don't ah sound like a kook? Who would have thunk it, right? I have you to thank for this."

"Me?"

"Mmmm." Lyla takes another sip of wine. "It was you who kept saying, or kept browbeating me, I should say," she laughs, almost embarrassed, "you were the one who forced me to look at my real beliefs. *Ah* had to stop deceiving myself. I'm a better person because of you, dear . . ."

I'm beaming. Proud. Flattered. Dying to jump her once we get back to the hotel. You would be, too. Not only is Lyla still beautiful and seductive, she's become a whole person, a woman instead of a caricature, and it's dark now. After dinner, we walk hand in hand through Times Square, through busy traffic, past Broadway theaters, the Majestic, the Neil Simon, past the Algonquin and the Iroquois Hotels and the Harvard Club to the Madison Club Lounge back at the Roosevelt Hotel, where we order cocktails.

"So, how is Esmé?" Lyla asks as I stir my gin and tonic. Her eyes are wide, expectant. "You Don't Know Me," a great old song oozes through some speakers and the room smells like lemons, lime and perfume.

"Oh, okay," I say, clearing my throat. "She's okay. She's still high-strung and neurotic."

"You two gonna get married?"

"No," I say dropping the word like an ax into wood. There's a significant pause. Even though she's gained a tiny bit of weight in her face and waist, Lyla's almost dangerous now, young Ava Gardner dangerous; Hedy Lamarr-Black Madonna-Little Annie Frank dangerous. Over her right shoulder is a portrait of Teddy Roosevelt. The bar area is filled with blue business suits and black one-piece zip-up dresses, blonde hair.

"How is your beatnik book?" Lyla asks. "The one about the beatniks and the priest?" She opens her compact mirror. Applies lipstick. I wonder what she *sees*?

"It's going okay," I say, "I heard from the Oblates. From the Catholics in Massachusetts. You have some pictures, you said. Photos of Stephanie and her boyfriend?"

"Yes, *ah* want you to see them but, oh darn, they're upstairs. Do you want to come with me up to *mah* room? It'll only take a second." She puts her effects in her purse.

Tatiana had been prescient. My little poison heart races, stirs like the wings of a sparrow, as I pay for the drinks and the two of us make for the elevator under the revolving ceiling fans, and up on the 17th floor, Lyla asks if I would *mond* very much if she slips into a camisole, then emerges from the bathroom in a shiny black thing over faded dungarees and I'm trembling again because Lyla is standing by the queen-size bed and smiling. And the perfume. A scent from the dream life seeping into the room like silky gaslight.

"Sweetheart, let me show you my tattoo," Lyla says before unfastening the top of her pants and lifting up her black camisole to reveal the blue dragon or snake inked on to her lower abdomen, just above black pubic hair. "What do you think? Isn't it nice? *Ah* had it done at a place over in Winter Park. It didn't cost much at all." Lyla lifts the camisole up a little more and I can see her lacy black bra. She jerks to one side and suddenly the top section of her right nipple—what, mathematically, would be called a chord—is exposed. Just a little bit of the circumference, a section of that deathless nipple, that aureole, just a pink and purple Islamic moon crescent, not much surface area but still a portion of eternity too great for the eye of man, pops out of her bra, a hemisphere, a semi-circle atop black frilly lace. I lunge at her and we kiss furiously for the first time in five years. I take off my suit jacket and throw it on the carpet. Her kisses are still sweet like manna.

"*Ah* never could resist *yooo*," Lyla says as I bring her over to the bed and probe her tattoo with my left hand. "No, no, dear, no." Lyla protests breathlessly, putting her hand between her legs. "We can't do that."

"Why not?"

"Because I'm engaged."

"What?"

"I'm engaged. See?" She lifts up her left hand to show me a diamond engagement ring. How did I miss that one? All those facets . . .

"For how long?" I ask. We both sit up on the queen-size luxury bed. I brush hair from her eyes.

"A few months. *Ah* know 'im from grade school. We just ran into each other outside the insurance office in Leesburg." Lyla points in some cardinal direction. She always referred to her personal landmarks as if they were just a mile away.

"And you're in love with him?" Lyla looks down like a lonely orphan girl, like a chastened child. "Are you passionate with him? Tell me the truth."

"He's a good man. He's so kind to Stephanie. He's good to me."

"Then, what is this 'come up to my room and see my tattoo' and all that?"

"*Ah* know, *ah* know. It's just that with you, *ah* had more passion than . . . that's the most passion *ah*'ve ever had. And *ah* will always love you. Always."

"I never stopped loving you," I say. She kisses me on my face like dew settling on grass. "I don't understand it. You hurt me so much. You almost killed me, you know that? I even went to a hypnotist to forget you."

"*Ah* remember. To get de-Lyla'd."

"Yeh. Samson'd and de-Lyla'd. I was in hell. I'm serious. You almost killed me."

"*Ah* am so sorry. *Ah* was so afraid you'd leave me for some young girl. *Ah* was in such pain, too." She looks down at the bedspread then looks up at me. "What brought you out of hell?"

"'M still in the wilderness."

I take her face in my hands and kiss her again. I guide her hand down to my crotch. "See how you affect me?" She touches me down there, over my dress pants, but only briefly. I'm just beginning to notice how rumpled is my only fancy white cotton shirt and my gold silk tie.

"If *ah* weren't engaged to be married, we'd be makin' love right now," the woman says softly. "But you should go. You must go. Please. Before *ah* get into trouble." We kiss again. I'm granite-hard. Her tongue and lips are manna, strawberry and cinnamon. D.H. Lawrence would say a flame was licking my body, from my balls up to the crown of my head and he'd be right. "Go now," she says but she's smiling.

"I have to call Esmé anyway," I say.

"Gotta check in with Mama, huh? Does she ask about your liaisons and soirées?" Lyla's voice is like a quiet prayer.

"I've given her lots of clues." I chuckle. "Seriously, I tell her everything. Almost everything. Hey, where are those pictures of Stephanie?" A stalling device: maybe we'll get in one more kiss.

"Oh, yes." Lyla stands up and walks over to one of her many suitcases and retrieves a snapshot of her daughter and a young man of about 24 or 25.

"Do you like him?"

"Evan? He's a good boy. He's bright and has already demonstrated his wisdom." She sits back down on the bed.

"What do you mean?"

"*Ah* mean it's already obvious that he derives strength from hard times and that he knows that it's not about him. Now, go, darling. Please go."

I give Lyla another quick kiss, grab my suit jacket and head for the elevator. I walk briskly through the lobby, out the doors on to Madison Avenue into the shadowless night and I begin to cry.

Never give all the heart.

THREE

Don't Be Afraid

"Magical realism? We used to call it poetry." —Joshua Moses

Cry, cry, cry, not like a baby, not lots of real tears, gasping for air crying, but, there's a coldness on the heart as I get on the F train near the big library, going uptown. Cup of desire. It's not loneliness, but rather, the fear of it. *When will you answer me, Blessed Lady? Saint Thérèse? When will you intercede and answer me with love, with passion and compassion, oh, Queen of the Atonement?? I'm calling out to you . . . how can you* ***praise*** *and* not *give* ***all*** *the heart? . . .* Lyla, Lyla, Lyla. Too much eternity. Too much earth. Why don't you forget about her and take a train to Lowell? Or hitchhike? Hear that confession? Stop making excuses and end this life cycle? Only one reason:

WHO REALLY WANTS TO STOP SINNING? Who really wants to be sane, after all? And the damn e-mail said that "he (Father Tom*)* ***is buried on the grounds here***." Buried on the grounds here!

Tatiana's sympathetic when, with almost unforgivable martian gall, I arrive at her door at about 10:30, although she does greet me with a kind of knowing smirk, a world-weary Cheshire cat quarter-smile full of piss and vinegar.

"So, she dumped you, eh?" the woman remarks as I drop like a lead ball on to her sofa, exhausted. "And now, you've come back to me. You know, I should throw you right out, don't you? I should have thrown you out long time ago."

"I know."

"And you got all dolled up, yes?" Tatiana walks toward me and sits down in her favorite chair across from the sofa. I'm despondent. "All dressed up in silk tie and jacket. Ha! Silk tie I bought for you. Yes, I remember it. Bought it at Macy's. Poor baby. You're so needy."

"*I*'m needy?"

"Well, yes, I'm needy, too, I admit it, but you sink I'm so attached to you when I'm not any longer. It's nothink but pain. Passion is pain. I'm telling you. In dee end, it's a vanity and self-involvement, I'm saying? You have to come out of yourself. You don't sink zis puny little self, your ego, is your true self, do you?" Tatiana says with a guttural laugh that recalls Pixie Morningstar. "For years, I *sought* America was paradise but I see now how unfair and unjust it can be. You are a self-involved country. Narcissistic. And narcissism leads to insanity. Really, it does. You go crazy. Ever notice dat schizophrenics and crazy people are completely self-absorbed and paranoid? Someone is on *dare* trail, keeping a file on dem like Soviet Union? Even *doze* people who are pathologically afraid of germs are really being egocentric. Don't get near *me*."

"Yeh, but you've been almost powerfully paranoid of late yourself."

"Yes, I have," Tatiana admits. The blue veins in her hands make them look like wet autumn leaves. "But I can witness it, too."

"This wise woman, Maggie, said that a book is your way of saying to the world 'this is who I am' and she's written four of them, all very successful. Archie says that, too."

"Well, who are you? Why are you so distraught, anyway?" Tatiana asks, calling from the kitchen. "Lyla? You really wanted hot date, no? What, she put you off and now you are down in dumps?"

"I guess I did have my expectations," I say. "I mean, all I'm doing these days is workin' and jerkin'."

"Well, you had your chance wiz me . . ."

"I know, I know," I say, running out of breath, head back on the cotton pillow. "But, there's something else." Suddenly, I recall, have an image in my mind of the outdoor noon-time memorial service I recently attended for a graduate of Grover Cleveland High School in Buffalo. Killed in Iraq. Class of '03. In Basra. The flag. The speeches. The uniforms. Taps. "*Those kids, those kids . . . killed on the sands of Babylon . . . When you're dead, you're dead, I guess.* Gone. *Unless.*"

"Unless?" Tania repeats from the kitchen, her voice quietly echoing as if bouncing off trees in a forest clearing. "Unless what?"

"Unless soul clap its hands and sing, and louder sing . . . for every tatter in its mortal dress . . ."

Tatiana brings the teapot and two cups to her coffee table and sits, pouring. "What? Are you thinking about dyink? You're morbid suddenly? You know, you may haf past life issues, I'm saying? Your left leg went out on you last summer. Let me look. Yes, it's still swollen. You probably had some accident in past life and it has caught up wiz you. So, what are you doing to do? Die to become free? No. You'll just haf dee same lessons to learn in next life."

"Will I have the same I?"

"What is wiz you?" Tatiana's dark Tartar brows are furrowed like an eagle's. Impatient. Disappointed. It's like five thousand years of Vedic wisdom weigh in on my question, borne of interminable, earth-bound self-involvement, you might say. *Have you built your ship of death . . . ?*

"Dee I is I, not you, I'm saying?" Tatiana says. "What you say 'I am' to is not *you*. Don't get all caught up wiz I. Gott is what matters. Gott is not your errand boy to make all your dreams come true. You hang out wiz these New Agers who tell you Gott can bring you money and sex and nice home in country but dat is vanity. You're not so great. You're not so evil, either. So, come out of yourself and relax a little. You're a warrior not a worrier. I'm not perfect. I have pains and wants but I accept sings as they are. Acceptance is very very important. Remember Govinda? He comes from cheap Scottish family and he would never pay for my dinner. Now, he's very generous and it's very attractive. There is nothink more sexy than the revised man, right? It's very attractive when someone transforms but your essential self never changes. But you haf to have acceptance."

"I revised you, Tanichka,"

"Me?"

"Remember? I told you for years to grow your hair long. You used to have it cut short like a helmet and now look at you. I've made you beautiful."

"You did?" she laughs. "Well, I'm glad you sink I'm beautiful. And you made me go out and buy black teddy, remember?"

"Tanichka, you're a true friend," I say, emptying my teacup. "Honestly. A real friend." Tatiana brushes her shoulder-length hair from her forehead. She can be self-defeating and contradictory and contrary—who isn't?—but she has wisdom. She's a plumed serpent in a rent-controlled apartment. We first met at one of the shiny satanic law firms on Lexington Avenue and, later, worked together on the 57th floor of World Trade Center One. Haven't called her in a while.

"Friend. Beautiful," says Tatiana, "very interesting but how come you didn't make an intention for Lyla? Or did you?"

"That's a good question. I must have forgotten. I was seduced by seduction. Funny. Or could it be that everything turned out for the best? She's a new woman. She remained loyal to her fiancé. Well, for the most part."

"Now, what are you going to do wiz all zis power, hmmm?" Tatiana asks like a mischievous child, open palms on the arms of her chair. "Did you ever sink you could intend somesing bad and it may come true?"

"Desire, desire," I reply. "Desire is the key. You're right, though. The falcon might not hear the falconer. Hey, can I sleep here?"

"Tonight?"

"Well, yeh."

"You're not goink back up to Mount Kisco? There are trains leaving Grand Central until late."

"I know, but I'm tired. Is it all right?"

"Well, okay. I'll get dee mattress from dee closet and some sheets. You can sleep here in livink room."

"Well, Tania, uhm, I was really kind of hoping I could sleep in your bedroom," I say. "With you."

"Wiz me?" she's more than taken aback. "What do you sink I am? You strike out wiz Lyla and come here expecting me to be your concubin?" She pronounces the word with a short "i." "You haf to have lots more money for me to be your concubin. Go get train up to Mount Kisco . . ."

"No . . ." I'm obstinate, hoping Tatiana will submit to the Beast or that she'll participate joyously, take infinite pleasure in one of those dreamy ether-infused fucks, a thousand nights of love, when she loses all her defenses and says 'I'll do anything you want' and you come *all* the way out and go *all* the way back in for a *loooong* time and she just kind of melts, like a snowflake, at the touch, as Updike put it. Who *is* that woman beneath or beside or on top of me? She was solemn and daunting in her suit jacket and pleated skirt but now she's on her back, naked, and has become a baby, an innocent baby whispering 'I'll do anything you say.' *She's become a completely different person. That's lovemaking. A most curious alchemy. From the crown to the kingdom.* What's that rondeau emanating from her hair? That aubade? That fado? Lovers parting at dawn. The alba . . . She touches my hand. The gopi handmaiden. The lady. Just to be in her presence . . .

Tatiana stands up and angrily takes my teacup, places it on a saucer shaped tray with the other cup and the teapot, and marches like a Hessian into the kitchen. "Is zis what you intended?" she asks from the kitchen. "Did you make an intention for me? Well, I'm not going along!"

"All right, all right . . ."

"So, are you stayink here or are you going back up to Joshua's? If you stay here, you sleep in livink room and behave yourself and don't dare come creeping like fox into my room in middle of night, I'm saying? I am only interested in being a celibate from now on. You must sink of me as you sister. I am not hot Slovak lover anymore, I'm saying? I am your sister."

I stand up. "Tanichka, I'm sorry. You really have been a friend and I've abused that. Really and truly. I'm sorry. Let me get the mattress and sheets. You're absolutely safe. Don't worry about it, okay?"

Even in the worst of times, Tatiana's place had been safe haven. The aroma of incense is ever in the air, the guru photos, though overbearing, are colorful and exotic, the little Vedic shrines, the bookcases filled with Balzac, Hamsun, Dostoevsky, Stendahl, Flaubert and, of course, Dreiser's *Sister Carrie*, make you feel as though you've found sanctuary. I take off my silk tie and rumpled white shirt and place them on the wicker chair under the huge picture window overlooking Central Park. Manhattan looks like a chocolate birthday cake with lit multi-colored candles. I unbuckle my belt and slip off the black dress pants and try to maintain their creases as I place them on top of the other clothes on the wicker chair. Tatiana'll surely have a T-shirt for me, maybe one without a guru's face on it.

Now, pretend that you're me again. As you're dozing off in the dark, you're touched in the middle of your chest by the wings of a warm, comfortable dream-bird, maybe more like a butterfly, and in your sleep, you feel that your consciousness has been elevated in some way, something in the manner of a vision, as dumb as that might sound. Can you see him? It's Hubert in his vanilla-colored beret and pond-green shades. You'd be expecting profound words and insights from the man, especially as he'd gone to the other side, so you'd ask, "Hubert, what's it like to be dead?" and let's say he shrugs just as he had on that fearful summer night so long ago. He doesn't look happy. A shrug? The voluble, eloquent, bombastic, ever-opinionated Hubert assays the subjects of life, death and immortality from the fucking beyond with a SHRUG of his gigantic shoulders???

"Hey, Hubert. Hubert. I miss the old days," you'd hear yourself saying. "Hanging out in the city. Running around the bars downtown. Tommy Milano's, Tim Riley's . . . the jukebox. Your place in Queens. You were Solomon. The fire's center. Before the yuppies took over everything. I would have ended up a grad school liberal if not for you . . ."

Then, suddenly, Hubert would become a child. A little bit like big-eyed Emmett Till, a little bit of a teddy bear; a schoolboy, clean-shaven, holding his textbooks, no beret, no shades. Hurt by the death of his mother but happy. Hubert would utter a word or two about Lowell, something unintelligible, but then he'd clearly say "don't be afraid," and "forgive Moses," before dissolving again into the comfort of the opaque night.

FOUR

E-mail to Joshua M

JoMo:

Did you know that when the Beatles performed on Ed Sullivan, not one crime was committed in the US?

The Beat will end the terror!

Rhythm restores order to the world (not routine, daddy-o, but rhythm).

Strike a note, a chord, and a resounding chord will be struck. Inside skull as vast as outside skull. Gyres run on . . .

Am really tired. Drove most of the night. Write soon.

Your humble & obedient servant . . .

P.S. Who opened for Patti Smith when you saw her at CBGB's? I was thinking it was Television, not Suicide. Fuck you.

P.S.S. Hubert appeared to me in a dream two nights ago and said "forgive Moses." What does this mean?

E-mail from Joshua Moses

Yo, Dude:

As I expected, you've gone over the deep end. First of all, I never saw Patti Smith at CBGB's, I saw her at Cornell, remember? I went with Christina to see Messner and we all went to the show together. It was the first time Christina and I actually slept together. During the concert, Patti left the stage and walked into the audience to watch her own show. She stood right next to me, like a spectator at her own gig. That was wild. She was getting out of her ego. An out-of-body experience. And Patti's brother, Todd, was passing out ear plugs before the show to protect our ears. It was a loud concert.

Listen: When I was working on that *moshav* in Israel, near the Sea of Galilee, my boss, Jerry, had me slaughter a pig, which I'd never done before and haven't done since. I slaughtered the pig one morning and Jerry came out to tell me that some famous artist had been killed in New York. I heard about John Lennon when I was in Israel. Maybe you're right. Maybe Reagan stepped into the White House over the dead body of John Lennon, I don't know. I remember that I stayed in Israel that Christmas. Miriam joined me and, as a matter of fact, that was the first time *we* slept together. We went to a Christmas service at the Church of the Holy Sepulchre. Now, here are two Jews, going to the Church of the Nativity in Bethlehem, then to the Holy Sepulchre for Christmas services in the old part of Jerusalem.

At the Christmas service, we're sort of ducking and burrowing our way through tunnels to the get to the chapel. Miriam bent down to scoot in and some monk pinches her on the ass. On Christmas Eve. In Jerusalem, at the grave of Christ, a pinch on the ass. Miriam went back to New York and I went up to the Golan Heights to work. Before Mim left, though, she gave me one of the first walkmans. The Arab kids we were staying with wanted to show their grandfather the walkman because they knew he'd say it was cursed. One of the kids, the rough-edged one, stole the walkman later and all it had on it were Beatles songs. Maybe the hood who stole the walkman will bring peace to the world with some obscure precedent from Islamic law. They're a very litigious, lawyer or mullah-based culture. Islam is a very legal religion, more legalistic than Judaism. He'll persuade the world that peace must reign, that the Jews have a legal right to Jerusalem, because he heard "All You Need is Love" over and over again on a stolen tape.

Can't stop babbling, babbling, and coughing, still, if you'll allow . . . It's very possible that Muslim culture will have a greater influence on us than any feeble attempt on our part to 'democratize' the

Middle East. Caliphate at Baghdad. The Persian and Arab poets. Astronomers. It's a pretty straight line from Ibn Turfail to John Locke and tabula rasa to the Declaration of Independence, if you follow my meaning. If we're headed for another Sixties, Islam is the keynote, instead of Hindus and Buddhism. Rumi's the man, right? A Sufi like Bin Laden. And you can forget about democracy in China.

To what, then, shall we compare this generation, and what are they like? They are like children sitting in the marketplace, calling out to one another. "We piped and you didn't dance. We gave our VH-1 confession and you didn't cry." Pull-eeze. The electric charge of our music was too much gravity for our parents' generation, anyway. Too loud to end terror and reverse entropy. I mean, let's not lose perspective. Blau told me that his father just didn't understand all the grieving over Lennon. 'I don't understand all zis fuss about John Lennon,' Zollie said after the murder. But if you'd spent your high school years at Auschwitz, you'd probably think the same thing.

Remember to RSVP for Marly's bat mitzvah. Bring Esmé.

Selah!

Your humble & obedient servant . . .

P.S. Hey, you were right: CBGB's is now a men's clothing store. No more CBGB's. No more Bottom Line. Or Gerde's Folk City. Or Chumley's. No more Tim Riley's Bar. Just dust and echoes. Gone.

P.S.S. Did you know that there was no word for 'blue' in ancient Greece?

P.S.S.S. Forgive me for what?

P.S.S.S.S. Lowell? When?

FIVE

A Nice Life

My muse by no means deals in fiction:
She gathers a repertory of facts,
Of course, with some reserve and slight restriction,
But mostly sings of human things and acts—
Lord Byron, Don Juan

I get back to Esmé's in damn western New York at about 9:30 or 9:40 but, strange for her, she isn't home. On a Sunday night. She'd left a note on the dining room table.

B,

I'm at the beach. Will probably spend the night.There are tacos in the fridge. Will you be around. Tomorrow night? Come by for Jeopardy!

E

I've begun renting my own apartment about four miles away but I'm still crashing at Esmé's most nights especially since the October storm which messed up my heating and electricity. All right, I'm a little attached . . . Still no check from FEMA, either. The beach is her mother's place just over the border in Ontario and I set my overnight bag down on the pine wood floor and look out from the back window in the dining room, to the bare tree branches in the tiny backyard, lit up by a neighbor's floodlight and think: the landscape here will never be the same. Those poor bent and ravaged maples, spruces, elms and crabapple trees, damaged like beaten children. A freaky autumn snowstorm, freaky even for this Great Lakes town and region, has taken its toll. Gabriel is the angel of winter but he hadn't even arrived when the snow came to set on the fully leafed trees. I walk to the refrigerator and peer in. I decide not to eat and walk up the creaky wooden stairs to the middle room where the computer is.

I take off the red windbreaker that Joshua Moses gave me, the one with the cable TV network labels stitched all over the sleeves, and sit down at the computer. The web site for substitute teachers is full. I'll have work all week and next week, too. Good. Why not do some writing before going to sleep? I'm jumpy, and memories, ideas and fulminations spill out of and over me like water over the side of a bathtub, if you can picture *that*. Almost effortlessly, as if channeling, I type up or input about four or five pages before my eyes give out on me. I'm pretty sure I sent out an e-mail, too. To Joshua Moses. When I wake up, it's 12:30—I'd fallen asleep in front of the computer screen—and I virtually sleep-walk to bed.

It's tough getting up and going early next morning but the fourth graders at P.S. 19, the Native American magnet school, are always great, worth suffering through the morning. For the social studies lesson, they're alert and cooperative.

"OK, kids," I ask them, "when did African-Americans get the right to vote?" A little boy raises his hand.

"When Bill Clinton became president?" he answers, his voice trailing off uncertainly. God, that's funny. The boy is serious. The names of these kids are great, too. In addition to natives, there are many Vietnamese students—Nancy Nguyen, Tommy Nguyen, Cindy Nguyen—and Muslim kids, Omar, Ahmed, Fatima, Mohammed, even Samson. (At Lafayette High School, my dad's alma mater, I had a student named Ulysses S. Grant.) It's fun to see the little girls in burkas and head shawls flirting with the East Side boys. The native names are remarkable, too, like mythology: Naomi Ground, Chad Nephew, Lafayette Keyes and, my favorite, Christopher Two-Guns. I drive back to Esmé's, arriving there just before 3 P.M. and am surprised to find her home. I walk up the creaky old steps and find her in the middle room.

"You're home early," I say to Esmé who's standing by the computer with her arms folded. The First Lady of Willoughby has a steely look on her face and her jaw is set tight like a tiger's upon siting prey.

"So, you did a little writing last night, eh?" she says tartly in her aristocratic voice.

"What?"

She walks two steps toward me, high heels click-clacking on the old pine wood floor. Then she gazes at the computer screen and reads: " 'Like a beast, I lunge at her and we kiss furiously for the first time in five years.' That's good. Very well done."

"What? *That*?" I protest. "That's fiction. Come on . . ."

"There *is* no fiction," she hisses. "Remember?"

"Look, this is all about 'you' and 'he' here. Let me scroll down." I reach for the mouse.

" 'You' means 'I' and 'I' means *you*," Esmé says pointing at my chest. "You met Lyla in a hotel and were 'dying to jump her'? You know, I take a lot from you but Lyla? Have you completely lost your mind?" I stand motionless like Joshua's iguana not even gesturing or blinking. "You left the computer on. Did you forget?" Esmé continues. "Look, you want to meet up with that whore in some hotel, you go ahead, but you're not staying here and you're not going to write about it on my computer. You're such a cunt."

"A cunt?" I repeat, blinking finally. "That doesn't make sense. That would be like *me* calling *you* a prick. It makes no sense."

"I don't care, you're not staying here anymore." She stretches her right arm out, perpendicular to her svelte ballerina frame and opens her palm. "Give me the key," she says. "Give me the key to my house."

"Oh, come on . . ." I protest sheepishly.

"You've got your own place . . ."

"But the furnace is practically shot and it's almost November," I say, voice becoming pleading and whiny and reed-thin. "It's all electric hook-up and the house wasn't even wired right. Let me just stay here until it's okay." Esmé sits on the old Kittinger chair underneath a framed Allentown Arts Festival poster and relaxes her jaw.

"You had a nice life here," she says evenly. "Nothing's perfect but you've had a nice life. You *had* to mess it up." How beautiful she is, I'm thinking, with her blonde hair pulled back from her forehead, her pink button-down sweater, black mini-skirt and black stockings. A sprite in an electric forest. "I know you see your fuck buddy,Tatiana, in the city. That doesn't even bother me. But that crocodile. Lyla. Ugh."

"She's changed, you know . . ."

"Oh, yes. A new woman. You probably want to take credit for revising her mind or something. Well, I don't buy it. Charity doesn't cover up for sins."

"Esmé, you're an atheist," I say, "and it's not charity."

"Well, pro bono or legal services don't . . . look, can't you stay at Archie's tonight?"

"It's cold and drafty there and that couch is hard."

"Lyla. I don't get it," Esmé continues almost obsessively, nose wrinkling like a kitten. "What? You just like her big breasts and her Southern belle act? She's bad news. She has age spots. And all she ever brought you was hurt and pain. Remember? I remember her in law school. How unreal does it get?"

I sure don't like hurting Esmé but I don't feel guilty. Bad about lying, yes, but I'm glad all this has come out and, who knows? Maybe I left the computer on and the file open purposely to force things to a crisis.

"Could you explain something to me?" I begin, gentle like a clergyman. "Someday, tell me how you can turn a man away, I mean, to the point where you won't even kiss him, then expect him not to kiss anyone else. Someday, please explain that. I've been crying inside for years now. Do you know what that's like? Crying inside?" She's silent, looking straight ahead. Esmé's the snow. The wind and the snow. Softer now, I begin again. "I'll get the heat and everything at my place going tomorrow. I think Johnny Half Breed knows all about that stuff. He says he can fix anything except his two marriages." I laugh. Esmé remains silent. "I'm going to drive around and give you your key in the morning, okay?" I leave Esmé in the room alone.

That night, after a drive through the old neighborhoods, I walk across the old hallway upstairs to Esmé's room, to what used to be our bedroom, feet snapping like punctured bubble wrap on the wooden floor, and slip into bed with her. She doesn't stir, is sleeping deeply like a child. Beautiful dreamer. Her breath is steady and light like ebb tide. *Esmé, Esmé, my love and my squalor. Queen of my song.* I kiss her on her pale velvet neck. In the morning, before sunrise, I light a stick of incense downstairs and boil water for a hard-boiled egg. I take a shower, then walk to Esmé's room and pick up my keys.

"Leave the key on the desk," Esmé says rather curtly. I didn't think she was awake. She keeps her eyes shut and points. "Go out through the garage door. Hit the switch and walk out under it."

"All right," I say. "Hey, Esmé, what about . . .?"

"Could you just leave?" she says. I walk down the stairway and gather my things.

Esmé, Esmé, while it was still dark, I lit some incense, a cigarette and the gas stove. Three flames, three testaments to, three reminders of you. The first one was for your father in Afghanistan and at Harvard and for your mother who took you and the boy home away from him in a saturnine puff of smoke; the second flame fired your limbs and you danced the danse macabre, isolated and alone, it's true, but you can still stand torch in hand, triumphant before a thousand clowns and I thought I felt the third pentecostal flame at 3 A.M. while you were still sleeping, a jerk in the legs that said 'tonight, thy soul is required of thee! Tonight!'

Then, as the sun came up, your eyes became bluer, the angrier you got; is this because the sulfur quit your blood and lighted on me or because the force that through your too-short fuse drives the flower, strives to ripen the raw green lawns of the world before you drive down to Broadway for work?

I'm still kind of in love with you.

SIX

The Answer at Last
(#9 Dream)

THE WORLD

Longing, longing, longing, love, love, love, baby girl who sleeps in my dreams, You, angel of my mental health, Little Flower, pussy love, do you ever think of me?

THÉRÈSE

Do I think of you? Can a pounding heart be said to think? Does the hand that trembles convey thought on its rosy fingers or did my breasts, once girl's breasts but now grown to full womanhood, form cold crystalline thoughts as they heaved up and down, sighing because they were no longer touched and kissed by your lovely mouth, my little brussel sprout? My lips remember, my skin remembers, the treasure between my legs ached for one word from you, one sight of you after my great blasphemy, after you became my Lord and not the Nazarene. I read my missals, said my rosary countless times a day, prayed to the Blessed Mother, confessed my grievous faults and sins, ate

the host of the holy communion, performed Stations of the Cross, but it was hopeless after your invocation. Ah! How sweet was that first kiss of Jesus! It was a kiss of love; I felt that I was loved, but, it was you, not humble Jesus who transformed me from a girl to a woman. I no longer wore the habit. Instead, I wore you. And, indeed, I became worldly. More worldly than anyone knows as I spent my heaven on earth, pining for you. Oh, what a crown I have woven. C'est dommage.

Everyone thinks I died at twenty-four, but I did not. I only died to my old life and my pussy has yet to dry for my dreams are still filled with thoughts of you and how you made me come as I'd never come before, as our Lord must someday surely come. Such power. You rammed me and rammed me until I came like a shower of roses from heaven. I left the convent and my little French town and traveled all over the world, acquired great wealth, spoke in many tongues, commanded men; when I said 'come hither,' he came, with a 'go thither,' he left my sight, and I now have estates, thoroughbreds, chariots, servants, I ride to hounds on wild Arabian horses, and yes, I had other lovers, men who spoke of empire, who commanded boats to spirit me away to their secret islands; they gave me gold for my wisdom, silver for my beauty, diamonds for the clarity of the stars in my eyes, one offered me half his kingdom if I would make love to him just once; there were merchants and traders, soldiers,

nobles, wayfarers, teachers, troubadours who could pluck the strings of pagan Apollo but not the strings of this woman's disgraced heart as I now see that our Lord wraps himself in darkness and disgrace as easily as he wears the garment of beautiful splendid nature . . .

I was more than a queen, I was a maiden king who drank wine under the moon of the Caribees, spied on the riches of Africa, traded in the markets of Muhammad, saw men rocketed into the heavens in Florida, I had the finest food, the most elegant clothes and silks on my back, I knew the mysteries of the north, the south, east and west, and even of the unseen cardinal points, and I was seen myself, little child, I knew what it is to be seen; I read the worldly philosophers and learned the magic arts, did battle against the powers of doctors, dogs and devils and, as if over night, suffering was no longer sweet to me. I sought pleasure and joy; smoked fine cigarettes in long, silver quellazaires and read dispatches with my ivory lorgnette. I even had women as well; I sucked from their unearthly breasts and kissed their lips and hair, drank nectar from their navels and pussies, a frightening music emanated from me . . . To you, to the World, I was a ruler, a monarch, an empress of pleasure, but inside, just a lonely girl left empty and desolate, for what does it profit a woman to gain the World but pay tribute to an empty heart? **Fin de siècle, ç'est vrai*****? And yet, even now, I look***

at my naked image and rejoice. So possessed is one at such times and points, one is dizzy with inspiration. I kiss my own hands and arms. I hypnotize all—men, women, the child, the pious, the heathen—because I am delicious. I have the smell and taste of a goddess, not a saint. I did not ask for these gifts, neither do I refuse them. I give them freely to such as I love and loves me. I could spend all of eternity with your head between my legs, with your wonderful cock inside me, but can't you relate to me now as a sister, rather than a lover?

THE WORLD

But, why, mademoiselle?

THÉRÈSE

Because I'm taken. Taken. But, my saint day is the day of your birth, your real birth: October 1, my saint day, the day of atonement, piety wed with worldly love . . . I ask you to cut the past away . . . here they are, the Freemason sword, the Knights Templar sword, the Celtic, the Claymore, the Excalibur, the **honi soit qui mal y pense** ***sword, take your pick. Scimitar. Dagger, harmonica, shilleagh, rod of Aaron, Catholic propaganda sword. It is you who needs awakening. Time to wake up. Réveillez-vous! Mourn . . . mourn for***

the glory that has left the earth, the world; get your horns back. Do it right this time. Not so aggressive; don't come on so strong. Say that I loved you as no one else could, that I offered myself as a victim of fire to your merciful and passionate love so that all sins and crimes might be forgiven and that you consumed this woman and loved her with an immortal love. Say that your gentle muse, the formerly innocent Thérèse of the Child Jesus, of the Holy Face, heals those who invoke her, those who PRAISE the Lady, that she is the patron saint of love and holy longing and of atonement, but also of Balance and Sanity. She is always your sister. Say that I never wavered in my love, say you consumed me heartily, say the World trembles when it gazes on something immortal, which is why you slouch toward Lowell. Just go there. To Lowell. Hear the Confession. Go sooner rather than later. Réveillez-vous! Allez! Look for me in Lowell. I'll be watching you. Allez!

THE WORLD

I call your name. Je t'aime.

THÉRÈSE

Je t'aime.

SEVEN

Dreams Are Wishes of the Soul
(The Key)

"She threw me out, Archie," I tell the old bearded Scotsman after a day of subbing at a school near the man's home. "Esmé made me give back the key to her house and everything."

"When was this?"

"Four days ago," says I. "Monday."

Archie's standing in front of his cluttered desk, getting ready to sit. He'd answered the front door to let me in, then had taken his automated stair seat up the one flight and is now ready for a fat *El Presidente* cigar that he'd bought with a hundred others at the Tuscarora Reservation or "the rez" up in Niagara County.

"How do you feel?" he asks as he sits down at the desk chair. I'm sitting across from him near the TV. "Depressed?" Archie grabs his ice pick and swares into the end of the cigar with scientific precision. As always, he licks the end first, then thrusts the whole thing into his mouth like a crack whore in the back seat of a Chevy.

"You know what?" I say. "I feel great. I had the key to Esmé's place for, let me see, about nine years. This is a good thing. I feel released. My left leg cramps up sometimes, otherwise I'm doing great."

Archie's big cow eyes set on the younger man a long second, then he smiles. "You'll have the key back in no time. Just wait. Don't mean to be harsh, pal, but you are a bit, well, pussy-whipped. Of human bondage, indeed." Archie puffs on his cigar with wicked delight and looks up at the ceiling, the way he always does when he's contemplating the ineffable or when he wants to give the impression that he is.

"No, no," I insist. "There's no going back. I *like* this. I'm not blaming Esmé for my, uhm, issues, but this is an important step. A symbolic step. And my new place is great. I've got heat now and electricity thanks to Johnny. I can't wait for you to see it."

"Are you leaving up the toilet seat, yet?" Archie asks with a deep laugh, belly shaking like Santa Claus. "Then, you'll really be a bachelor." Archie has two sides that occasionally seep out of his mortal Scottish coil to mix in with the cigar smoke: one side is the backslapping, gruff, ribald, even ill-mannered freemason, the other is the reflective, philosophical father or uncle giving out sage advice. Archie's countenance turns serious, almost grave. "You know," he says, "I took a vow of celibacy years ago because I was being ruled by my gonads. Maybe it was my ex-wife. I ended up hating her but I was trapped. You know, I never felt that I actually proposed to her. It was a voice speaking with my voice, speaking through me. Honestly. But once I proposed, I felt honor-bound to go through with the wedding. And she was beautiful, extremely intelligent. A Jewish lady. But she drove me nuts. After we divorced, I got into drink—I was drunk all the time—and started smoking hash. I was miserable. And all I thought about was women."

(Good line, Archie: *I didn't propose, Miss. It was a voice speaking through me.* Gotta remember that one.)

"That's the thing," is my reply as the window fan sucks cigar smoke out of the cramped room. "I don't think you have to become celibate to come to terms with the beast within. You know, I had a very interesting time in New York. I was . . . well, let's just say I want my horns back. Someday, I'll get to Lowell."

Archie harrumphs like an old buffalo. "What do you mean? Horns?"

"My sanity," I say with resolve, "my mental health, my equilibrium, my power, my genius. My crown. Remember when Beelzebub gets his horns back? At the end of the Gurdjieff book?"

"Gurdjieff!" The old man's snort's like an oak hitting hard ground. "He had no integrity. He did dishonest things. Steiner wouldn't even meet him, you know. Wouldn't even walk down the stairs to shake his hand. To do the serious work, one must have unimpeachable integrity. One must always be honest."

"Yeh, but Rudolf Steiner was pure," I say. "Vegetarian. Like Hippolytus. Gurdjieff was a different kind of animal. What I'm saying is really very similar to your idea, to your saying 'lift it up.' Why do you think Michelangelo portrayed Moses with horns coming out of the top of his head? He lifted up the serpent in the desert. Not that the Bible is anything but fiction . . ."

"Fiction?"

"There's no historical proof that any of the events happened, that any character in the Bible actually existed. It's a huge revision." I laugh. "An emendation. But, listen, I don't care. The Bible is true psychologically. I'm talking about accepting the beast aspect of the self; a beast with a sense of 'I am,' because, let me tell you, I'm fucking through with the schoolteacher act. No more working on Maggie's farm. I've had enough. Gimme the morning star."

"Hmmm," Archie's face has an intense look. "You know that I was in the Air Force with Johnny Cash, right?"

"Yes, I know."

"He was a top radio man back in Germany where we were stationed and I knew him pretty well. And, honest to God, pal, I got that saying 'lift it up' from him. From Johnny Cash. If we were in a tough spot or if someone acted like a shit, he'd say 'we'll just have to lift it up' or 'lift *him* up.'"

"No way!"

"Honestly."

"Shit! Did you ever meet up with him again? After your stint?"

"Yeh," Archie says. "He and his wife were playing at Melody Fair in the late 60s and, somehow, I got backstage and he was out of it, man. I don't think he even recognized me. Lots of dope, I think." Archie lets out a dense almost blue stream of cigar smoke. "We were born the same year. 1931. He was a spiritual guy, even back then, but became depressed. Hell, what can you do if you've made a living out of being the Man in Black?"

"What was it like growing up in those days?" I ask him. "In South Buffalo?"

Archie attended the same high school in South Buffalo as Warren Spahn, the greatest left-hander ever to pitch in the major leagues.

"Oh, it was still country back then," Archie says. His black eyebrows form a perfect V against his white hair and whiskers; looks like the wings of a jackdaw in white snow. "Our house was a converted barn on Buffum Street right at Seneca Indian Park. We had some goats, chickens, and over 25 acres of land. Seneca Street was pure sacred Seneca land once. I used to sit up in my bed when it was still light because my father made us go to bed at 8:00 or something no matter what it was like out. I'd hear the other kids playing outside. Hated it. I also heard the natives chanting, heard their celebrating and mourning in a kind of clairaudient way. Indian burial grounds. The Iroquois confederation. The legend is that the great peacemaker was born of a virgin and got the tribes and nations to bury their weapons under the tree of peace and you know what the arts of peace consist of? Saying the right word. The healing word. You know why the tribes got so violent that they needed the great peacemaker? They forgot to be thankful. Grateful. They became cannibals. That's the legend. Healing was never about surgery or pills, it was a mind thing. The Muslims, too. You should talk to Johnny Hill about this stuff, pal. You should. Anyway, my old man really rode me hard. He was all form, you know. He cared a lot about status and appearances. He would slap me if I spoke with a South Buffalo accent, can you believe that? No flat 'a's. We had to speak proper."

"Did you swear as a kid? Did you curse and cuss?"

"Oh, yes."

"You said 'fuck' and all that?"

"Certainly. We knew some words. Not healing words, though." He laughs.

"What about 'cocksucker' and 'motherfucker'?"

" 'Motherfucker' was a word you heard in the black communities." Archie clears his throat. "I didn't use that word growing up. But 'cocksucker'? Yes. Of course. I called Dutchie Maier a cocksucker in high school and he never let me forget it." The two of us chuckle and hiss like barnyard animals. "But never in front of my father," Archie continues. "He would take the strap to me. If he heard gutter talk from any of us or if we got out of line in any way, we got it with his belt. One time, I came home at five in the morning, just as it was getting light, and he was waiting for me. I was scared. I was about sixteen and I'd been drinking. My dad went after me with his belt but then I realized that I was bigger than he was and I stood up to him. I said 'don't you lay a hand on me again or I'll knock you into next Tuesday' and he didn't. Never touched me again. Things were never the same after that. Suddenly, the darkness was scared of me instead of the other way around. And the sun came up right after that."

"Have you ever tried to revise your own past?"

"Oh, sure," Archie says taking another puff of his cigar. "I don't believe those who say 'I regret nothing.' We've all made huge mistakes. Now, we're both writers, so we understand revision. We're revising all the time." Archie smiles and his cow eyes become little narrow slits, like the holes on his father's leather belt. "You take a situation or a person and make 'em less sleazy, less debauched than they really are, less trashy, as Dylan puts it, but it's more than that. You forgive the past. Bless it. That's remembering well like the muse. Creeley says don't clean up the muck but you have to. You have to. I know *I* have to. And revision isn't reinventing yourself as they now say. The actor reinvents himself. The playwright revises. Creates if you will. The director revises, too, if he's good. Reinvention is a mask. Revision changes the past. It's part virtue, part virtual reality. There are 800 free energy patents online right now, *eight hundred* inventions from water pumps to sports cars that emit more energy than they take in, in other words, they're powered by etheric energy which belongs to us. Our servant, as it were. Not our master. That's how powerful we are. You just have to modulate, change key, vibrate at a higher frequency to beat gravity and time. But Tesla was working on a death ray, too, so you have to be careful how you use your power. The war gods are watching closely. Defy entropy, change the past, give out more than you take in, that's what it's all about. Revision is the real deal, my friend. Revision raises the dead." Archie chuckles. "Now, let me ask *you* something, pal," he says, leaning toward me a little like a doe waiting for a crust of bread, but not quite as innocent. "How and why in the hell did you decide to become a public school teacher?"

"In a dream," I answer, not mentioning the anxiety that went into the decision, the insecurity that informed it. I'm staring at an old reel-to-reel to the left of Archie's desk. "I was in a shallow sleep," I say, "and a voiceless voice, the feeling of a voice said 'go teach.' I'm serious. Was it the goddess speaking to me? Urging me forward? I don't know."

"Then, that's it," Archie says. "The Cayuga say that dreams are wishes of the soul. Tesla dreamed his inventions full-grown, fully completed. But you don't want to yell at kids all day long, do you? For the next twenty years? No. Why don't you teach revision and redemption and all that stuff we're into? You keep saying you need a calling, a sense of purpose, but you can write and your lectures are good."

"Free speech I call them." I laugh, taking a dig at Archie's promoter-take-all arrangement with the Unitarian Church.

"I'm serious, pal. Be an apostle. Be a healer. Write a book or a play that inspires people. It can't all be about you. In fact, it's never about you. Now, that's sanity. Just do it. Promise me, okay?"

"I promise."

"So, how is that Kerouac project coming? You're going to Massachusetts?"

"I'm writing a lot," I say. "I e-mailed the Oblates, you know, my Uncle Tom's order. He's buried near Kerouac. I'm broke, though. Can't go now."

"Don't delay," says Archie, low register. "Now's the time. You don't want to be Hamlet, not in the end. A book requires concentration and isolation. Real focus. Thought. Work. And imagination. Don't disrupt the process."

"I was thinking of skipping the trip. I can travel to the Lowell of the mind, you know, and not even go to the physical location. Imagining creates reality."

"No, no," says Archie. "A book is saying to the world, 'this is who I am.' Take the trip. Get your emotions in motion." He laughs. "Lift it up, pal. Now, I gotta go take a shit."

Archie stands up, the big Highlander, the indomitable warrior, and walks to the bathroom. What a life. Only nine years younger than Kerouac. Just five years younger than Ginsberg. In the Air Force with Johnny Cash, reading short stories and plays over the radio in the mid-50s, a book seller and health food store owner in Toronto, a pilgrim at Findhorn where he hung with Sir George Trevelyan, the poet in the purple cape and cane, long silver hair, silver clasps on his cloak. On a wall in Archie's living room is a black cross with artificial red roses "growing" from its center. Life out of death. *I used to be afraid of the darkness, now the darkness is afraid of me.*

Am thinking now of a kid at South Park High, Archie's alma mater—yes, it's really called 'South Park,' located near Cazenovia Creek and the Buffalo River. He was a tall kid in the Junior ROTC program there, a kid who stood ramrod. He kept yelling out "hoo-hah," one of the mottos the Marines use, probably of Native North American or perhaps Chinese origin, like "gung-ho." The kid wore a khaki green shirt and pants and was psyched to go to Iraq. Full of jargon and bravado. That was back in '03, just before the war began, before the looting of Babylon, when the Darkness was going to be taken back to the shed where Sergeant Joe Pesci could kick the shit out of it. Or the daylights.

Right.

Don't remember the kid's name but I'll read obituaries occasionally, death notices of kids killed over in Iraq and the notice will say 'graduate of South Park High' or of Riverside Tech or of Grover Cleveland High, places where I teach. *Why couldn't I have reached them back then? When they were alive? It's so much harder now.* I recall that memorial service at Grover. Spring day, sun bright like Atlantic City. Reminds me of my Uncle Bill who came home from Okinawa and for weeks, just stared out the sunroom window on to Lafayette Avenue, straining to hear the voices of war's dead ghosts in the silence. Never talked about it, though. Wouldn't say a word about Okinawa. *No one says the healing word until the man is dead.*

"Pardon my indiscretion," Archie says when he returns from the bathroom. "That was not an elegant thing to say. I'm sorry. One shouldn't talk about bodily functions."

"Oh, don't worry about it."

"Hey, are you coming by tomorrow? We're going to have a little barbecue out on the porch if it doesn't get cold. Mama Rose is coming. Johnny Half-Breed. Think you can bring some of your lamb?"

I reach for my red windbreaker, which I'd placed on the couch next to the roll-top desk. "I can't," I say. "I have to move my things. Most of my clothes and books are still at Esmé's."

"At Esmé's, eh?" Archie sits down behind his desk and smiles, eyebrows raised, deep sonorous voice, the voice of the world. "You'll have the key back in no time. Just you wait. You're so pussy-whipped." The old-timer winks. "Well, call me this weekend anyway, okay, pal?"

"Okay," I say.

"Promise?"

"I promise."

EIGHT

Before the Secret Working Mind

(99 Truths)

"We can never get close to the truth except through lying"—Abbas Kiarostami

Have only about three cardboard boxes in the backseat of my Pontiac as I drive to Esmé's, thinking about my strange, gotta be resolved in some way soon relationship with her which is almost completely devoid of true redemptive, hot, wet passion, although it's often tender and affectionate and the girl kind of lives in my heart. To intrude or not to intrude: that is the question. To be intruded upon or not. That's another question. Vagina as gash/wound, bloody Maya Lin intrusion into the coffee brown earth-soil. A war?

Lust. Illustrious. Luster.

Blau always said 'everything is in the embrace. *Abbraccio.* Arms outstretched.'

Clothes off. Unashamed.

Imagine you're in law school, when Esmé would knock on the door of your study carrel on the second floor of the law library and surprise you with a cookie or an apple, then you'd unfasten the top of her faded blue jeans and you'd fuck standing up, her round alabaster flask ass resting on the desk, one time as she intoned *how do I love thee? Let me count the ways. I love thee to the depth, breadth and height my soul can reach when feeling out of sight* . . . maybe some of the other future attorneys heard the belt buckles coming undone and the zippers unzipping and the low murmur and violent gyrations of new love, happy love, along with a Portuguese sonnet or two and stopped to listen . . . or maybe they muffled their ears as they plumbed the depths of contracts law, civil procedure, constitutional torts and anti-trust law in the carrels on each side of you.

I know what love is: it's kind of about you, it's kind of about me and there's this other thing, a third thing . . .

Esmé called me 'Big Daddy Spoiler' and said "you have to go to New York City this summer and make lots of money so you can come back home and spoil Baby," meaning her and I would say "Esmé, you are a big fat baby," because she's so thin and "you have always been a big fat baby and you will always be a big fat baby. Should you be unable to fulfill your duties and obligations as a big fat baby, one will be appointed in your stead until such time as you resume your duties as a big fat baby" but now I just exclaim, practically cry, "why can't you at least go on *Oprah* and weep and say 'I've lost all interest in sex and I'm afraid of losing my husband'? but you don't even care to do *that*! Gawd, you run here, run there. All these ingenious ways to keep love out of your life."

"I do care," she answers.

"That's right," I usually sneer at her. "You're a healthy, vital, vibrant sexy woman who's just with the wrong man. Okay. Why aren't you out of your mind? Why don't you cheat on me like I cheat on you? Why aren't you coming home late on week nights and why aren't you making clandestine phone calls at all hours? At least read a book on the subject or talk to a counselor."

Usually, Esmé becomes silent at this point. The litigator's without an argument and I don't help with my finger-pointing and stubborn insistence that counseling and therapy are elaborate scams that've never helped anyone.

"You think sex expresses love," Esmé once said. "Sex expresses sex. You and I have something greater than sex. We have a real friendship. We can share our thoughts and feelings. We finish each other's sentences. I know, I know . . . you find beauty in the body and in passion. You pretty much idolize women, don't you? You idolize their bodies at least, but I can see beauty in other things. Music. Ballet. In ordinary things like a dinner table or an antique chair. Look at kitty. Just the way she walks with all her mystery and secrecy fascinates me. Look at her eyes. I'm more comfortable with the natural rhythms of life."

"You sound like Josh, Josh Moses," I say. "He says 'not everyone has their sex drive turned up to ten.' I don't buy it. Not at all. Everybody has a hungry heart. But, now, you have people afraid to French kiss. Afraid to kiss! Crazy, man."

"Who have *you* been seeing?" she says. Chuckles. "Too often, sex is about power and ego," continues Esmé. "There's a lot of falsity to sex. I don't like the rhythm of it."

"Sex isn't about the ego," is my clever rejoinder, "it's about losing the ego. It's nourishment for the dead."

"Well, you can't fuck your way into the World to Come," says Esmé, "or into sanity, you know. You can't. There's more to men and women than just sex."

I drive up Esmé's driveway at about one o'clock, snatch the cardboard boxes out from my back seat and ring her doorbell. Looking to my left, I see the old red mill in the distance. This is Esmé's domain; seems as though Esmé authored the mill, this scene, the entire village; the waterfalls, the ice cream palace, the escarpment, all pieces of the woman's memory. This is her dream. Like one of her line drawings; near-perfect, meticulous sketches of Willoughby and of Allentown, the bohemian section of Buffalo. It's not winter yet . . .

"Hi," she says at the door. "I got some of your things together."

"Good," I say, placing the boxes down on the floor. "What are you doing now?"

"Just work. A settlement agreement and release." She has documents strewn like pottery shards all over her antique desk. "The usual scintillating material. A great way to spend a Saturday. This guy has information I desperately need and when I ask him questions, he just interrupts me and answers his own questions and this goes on and on."

"Who's this guy?"

"Oh, just this guy. An attorney."

"A new beau?"

"You're impossible. One-track mind."

Upstairs, I place some books in a box, a ream of papers, CD's, personal effects and after filling three boxes, place them in the back seat of my Pontiac. I walk back into the house and sit on Esmé's couch, thinking about the crimson red drops of menstrual blood I still thrill to see on the tiles of her bathroom floor, red like cinnamon jelly beans, as I look from the shower. *Things* . . . Joyce Carol Oates says that the house is the mother's body. A dangerous place? Esmé's back is to me as she works on her settlement agreement and release. She turns to face me.

"Hey," she starts, "about your manuscript."

"I'm sorry," I say.

"No, I mean . . . were you really that depressed? Are you really that unhappy?"

"Well, it hasn't been easy. You know how life is. A prison sentence. I never thought, even with all my crimes and stupidness, that I'd be brought so low."

"You really had a roommate named Ramona? You really had sex with her on your living room carpet and made her run away?"

"Yeh, that's all true. Except her name isn't really Ramona. She's at Columbia now. Law school. I ran into her a few years ago."

"Get her phone number?"

"No, no, no. It's not like that. But we may become Facebook friends." I pause. "If it's okay with her."

"You call her 'a minor deity.' You must have liked her."

"Yeh, I did."

We're silent for a few seconds. There's a quiet passing of mortal time like in those hip indie films in which the couples never touch each other, not anymore; so hip they don't even kiss! *Soooooooooo* hip. Paralyzed sweetness, as Katie Roiphe puts it.

"Your writing is kind of egocentric," Esmé says like an earnest schoolteacher. "You could be more humble and not write so much about sex. You must think you're some kind of lothario. Somebody's getting the best part of you, huh?"

"No, actually, I'm beginning to think I'm an inept lover," I say. "Completely inept. It's not about me, you know? Besides, you shouldn't be too humble. 'Don't be so humble. You're not that great.' I love that."

There's another pause, like the turning of a page, then, like fingers on white Easter gloves, sunrays steal through the wooden shudders and rest on the coffee table. "I can't believe you put so much faith in dreams and thoughts and all that," the lady says. "Hubert appears like a ghost? Was that a dream?"

"I don't know. But I did see him and he did say 'hate and unforgiveness are like hot ice to me' or something like that, like Norman Mailer speaking from the beyond. 'Your anger hurts me' or something similar. He also told me to forgive Josh. Josh Moses. I guess it was a heightened state of awareness." I laugh.

"Forgive Josh? What for?"

"Oh, I don't know. Everything." I laugh again.

"You know what your problem is?" Esmé says with a blue pen touching her chin. "You should have been more responsible when you were younger. When you were in New York City. You should have reined yourself in and taken advantage of your connections when you had the chance."

"You're only partly right," is my response. "I gave up my horns, that was my first mistake." *Before the secret working mind, profane perfection of mankind.* "I thought I had to become like everybody else but, you know, who needs civilization? Better to be a civil disobedient." I pause briefly. "Wanna know what my second mistake was?"

"What?"

"I wish . . . ah, forget it. You hate all that sappy stuff, anyway. It'll sound like a TV script. A bad TV script if that isn't redundant. No. I'm Ingrid Bergman in *Casablanca*."

"What? Tell me." Esmé's eyes are blue as her pen, blue as perch.

"I wish I didn't love you so much," I say. "I'm serious."

"Oh, Beast . . ." Esmé says. She walks toward me and sits down to my right. "You're such a boob. Nobody talks about love anymore. Such a strange man. What's love to you? An old song? *I'm Confessin' That I Love You? And Then He Kissed Me?* You still love Lyla, though. *Lyla*. And who else?"

"That's different and you know it. And what are you doing with me? You can get any man you want."

"Yeh, right."

"Oh, so you settled for me, then? That's an insult to both of us. You're a trophy. You can call your own shots. I don't know why you call me up and why you can't make the break. You can do much better than me."

Trophy, trophy. You're my trophy. With love and squalor . . .

"Don't say that," she says. "You know, I look at myself in the mirror and I don't even know myself. I hate my haircut. I need a nose job. I'm just disintegrating before my eyes."

"Of course."

"I'm serious," she says, her deep voice becoming high and thin like wheat blowing in autumn wind.

"You know, you *are* beautiful," I say.

"Is that a lie or one of your 99 truths?" she chuckles. "Am I really beautiful or is it, like, everybody's beautiful inside?"

Esmé laughs a laugh you would expect from a woman who's witnessed a drowning. She walks back to her desk chair and sits down. "In your writing, you're going to revise everything anyway, aren't you?" she says. "Change everything and make it better?"

"Well, not better, exactly, but, yeh, the whole damn world needs revision."

"Then," she asks matter-of-factly, "how do I know you're not going to make everything up?"

NINE

Made To Mourn

"The world keeps dreaming, dreaming of spring."—Tom Waits

Thanksgiving and Christmas and Hanukah come and go. The snow, the first since the October storm, doesn't arrive until February and it falls lightly and quietly at night leaving the ground and wounded silver maples, elms, birches, willows, spruces and oaks dusted on a dozen cold mornings, making it a polite, somewhat considerate winter, though windy snowstorms do visit occasionally. The secret passion of a virgin. March arrives, and it would be understandable to be excited, to anxiously look forward to Lent and to Easter and to the Pesach (and to March 12, Kerouac's birthday), the feasts of freedom and renewal because sanity is a feast, a kind of ritual—if you have to do the 12 steps, do the goddamn 12 steps—freedom and release—and yet, I haven't stopped being Hamlet, because nearly five months have passed since that e-mail from the Oblates and I still haven't journeyed to Lowell; haven't resolved the situation with Esmé, either: it's like I'm still on the cross, or in the tomb, the place of the skull.

Resurrectile dysfunction?

Am thinking of ringing up Blau, the Sage of Lake Michigan, the Sometimes Suffering Son of the Holocaust, the Man Named Blue, when he suddenly calls. What would Blau do? What would he say?

I've known men and women named Gelb, Roth, Weiss, and Schwartz but Blau, to be sure, will be able to play the Chicago blues for me.

"Hey, man, I'm comin' east for the Pesach," he says, his nose stuffed up with a Windy City cold. "You gonna be in New York?"

"I don't know."

"Well, why don't you come to the *seder*? Come for the second night in the Bronx. You remember how to get there, right? Just take the 5 train to the botanical garden. We'll play some hoops, okay?"

"I'm there. Definitely."

"Good," Blau says. "Now, what's going on with the Kerouac project? What's happening?"

"I got two e-mails from the Oblates in Tewksbury. Near Lowell. I heard from them just before Christmas. My great-uncle was buried in back of the novitiate but I don't know when I'll be able to get there. I'm getting discouraged."

"But why?"

"Oh, fucking Moses. He says it's near impossible to get a literary novel published now. A half-dozen novelists dominate the field. I wonder if he knows how much it hurts to be dismissed like that. To be treated like one of the poor relations. Never asked to be on staff. And for what? To be bankrupt? Mister Passionate Mercy . . . "

"Don't you see that he's intimidated by you? By your passion and conviction? Even his mother. Gabby loves you, man. Sometimes I think she likes you more than she likes her son."

(Blau may've been right. Even in these awful subdominant times, Gabby is like some kind of blessed mother, sacred heart burning for those she loves best.

"Why aren't you married yet, Bubi," she asked at Josh's place in Mount Kisco as Harry picked out "All of Me" on his ukulele. Gabby was wearing a black skirt that was almost a mini-skirt. "You're smart, you're handsome. I don't get it."

She called me handsome . . .

"If you don't get snapped up soon," she said with a wink, "maybe, *I'll* marry you.")

Blau continued. "Josh is good at covering up the wounds," he says, stifling a cough. "You display your wounds for all to see. Frankly, I never knew you were so affected by this. I can hear it in your voice. Look, I've got an idea. Why don't you write a book about how hard it is to publish a book. I'm serious. My uncle Emmanuel did that. It's still in print. I forget the title."

"You could do that," I say. "I'm too dependent on Moses. What the hell does he know? Why should I take his advice? I don't write for Josh Moses, I write for The Goddess. He's given me a lot of work, though, Mo has. I have to admit it."

I can recall JoMo's response to my novella a few years back, something called *The Last Sane Man*: "not cohesive. Predictable. Just another 911 saga." *They Asked Me How I Knew: The Hemp Diaries* was, according to Mo, "fragmented. Not enough character development. Needs revision."

Revise *this*.

"Just remember one thing," Blau says, his velvety nasal voice made just a little sluggish by his head cold. "You are the story. The story isn't out there. *You* are the story." Blau sneezes. "And you have to go to Lowell, man."

"Yeh, I guess so. But, I was thinking of making it a journey of the mind, you know? No need to actually travel. To get on the road. The road is inside, too. I guess. Besides, I'm broke."

"Don't guess. Lowell is not that far from you. You can't not go. I have twenty-one years experience as an editor. Lowell is the unknown and the unknown is the best fucking part of the story. Look," he says, "I gotta go. The baby's crying. Call me when you get to New York, okay?"

"I will," I say. "Feel better."

As I hang up the phone, something becomes clear for the first time: While Joshua Moses is the yellow of the flame, Blau's the blue, the steady blue calm inside the golden fire, close to the source. Like Hubert, but not: Blau doesn't flare up easily. Sanity amidst the flames—that's Blau, even if he always was a bit of a scene maker. Always had the right phone numbers, the right parties, the right contacts; always had some place he had to be, cruising around Manhattan with the staff of *Island* magazine. *Pretty classy*, he'd always say. Gotta make a phone call, Slick. No time to lose. *Hee-hee, that's our Blau,* yes, Blau's the blue sky under which brilliance comes out to play like an innocent kid, even though the ancient Greeks had no word for 'blue.' He always gives his friends permission to shine, license to reflect the light of the golden dawn. Fuckin' Blau. He'd give you the morning star if he could.

Next morning, while driving to the Native American magnet school, while riding along Scajaquada Creek, my muffler goes out and the engine becomes so loud, it's deafening, ear drums punched with an iron fist. No way am I going to drive down to New York City with an engine that loud. I call Archie during a break.

"Is Johnny Hill going to be around today?" I ask him.

"Yeh, in fact, he's coming by for lunch and a game of chess," the old-timer growls.

"Could you ask him to stick around until 2:30? I need him to look at my muffler."

Archie says 'sure,' the old lion, and when I arrive at the blue-gray two-storey home, paint peeling from the guard rail, on Elmwood Avenue—tattoo shop and pierced bikers next door—Johnny is all set to work, having lost the chess game to the big highlander. The half-breed gets out a measuring tape along with the other tools he keeps stored in Archie's basement and says "you need to get two and a half feet of flex pipe, two and a quarter inches round and two muffler clamps, all for about twenty bucks. But I'm gonna charge you sixty bucks for my labor, dude, all right?" says Johnny under the crisp blue early spring Monday afternoon sky. "You know I treat you good."

While Johnny works on the car in the lot back of the house, I walk upstairs to see Archie but he's already started in on his afternoon nap. Like Ham from the Bible, I peek into the old guy's room and see him dozing like drunken Noah and, fortunately, I don't see or uncover his nakedness, but I'm getting nervous because my bank has started putting the screws on its customers—for example, I deposited $500 on Friday and here it is Monday and, sure enough, when I tiptoe away from Archie's room and walk down the old wooden steps and across the street to the gas station to use their ATM, my balance is $17.58. How'm I going to pay Johnny Half-Breed? The guy does great work and he's always desperate for cash, buying drinks all night for bikers and tattooed party chicks in the pool table bars along that immortal dream called Niagara Street and besides, he just might beat the shit out of me. There's always that.

"Johnny," I tell him, "I don't have the cash. I'm going to have to borrow it from Archie."

"Okay," he says, "but tell him you're only giving me twenty. Otherwise, he'll be all over me. I owe him."

Johnny says he'll be finished with the muffler and catalytic converter in fifteen minutes and asks me if, afterward, I might drive him over to Black Rock to see a guy who buys his food stamps. Johnny's flat broke.

"Man, your bank is bad news," he says as he holds a burning, hand-rolled cigarette out my passenger window. "When I had a bank account, I'd get the money next day." Johnny looks out his window. "This used to be the Italian part o' town," he says. "Now, it's just a bunch o' ragheads and Africans. Hey," Half Breed Johnny exclaims, pointing to a yellow-brick art deco structure on Tonawanda Street, "that was my first job. Machine shop. I loved my job so much, they used to have to tap me on the shoulder to tell me to go home. The time just flew by. You got one life, you might as well do what you love, otherwise, it ain't worth it. Out in Vegas, I made a thousand bucks a week but had too many DUI's. I lost my license, couldn't work, starting pimpin' and sellin' crytal meth. Don't tell Archie, though." Johnny runs a hand though his auburn pony tail. "He'll kill me. In Vegas, I had two ex-Green Berets for bodyguards. I had shots fired at me. Twice. One almost got me when I was runnin' out of a motel room. I ran down those steps like a bear for the forest. Hey, your engine is still noisy," Johnny says. "I could only get a pipe two and half inches in diameter. It's too big and not tight enough to quiet your engine. I'm not satisfied with the job."

How much more is this going to run me? Then, almost from out of nowhere, like a putrid odor coming from a restaurant dumpster, a pronounced feeling of inadequacy and inferiority comes to me: here's Johnny, robust, deep-voiced, self-assured, able to fix anything but his first two marriages—he rewired my house after the October snow storm brought down the power lines—strutting with macho confidence from the spare parts shop to the car, around and about the streets of Black Rock, too, and it all makes me feel insufficient, immature, weak and effeminate like some Bourbon fop from the 18th century. Fat. Feckless. Hornless. Even worse: a beast with no sense of itself. Without horns or genius. The half breed has grown before my eyes, from a sort of lovably hapless hanger-on to an Onondaga warrior—barefoot Onondaga, that is—with his hand-rolled smokes, ruddy face and long chestnut mare pony tail. It's as though I've been eclipsed. I don't even know if my car has four or six cylinders and having lived in New York City for over a decade is really no excuse, but Johnny's a genius mechanic, a builder, a fixer and a leader as well as a hustler and whoremonger. He's Steelkilt the Canaller from *Moby Dick*, the Lakeman and desperado from Buffalo, a tall and noble animal with a head like a Roman, but with long hair. That's who he is. He doesn't just talk about revising and changing the world, he changes it. He fixes it. And if a mutiny's called for, he mutinies. Johnny starts ragging on Archie.

"I'm tired of being played," he says, his accent a decidedly Great Lakes one with its flat 'a's, flat as the frontier and the prairie. "He talks down to me, man, and thinks he can budget my funds. Archie's always askin' me 'where are you spending your dough?' Hey, whores cost money! I don't have time for all these rituals. I want her clothes off as soon as we get to her place. That's it, man. I've been workin' on the first floor at Archie's for months and you seen what a great job I've done. But the old man is nickel-and-diming me. I don't deserve that. I put in that bathtub, the tiling, the washer and dryer, all the cupboards downstairs. Anyone else would be charging him a hundred bucks a day. And don't tell me he ain't got the money. That man has cash stored in every pocket. Cheap Scotsman."

Johnny's pitch is building, is becoming menacing. Reminds me of Hubert and even of Ira Bloom as he assails Archie and 'the system' and I'm getting a little scared because Onondagas, barefoot or otherwise, aren't the warriors that the Seneca are, but they're the ruling tribe of the Iroquois nation and Johnny's formidable. The tree of peace may well be the way to end all terror, but right now, Johnny's transforming into the terrifying warrior and I'm half expecting him to come out with Hubert's blood-quickening threat, 'you wanna die tonight? Is that you want? You wanna *die* tonight, motherfucker?' As nothing is more seductive than leaving town, nothing is quite so fearful as returning to your hometown and now, if you'll just be patient with me, I feel as though I'm entering that liminal, subjective, which is to say in this instance, paranoid state. Now, here's the proposition: those who control the vectors of power, of political power, economic power, even police power, can lord it, lord this power, over the great unwashed, the poor, the beaten-down and the vanquished which translates into a class thing: the 'well-bred' wealthy man can intimidate the poor man, the ill-bred, the "half-breeds," with his sumptuous vocabulary, with his impeccable taste in clothes and wine, with his car, his stupendous home, his knowledge of painting, literature and exotic foods; with his access to other worlds, other modes of being, his direct bloodline connection to the gods back in Egypt and the alien gods in the Book of Genesis, the bright morning star, therefore, how can the poor man respond? How *does* he respond? What is his strength? *I can take your life* he says in all but words. With his every glance and gesture, the message is clear. *I can kill you and I have nothing to lose. Show me some respect.* Now, the rich and powerful man can also take your life, and he does—and many a poor person is rich in imagination and genius—but the rich man has more to lose, it would seem, and can't be as frank about it; about taking your life, that is—that's the proposition—there's an equality to it—but I feel woefully inadequate and ineffectual, anyway. Johnny probably sees me as a mark. Nothing more. Just an easy touch, just one of the whites who barely knows his ass from his exhaust pipe. This guy doesn't even look under his hood, he's thinking. Doesn't make cabinets, fix faucets, weld, shellac, tend plants, brew his own beer, paint his living room, play chess, bind up wounds—Johnny claims to have removed the bullet fragments in his arm himself after he was shot in Vegas and I believe him—nor even bet on the ponies at Fort Erie Raceway. What good is he? A friend of Archie's, I guess. That has to be what he's thinking. The entire Iroquois Confederacy, the people of the hill, have nothing but contempt for me, that's what I'm thinking. Johnny has the earth mother, the grasses, the waters and springs, the maple trees, the three sisters, corn, beans and squash; the birds who sing to the Creator, the virgin birth of the Great Peacemaker, Dekanawida; the counsel of Handsome Lake who once met with Jefferson (*Thomas* Jefferson), the Thunder Beings who live in Niagara Falls; Hiawatha, the arching sky, elder brother the sun, the great tree of peace, the vault of heaven, the ability to take my life and a great tool box and all I have is a noisy old Pontiac and a little cash to make him happy. That's who I am, I'm thinking.

"Can you find me a pipe that's two and a quarter inches round?" I ask Johnny, finally, as I pull up to the house in Black Rock. Sounds like my voice register has dropped an octave or two.

"We'll have to do it tomorrow," Johnny says. "Unless it's pouring rain, I'll do it. But drive me over to Vermont Street after I talk to my man, okay?"

I park my car on the left side of the street, at the curb, and wait while Johnny jauntily walks up the steps of the modest two-storey house and sells his food stamps. Black Rock kids drive by on bicycles; Polish kids, Hispanic kids, black kids. Others walk. Young mothers with toddlers stride by my car leisurely under the steady affably lazy blue sky. This, also, is who I am, I'm thinking. *I am, I am.* This is here, this is now, the self pushed out—the world is a reflection of the one indivisible self, the one soul in its infinite permutations like the Tuscarora rainbow. Accept yourself. No need to revise this. All is as it should be. I'm conscious of my breath—in, out, chest up, chest down. All I have is this moment. Admit impediments, that's how the light gets in. Suddenly, Johnny comes running down the steps of the house.

"Start up the engine!" he shouts. He jumps into the passenger seat as the noisy engine revs up.

"Hey, what's going on?"

"Undercover cops on the corner. We could see 'em from the second floor."

"So what?"

"Well," Johnny starts, "my man sells some weed and crystal meth on the side. Let's get outta here!"

"Oh, *great*."

My engine sounds like an opening drawer full of knives and forks as I pull away from the curb and speed toward Niagara Street. I'm hoping that none of my students are in the area to witness this ignominious escape, in fact, I think I can see Christopher Two-Guns from the Native American school in my rear-view mirror. Maybe I just imagined it because Black Rock isn't Christopher's neighborhood.

"I'm going back to Archie's to get you your money," I say to Johnny as he turns on to Vermont Street. "After I drop you off. I've never borrowed money from Archie so that'll help. I'll tell him that I need twenty-five bucks for you and thirty-five for gas and I'll promise to pay him tomorrow."

"All right," says Johnny as I pull into a parking lot somewhere on Vermont. "I'll be back in an hour or so. You talk to the old man and give me the cash when I get there. Thanks for the ride, man."

Archie reprimands me a little when he comes down

to the front door to let me in. I'd rung the doorbell twice. Maybe more.

"I heard ya the first time," he says with a boyish, playfully antagonistic smile. Archie's frame fills the doorway. "The buzzer was fixed and is back with a vengeance. Johnny fixed it."

"Sorry," says I. As I climb the old staircase and as Archie rides up on his automatic escalator chair, I begin to work out a strategy to get the old man to lend me sixty bucks so I can pay Johnny Hill. I decide to focus on the fact that we've known each other for four or five years and in that time, I've never asked to borrow money. I'll bring up our first meeting and even flatter Archie, say something about his wisdom and prescience. I'll be especially careful to avoid any disagreements or fights. I'll be particularly nice and pleasant. (Besides, I'm thinking, he still owes me for the Course in Goddamn Miracles talk.) I get upstairs and look out across Elmwood Avenue and notice, over the Celtic cross, through the picture window, Rick James's brother, in a windbreaker and shorts, trimming his hedges on the other side of the avenue. Rick James, of "Super Freak" fame, was from Buffalo and his brother, Jesse, lives across the street from Archie but his name isn't Jesse James. It's 'Johnson' or maybe 'Jenkins.'

"Were you downstairs with Johnny?" Archie asks as he settles down into his leather-bound desk chair. "How's he coming with the kitchen?"

"We ran over to get the flex pipe and clamps but Johnny's not satisfied with the job and neither am I," I say. "It's still noisy. I can't drive to New York in that thing."

"Should have used stainless steel," Archie says knowingly. "Where *is* Johnny?"

"I dropped him off at Vermont Street."

"Vermont Street?" Archie shakes his head like a punch-drunk prize-fighter. "You mean, you did all that today? While I was sleeping?"

"Yeh." *Mendacity. I can smell it!*

"Didn't know I slept that long," Archie says. "Wow. Sorry. Can I get you some tea? Coffee? A cigar?"

"No, no," I laugh as I sit down across from him. "You know, I can't pay Johnny. My bank is really squeezing me. I just put in $500 on Friday and I still can't get at it. I've got seventeen dollars and fifty-eight cents." (This was *just* pre-subprime meltdown.)

"You gotta change banks, pal," Archie says as he picks up a big cigar. "How much do you owe him anyway? Johnny is just so irresponsible with his money."

"Well, I'm going to pay him twenty-five but I need thirty-five more for gas. Man, the price of gas . . ."

"Yeh," Archie licks the end of his cigar and lights it. He takes a few deep puffs. "This is crazy. I don't drive anymore unless I absolutely have to. I don't like to drive at all at night. I just can't see. Gettin' old, pal."

"Oh, no," I begin. Flattery's a long road. "Well, yeh. I mean, how long have we known each other, Archie? About four or five years, right?"

"I think so." He lets out a goose gray puff of smoke. Mirage gray. Kaopectate gray. And thick.

"I remember when I first came here," I'm saying. "But this was way back. I was still in law school, remember? We didn't really become friends until much later. Mike and Beverly brought me here. I was going out with JoAnn. Remember?"

Archie smiles. "JoAnn," he repeats the name as if harboring a great tender memory. "She remarried, didn't she? To a superintendent of schools somewhere." Archie's Burl Ives, Lucien Carr, Dave Van Ronk, Falstaffian face is transformed by a particularly lascivious smile. "You know, she came on to me once," he announces softly.

"She did *not* come on to you," I spit out. Archie's smile vanishes and he looks angry and forlorn. Hurt like an abandoned puppy. I'd resolved to be as pleasant and as non-confrontational as possible, but this is too much, because this is the man of unimpeachable integrity, a lie will never pass his lips, don't you know. Archie looks at me finally.

"I'm not going to tell you anything anymore," he says. "You just distort what I say. And deny."

I start laughing. "Oh, c'mon, Archie. Don't take it so seriously. Everybody revises. Everybody lies."

"Not everybody."

"*Everybody*," I say. "The most dishonest thing you can do is insist that you never lie. I lie. All the time. But I admit it. I lie to Esmé. A lot. But JoAnn did not come on to you."

"She did."

"How did she do it? Did she lift up her sweater?" I motion as if lifting up a garment I'm wearing. "Did she let her skirt ride up a little too high? Did she . . . lift it up? Or did she say 'Archie, will you take me home and screw my eyeballs out?'"

Archie smiles enough for his big cow eyes to disappear but then he turns serious. "You are so crude," he says. Everything in the room smells like smoke.

"I'm a profane man. Like Mozart. Insolent, too."

"Well, stop it," Archie says. "Lift it up. I know people who are pure spiritual seekers. I knew people in Toronto and at Findhorn. They are eminently truthful."

"They never lie?"

"I don't think Rudolf Steiner ever lied."

"Oh, I'm sure he did. Everybody lies. I'll bet even Jesus of Nazareth lied at least once. You know, 'your wine is really good, Lazarus' when it was really awful. Ha! Like those people who say 'I don't see color. I just couldn't be racist if I tried.' They're the worst of all sometimes."

"Oh? Now, you're saying I'm racist?" Archie has blood in his highlander eyes.

"No, I'm not. You're not racist," I respond gently now. But then the Beast bears in. "But, truth be told, JoAnn said she couldn't hang with you anymore because you got a little too touchy-feely with her."

"Look, pal, I have enough experience with women to know. We hugged and I could tell JoAnn was interested." Archie looks away and puts his cigar in his mouth. Even the mighty men of old are at a loss sometimes.

"Well, what did she do? You said she came on to you. Did she start gyrating her pelvis into you when you hugged? Was she grinding into you?"

"You know, I'm going to have to ask you to leave. I can't believe you would talk about JoAnn in such a crude way."

"Oh yes, you're shocked, shocked. So, she came on to you and you turned her down?"

"Yes."

"You *turned her down . . .* ?" I repeat with mock incredulity. "Why? You always liked JoAnn."

"I didn't think it was appropriate."

"Why didn't you call her afterward?"

"I just didn't."

"So, you turned her down. Was she sad? Embarrassed? Angry? Hell hath no fury, you know."

"Look, why don't you just drop this? I'm in a bad mood. Let's talk about this some other time." Archie stands up. "Please just drop this," he says as the two of us walk toward the staircase. "But I don't think you should talk that way about JoAnn. And you talked to her about me?"

"Hey, I just said 'do you ever hear from Archie?' and she told me what happened."

"Well, you weren't in the room, my friend." Archie activates his automatic stair seat and descends to the hum of the machinery. I follow, and now the two of us are standing in the alcove. I open the front door. "I would never speak so disrespectfully of JoAnn," he continues, his voice unsteady and indecisive like suburban sprawl.

"I'll tell her," I gibe. Archie smiles slightly. "But I haven't spoken to her in eight years," I say.

I walk down the front steps as Archie closes the front door and get into my car, which is parked directly across the street. ***Great: now, Archie and Esmé hate me as much as I hate me.*** This is like the time Hubert cast me out into the wilderness for my insolence and perfidy. I'm a violator. *Mendacity . . .* ! As I pull away, I realize that my front right tire is completely flat. Must've hit that sharp curb directly, the curb in front of the house where Rick James's brother lives. No way can I get on the expressway with this flat, so I make a right on to Bidwell Parkway and park in front of the Buffalo Seminary just before Soldiers' Place. It's still light out. The sky is pellucid. I open my door, get out of the car and suddenly feel a sharp pain in my left calf, the same pain and pull that had laid me up for nearly a month the previous summer. I try to walk but fall to the ground. My calf feels like an open hand suddenly closing into a tight fist. Got no cell phone. I force myself up, then limp to the corner of Bidwell and Elmwood, to a phone booth there. The air's warm but the trees overhead are still leafless, in fact, they're ghoulish against the blue sky and look like amputated limbs. Some branches are still strewn about the parkway. Fucking October snow storm! I know I keep harping on it, but everything's been ravaged by the virgin snow's brutal dream. Even Al Gore mentioned the October storm when he spoke at the university last week. I arrive at the corner and realize that I have no change. No money at all. I limp to a laundromat on the other side of Elmwood and ask to use their phone. They say 'yes' and I call triple A. They'll be there in forty-five minutes, they say. Then, I call Esmé.

"The guy's here," Esmé says with a dollop of sympathy. "The guy who's doing the floors. Upstairs. I've been waiting forever. I can't come. Did you call triple A?"

"Unh-hunh."

"Well, they'll help. I'm sorry. I absolutely can't drive over there now. Sorry. What about Archie? Can't you call him?" I tell Esmé what'd transpired between me and Archibald. "You've got to let stuff like that go," she says, her voice rich and aristocratic as always. "What's the difference? If an old man wants to think that a young woman was trying to seduce him, what do you care? Let him think you believe him. Let him have his fantasy. What a waste of time. You guys. Always fighting and disagreeing and posturing. Do you ever just shut up and enjoy each other's company? Just breathe? Everything with you is politics and ideas and philosophy and cerebration and on and on, clacking, clackety-clack. Can't you just forget your competitiveness and your cultural references and cycles of history and all that . . . involvement and just be? You're too much . . ."

I hang up and limp back to my car. It's starting to get dark. I feel inadequate again, absurdly inadequate. *How come I'm not helping Esmé with her floors? I'm useless.* I open the trunk of the car to look for the donut, the spare tire, but I've got so many blankets and papers and books and cassette tapes in there that I'd have to empty out the entire trunk to find, then open, the nut-and-bolt fastened jobber where the donut's stored. I hobble toward the back seat and put one of the blankets and some papers on the seat but realize that it's hopeless. Too much stuff. *Damn, what would Johnny think? I can't even change the fucking tire.* I close the back door on the passenger side, hobble to the trunk and close it, then feel another intense throbbing pain in my leg. I try to walk but fall to the ground again like in one of the goddamn man-was-made-to-mourn Stations of the Cross, fall right to the pavement in front of the seminary.

I crawl over to the park there, to the grass from the pavement, and shudder, literally shudder, thinking of all the things I've done and said in my life, all the people I've hurt. I remember Hubert, at

Joshua and Miriam's place in Battery Park City—way back, one hot balmy summer night in Manhattan, Hubert had screamed "I'm a hollow man! A hollow man who can't love! Can't love!" That night, he shrieked for all humankind it'd seemed; cried out for everyone living in bondage and I was unable to hide my tears. Then on that other night: *your anger and hate hurt me like a fire in my soul*. It's like everything is a Lie. My whole life is a lie. Wounding old Archie . . .

I pull on my left calf and feel the muscle almost fall back into place. It's still sore but not as tight now and I'm sure I'll be able to walk again in the cool early spring air. I roll up my left pant leg and put my hand on the calf. It's red and swollen and warm, almost hot to the touch. Suddenly, I feel nauseous. Fuck. This isn't a clot, is it? You fat *fuck*! My head is tingling and I'm short of breath. I've got a fucking blood clot and no health insurance! *I'm dead! Dead*! If you don't take care of a blood clot, you're leaving town in a big way. I get up on my feet again but can't stay balanced; feels like blood is rushing to my head, a tempest in the mind. My legs are weak, weaker than the heart of a racist.

Then, something truly weird and ghastly happens.

Imagine you're me: You lay on your back and fall into some kind of liminal state, not quite a dream but you're not conscious, either. Your vision's decidedly not filled with golden light and with lost and late relatives and friends. Head's throbbing. You've never felt pain like this before. Never in your life, not even after drinking seven shots of whiskey at a high school party. Pounding, pounding like a hammer on a nail. You're in a place of true, profound helplessness, beyond tears, beyond even dread or the blackest night. Head throbbing. Immobile like Bobby Kennedy on the floor of the Ambassador Hotel kitchen, clutching his rosary. ***Help me, Saint Thérèse, please. I call your name.***

Is this what happens when you refuse to praise?

Feels like a thousand-pound weight is sitting on your head, like you're drowning in your own blood. Trapped inside your skull. Meeting your doppelgänger at last. *Pain, which cannot forget.* You're conscious of cars passing by, but of almost nothing else except pain and terror and of the need to breathe. *Breathe.* Life. Breathing. Maybe Archie's using some anthroposophic voodoo and Tesla's death ray to get you back for challenging him.

THINK your way out of *this*, you bastard.

The pain's monstrous, hideous, enough for one town, for one slaughtered village at least—no kidding, you want to cry, you're helpless, *helpless*, supine in the city of the dead, terrorized and terrified—but then, the moon comes out, the beginnings of a horned crescent moon, looks like a chalice, and you can't tell if it's waxing or waning. Can't quite see it, either. It's in the corner of your eye and begins to grow, an orb glowing by the window of your skull; growing, growing, drops of moonlight falling like silver rain on your head and face.

You begin to regain consciousness. You're foggy-headed but out of pain, finally. Oddly, though, there's no "I" anymore as in "I feel better." There's no sense of self. There's only the whiteness of the moon, skull-white, and yet, you open your eyes and are shocked to see no moon—and you don't use the word 'shocked' easily. You sit up. Holy shit. You'd fainted and hit your head on one of the big branches in the park. Have vomit on your pants. You look in all directions. There's no moon but, looking west toward the river, you can see a little golden glimmer of the sun in its last throes, light dripping off the sky like hot butter. The evening star, the last faithful mistress. You feel the back of your head and there's a bump there but only a small one, like a bubble on a sheet of plastic. Your head still hurts a little. You look at your leg. The swelling's gone down but it's still red and warm like an underdone lamb chop. You're just happy to be in the world again, back in the slough of despond with seventeen dollars and fifty-eight cents in your checking account. The odor of vomit wafts up to your nose, but you know exactly what you have to do now.

PART IV: DOMINANT CHORD

The Greatest Confession

ONE

On the Road

Sure hope this bus ride to Lowell won't be an air-conditioned nightmare as everything's air-conditioned nowadays, even office spaces in the wintertime, even busses in early spring . . . My Pontiac's in the shop, maybe for good, and a bus trip isn't such a bad thing, really, if your neck is protected with some inflatable pillow, which I don't have, but, either way, I'm on the road, the seductive road, and fortune attaches to a body in motion, the mind is at its best. Allons! Allons! The unknown awaits even when you travel to familiar places and have no pot in your bag. New England . . . My head still hurts but the sky's clear and blue and it's always nice to pass through Albany for sentimental reasons. I pull out my new cell phone and dial Josh Moses. No answer. Voice mail. I call Joe Valentine, another friend from Albany—the Italian Bogart I used to call him because he has those sad, skin-draped, sepulchral eyes and that tight-lipped New York-inflected insistence. Like Moses, Joe has read everything twice but Joe always stood deeper in his shoes than Josh, more bull than bird. And he's a Kerouac fan. Back at college, Valentine adored all of the new wave and power pop music of that era (*nya-nya-nya* music he called it) and one afternoon in early spring, he charged into my room where I was napping.

"Did you hear what happened?" he said breathlessly as he nudged me on the shoulder. "Reagan was shot and the Buzzcocks broke up."

"You're kidding," I said, pinching out the sand from my eyes. "Really?"

"Really, man," Valentine said. "The Cocks broke up."

Within a few years, though, Joe became quite serious and focused, a soldier in the good fight; began teaching English to Salvadoran refugees at his church on Long Island, studied Spanish until he was fluent, met and became betrothed to a lovely coal-black-haired Salvadoran woman named Maria Concepción or Connie as she's known, and before long, was finding homes in Nassau County for poor Salvadoran families. Sometimes a dozen or more refugees—men, women, kids and old folks—lived in one split-level with a lush green front yard and a driveway on majestic, insular Long Island. They still do. The Sanctuary Movement. Liberation Theology. Every Saturday night, Joe and Connie gave parties at their home in Sea Cliff where we all danced, drank mescal and sang songs from El Salvador and Peru.

(When Tatiana once complained to Connie that I wasn't sufficiently interested in her, that I wasn't really in love with her, Connie suggested an old Salvadoran aphrodisiac.

"Put your underwear over his head," she said to Tanichka.)

About a dozen years ago, Valentine was diagnosed with MS and now he shuffles and stumbles from Penn Station to his job just below Times Square in Manhattan; bobs back and forth like a wind-up toy, like a drunken marionette, jerks this way and that with his nickel-and-chrome plated walking cane, a god all but struck down by this curse, by this ghost disease, his myelin sheath worn and frayed like an old electric wire. The signals from his brain don't connect to the muscles, but instead, go nowhere or spill out into the unorganized ether, so, when I'm in the city, in New York, we meet occasionally for drinks and maybe dinner at an Irish bar near Penn Station so that Joe doesn't have to walk over much, then I take his arm and escort him down Seventh Avenue, down the escalator steps to the Long Island Railroad, and you know, sometimes I want to cry, but there's a hurt too deep for tears. Try telling Joe Valentine that illness is a blessing as Steiner said, or that losing your limbs, your physical body, means gaining in soul and spirit as implied by Steiner and I.B. Singer and by Robert Browning ('grow old along with me/the best is . . .').

"Health isn't everything," Joe says over a mug of dark beer, "it's *each* thing."

"Cancer's for pussies," he says at another meeting near Chelsea. "I've got MS."

Not long after quitting grad school, Joe and I planned a trip to Nicaragua when Ortega was in power but backed out at the last moment, not out of cowardice but out of bureaucratic resistance as the saying goes and we flew, instead, to Spain and Portugal where Valentine inveighed against Reagan, William S. Burroughs and the Koran as we gazed in awe at Goya's work at the Prado in Madrid, then, in Lisbon and Portimao, Joe turned me on to *fado* music, 'fate' in Portuguese, music so melancholy, it leaves its silhouette on the the heart; it's like the blues but with some purple and red in its fateful strains and there's usually a promise of some kind of redemption. The troubadours can tell you, my man, the trovadorismo: *Fado* is mood indigo. Fado is the trill of four gypsy stringed instruments mourning. The zither. Portimao and Lisbon. Vienna. Newark. First heard Jonathan Richman and the Modern Lovers with Joe, too. *I love New England best, although I might be prejudiced . . .*

"This is like a pilgrimage, isn't it?" Valentine says from his Long Island home. "A pilgrimage to Lowell."

"I had to do this," I reply. "This can't just be a journey of the mind. But I have to admit: I'm more excited about seeing my great-uncle's grave than Kerouac's."

We talk more and the woman in the seat in front of me becomes perturbed. She wears her dirty blonde-hair painfully short; wears big round, wire-rimmed glasses and ear buds. She removes the buds from her ears and turns to face me.

"Excuse me," she starts with an authoritarian slant in her voice, "but the driver specifically said there is to be no cell phone use on this bus."

"Except for an emergency," I respond. "And this is an emergency."

"It doesn't sound like an emergency."

"How would *you* know? There are emergent issues here," says I. "What if I were talking to someone next to me? Would you object to that?"

"That's different," she says. "One-sided conversations are annoying. There is no cell phone use on the bus and you know that."

"Well, you'd better call a constable."

"I'm going to have to say something to the driver."

"Uh-oh," Valentine says on the other end. "Should I hang up?"

"No, no," I say. The insolent beast emerges. "This uptight bitch in front of me is making a stink but what's that to me?"

"I heard that." She turns around again to face me. Her hair is real short and combed to the side, a lamentable style choice, I mean, a pretty face like that . . . "I'm going to demand that you stop talking on your cell phone. The driver specifically said . . ."

"Oh, talk to the hand, lady. Fuck off," I say, but I say 'fuck off' with hesitation, kind of quietly, kind of between my teeth, like winter wind snoring through the door jamb. The bus pulls into Worcester where my father's father's father, Uncle Tom's father, was born in 1854. No wonder he left town. Everyone here looks gaunt. Cadaverous and bone-white. There's a pack of nuns in the station and my short-haired nemesis joins them. Holy shit, I told a nun to fuck off! The beast scares away another lady. I call Valentine again.

"Joe, I think I just told a nun to go fuck herself."

Valentine laughs. "Well, who else is she going to fuck?"

"Yeh, but, I feel . . ."

"Hey, look, man," he says with New York City intensity, just like Bogart, "don't worry. I went to Catholic school for twelve years and they can take it. Everything is upside down anyway. Hitler was a Catholic. Jesus was a Jew. The Virgin Mary didn't even die a virgin. Hitler died a virgin. Take it from there."

Have to revise the scene on the bus and forgive all parties, not least, myself. *Lift this up, cast the negativity out on to the brush on the side of the highways of the American Revolution. I am a pilgrim* . . . Leaving town, leaving home to get home . . . I expect Lowell to be dreary and depressingly industrial, mirage and smoke gray, but Mill City, cradle of yet another revolution, the Industrial Revolution, is actually very New England charming with cobblestoned streets, colonial homes and cafés. So, this is Parnassus? Maybe it was just Jack's Lowell that was dreary; *this* Lowell is kind of a delight. The world before electricity.

So, this is where The Road began . . .

I get off the bus at the Robert B. Kennedy Bus Transfer Center. Who the hell was Robert *B*. Kennedy? The city fathers didn't make a mistake, did they? Like Archie Bunker: Richard *E*. Nixon? The sky is still a deep blue with a few wisps of cloud. Bette Davis born here, too? How flinty. I flag down a yellow cab on Gorham Street and the cabbie, a tall, dark-haired, black-eyebrowed French Canuck most likely, suggests a motel on Main Street in Tewksbury which he calls "Tooksbury." 'Took:' rhymes with 'book.'

"You'll find the novee-ate . . . what do you call it?"

"Novitiate."

"Yeh," the driver says, "you'll find it easy from the motel in Tooksbury. It's right off Main Street, about two miles from the motel."

The driver doesn't appear to be one of the cognescenti, but he's tuned into something, you can see it in his groovy flannel shirt with its green and yellow geometric patterns. Tall gentleman with black eyebrows, a full head of Cajun crow-black hair. He drops me off at the motel entrance.

"Thanks for everything," I say as I hand him a five-dollar tip. "Maybe we'll meet again. What's your name?"

"Gerard," he says. No revision, no lie. That's his name. Swear to Godddd.

I check in and leave my bag in my motel room and walk out on to Main Street, going east. Tewksbury's also very charming but more modern than Lowell as there's a strip mall or two on Main Street. It's unseasonably warm. I find Chandler Street 'easy' as Gerard had predicted and the Oblates' building is on the left under pine and willow trees that nod in the wind, up then down, like a row of street junkies. There are about 150 gravestones on the grounds, which makes it easy to locate Uncle Tom's final resting place. The Grounds. All the headstones are the same size and shape like manicured unpainted thumb nails; all of them are equal, as it were, small, smooth, curved, unpretentious, and I'm surprised because I thought Uncle Tom's would be a little distinct as he was once the much beloved master of novices. In his obituary photo in the *Oblate World*, sent to me by Ms. Saunders, Father Tom resembles some of my cousins and looks not at all like Justice Scalia. Thinning hair, lighter, grayer hair than I'd imagined, wire-rimmed glasses. The obit says that Tom "was laid to rest in the grotto cemetery at the Novitiate where each day the novices come to pray for the departed members of the Province." The man is also praised in the article for his "maturity of judgment, kindly heart and fine community spirit." It's unsettling to think that I'm very much like Father Tom, because I'm forty-ish, unmarried, no children, poor, a teacher of novices, as it were, and, you know, when you've sublimated all your tellurian desires on to a woman you either never meet or lose when you do, it's . . . Anyway, I'm not sure about the kindly heart because my heart feels like a dog trapped in a hot room.

"To Father O'Brian," the obit continues, "was given the singular privilege of being born on Our Blessed Mother's own birthday, September 8." Tom shared a birthday with the blessed mother but never knew his own father. Most Catholics are the whiny children of the blessed mom but who doesn't want to be her lover, too? Her equal. *Don't be a naughty baby/come to Mama, come to Mama, do . . .* What did Sis say? Thérèse? *Do it right this time.* And Little Annie Frank? Little black-haired Annie Frank . . . Precocious girl. The ghost writer, writing in the woman language: she's here, somewhere, asleep in my soul and I wouldn't just say a thing like that.

Mary would like me, would love me, wouldn't she? She's a Jewish girl. She likes cerebral men.

Previously, before seeing his mug in the obit, I'd seen Tom's likeness only in photos taken when he was a very young child in a tarboosh and knee-breaches and as a young man on the town, at an arcade, actually, with his brother, wearing a white straw hat and suit before 1910, accompanied by a dame in a hoop skirt and parasol on the boardwalk. Big sexy hat on the girl from the Edwardian era, hour-glass figure, a face creamy with confidence and ready for the 20th century, the girl's that is, and Tom's face is flush, imbued with vitality and even mischief—looks exactly like my cousin, John Tabolt—the eyes are bright but soft, the bodies taut and lean like guitar strings. Tom gave all this up? For Mary? Who *is* this Jewish woman, this lady, more seductive than the road, than the aura left behind when you leave town?

The sages say that

Mary means ‘the sea’
As in *mar*, marine, marina
And *Memere*, but it’s not
Your name I think of
As I watch your chest
Rise
And lift, then recede
Like the rapturous
Tide.
I don’t know what it is
About you that is
Liquid exactly
But if you put it
In a cup and
Place
It on the
Table in front of
Us, I will
Drink it
Until
I, too, am
Full of
Grace.

The living come to the earth through the woman’s vagina; all suck on the mother’s breasts—another reason two straight women can cuddle and French kiss, but there’s something about Mary. Golden blood. Drawn forwardddddd. I look again at the tombstone and read the inscription. *Rev. T.F. O’Brian, OMI. 1889-1943*. Tomb, womb, Mom, Om. I am. Tom. The sky is kind of purple, like it’s

1999, like *fado* in the early evening. It becomes darker. I call my father up on my cell.

"Dad, you'll never guess where I am."

"I can't, son. Where?"

"I'm at your uncle Tom's grave in Tewksbury, Massachusetts."

"Uncle Tom? No kidding. Are you alone?"

"Yes."

"Well, you be careful, son. Why are you in Tucksbury? As part of your writing project?" Wait: even Dad says 'Tucksbury.' He must know it.

"Yeh. Listen, Dad. I've never asked you . . . how did you feel when Tom died? You liked him a lot."

"I did like Tom."

"He died suddenly, didn't he? How did you feel when he died?"

"I was overseas at the time," my father says, "I was out of the country. He died in what year?"

"1943."

"What month?"

"April. April 15."

"I can't recall the details, son. I could have received a letter or maybe somebody told me over the phone. I know that I sent a letter saying I'll be home for my sister Claire's birthday, which is April 26, but they censor that shit. The war was on."

Dad had worked for Curtiss-Wright aircraft as a foreign representative and traveled to Iraq, Iran and to South Africa before enlisting in the Army Air Corps in 1943, just two months before Tom died. Saw the Tower of Silence charnel place in India. Blood and rain washing down the drain pipes of eternity. Was 28 days from active duty in the Pacific when the A-bombs were dropped on Japan, which means that nuclear weaponry probably allowed my dad to live past the age of 26.

"How's Mom doin'?" I ask.

"She has her good days and bad, son. You know how it is. How's yourself?"

"Good. Hey, how about Teddy Kennedy? I feel bad. The last Kennedy brother."

"Yesss," says my dad, sibilant as a siren. "I feel bad, too. But he lived a full life." At 90, Dad has some perspective on fullness and life, I venture. You're up, you're down; you provide and provide and you keep smiling always. Part Tom, part John.

My father is America.

My father is the world.

Too.

"What is it about the Kennedys and their heads?" I hear myself saying. "Two are shot in the head and Ted has brain cancer. Trapped in his skull. John Lennon was shot through the heart."

"What's that?" My father's hearing aid squeals, piercing pin-like the skin of the moment. Bullet-like . . .

"Oh, nothing. Hey, Dad, how did you *feel* when Tom died? Your uncle Tom. Everybody loved him."

"They did. They did. I just can't remember, son. I just can't."

A soft fragrant wind blows over the yard from the west. The smell of fresh water. My father doesn't care about Jack Kerouac. He doesn't need him. The purple sky becomes black and despite a pinch in my left leg, I walk the two or three miles of brush, weeds and concrete back to my motel in the dark.

The following morning, Sunday morning, I shower quickly and head to Main Street again with my thumb out, thinking there's no way in this, our 21st century, cars'll stop for a hitchiker, no way at all, until a young dude in Bootsy Collins shades and a green and gold wrap around his dreadlocks stops his cranberry red sports car and I get in—his name is Victor, he's from Ethiopia, and he once lived in Buffalo, where he attended the university and knew someone in one of Creeley's classes.

"How did you like the snow in Buffalo?" I ask Victor whose disposition is as sunny as the day.

"Ah, the snow," he says, "like huge mountains of water and ice."

Victor drops me off at Chandler Street and I retrace my steps to Tom's grave. Originally planned on going to Lowell first this Sunday morning but I suspected I'd never get to Father Tom's in the day time unless I journeyed to the novitiate early and there was the prospect of attending mass, too, although church services of any and every variety make me sick, even African Methodist Episcopal services with amen corners and tambourines, hallelujahs, brilliant choirs and flashy preachers—if God equals sex, then organized religion is an abomination—still, I decide that attending a mass in the Oblate chapel is in order, after all. I walk to Tom's grave under the azure sky and the pines and look at his tombstone. This man never knew his father. A pine cone has fallen and is resting against the left side of Tom's stone as if it'd been waiting for me. I pick up the cone and place it in my coat pocket. I don't pray, I don't kneel. Next to Tom are the gravestones of the Reverends P.F. Murphy and J.P. Flynn and J.W. Burke and J.H. Doherty. Their

Celtic catholic spirits are silent this Sunday morning. Can't even hear them breathe.

I walk from the cemetery across the yard and into the novitiate building, which can't possibly pre-date Elvis Presley or *The Dharma Bums*, and see no signs of life as I pass beatific portraits of starry-eyed Mary and a pale androgynous starry-eyed Jesus, always looking up to the sky like Little Richard, and, DAMN, ever wonder why the Savior is depicted among Catholics wearing scanty, seductive clothing—loin cloth, cut stomach—while his mother's always wrapped up like a Muslim girl, like shrouded moonlight? Like the resurrected Pixie? What's *that* about? (The Intemperate Muse Says: It's possible that if the world were allowed to see the Virgin Mary in the stages of undress that one often sees her son, the world might be a little better off. It is possible.) For years and years, these men have been cloistered together in order to venerate the Eternal Woman, the idea of feminine divinity—acting and talking as though they love the mother even more than they love the son—yet no women are allowed into the inner sanctum, because what they really seek is the suppression of that divinity, no doubt about it. Too much power. This is what Cleopatra-haired Miriam Moses once said about pregnancy and going into labor: "there's a big storm coming and you're it."

There are no signs of life here in the novitiate, not until I get to the small dining area where tables are being prepared for breakfast, two American flags at every centerpiece. From the kitchen, you can hear Patsy Cline singing "Faded Love" on a small radio.

"Hello," I say to the woman, Wanda, who's toiling in the kitchen. "The novitiate's now a retirement home for the Oblate fathers," she says. "Many of the retired priests had been novices here in Tooksbury, forty or fifty years ago. They were ordained and went to the Ivory Coast or to Brazil or the Philippines, then returned to Chandler Street, to the new building built in about 1961." Kind of like retiring to the dorms, to Colonial Quad, I'm thinking. Like being eighteen again. An immature concept of heaven, as JoMo would put it, but I'm close to home. Almost there. Wanda takes me to meet one of the priests, Father McMahon, who is corpulent, unshaven and clearly upset at being being disturbed so early. He leads me to his office where we both sit.

"I know the name 'O'Brian,' yes," Father McMahon says. "I was master of novices, too, but I didn't know him. 1943? He's too old for everyone in here." The good reverend-father scratches his head. He looks like chocolate and marshmallow. "There is one priest here who was ordained in 1939, Father Hanlon, but he's . . ."

"He must be about ninety now."

"Yes and I can't let you invade his privacy," says the priest, still scratching the crown of his nearly hairless head. His voice is like traffic out the window. Distant, indefinite. "I have to insist on that." He looks at his watch. "And I have to say, also, that coming here at 8:15 in the morning like this is a bit much."

Huh? It's a Sunday morning and this cat isn't even seventy, so, what the hell's he hiding? The great world snake he brandished for his little novices, pure as the *nieve*? We've got a Father John on our hands, I'm thinking, a great world-class prick, like Father Timothy, a red-haired priest from childhood who, after one confirmation class, began brushing back the hair from my forehead as he gently spoke to me in a darkened corridor.

"I'm sorry, Father," I say. I hesitate, then stand and offer my hand. Never did get along with other Irish Catholics. "Thank you for your help." Father McMahon stands up.

"All right, then," he says with an obligatory smile. "God bless you." McMahon leads me to the lobby and leaves for his room, taking the decayed musty air with him. *I hate the church,* I say to myself as I leave the building. Protector of child molestors and Nazis. The strict constructionists. Don't want to be *too* insolent: some priests and nuns are okay, are honorable, know what justice is, but the devil has a home in the church, to be sure. *Écrasez l'infâme!* I walk back out on the grass toward the plots and headstones and see this engraved on a marker:

Oblates of Mary Immaculate: Constitution 43

We will keep alive the memory of our deceased and not fail to pray for them, faithfully offering the suffrages prescribed on their behalf.

At the north end of the cemetery is a little shrine honoring the Oblates of Mary Immaculate buried at Holy Cross Cemetery in Lackawanna, New York, home to sleeper cells, the deserted Bethlehem Steel plant, and to Steelkilt the Lakeman, and there, on the honor roll, is Tom's brother, Reverend John O'Brian, the mean priest, the bad uncle, the prick of conscience himself, the inquisitor, the one who aged without grace like dust in the wood grain. I walk back toward the building, walk into the chapel for nine o'clock mass, take communion, and leave.

TWO

He Honored Life

I'm standing on Main Street, on the shoulder, and, much to my surprise, another car pulls over to take me back toward my motel and to Lowell: it's a woman, thirtysomething, with tar black angel hair, thin strands like the pasta, and, again, I climb into a stranger's automobile, here in the uptight 21st century.

"Hi, I'm going to Lowell," I say. The woman's barefoot and talkative. Her name is Angela. No revision. No fiction. No lie. That's her name. A Lowell girl.

"Angeleeka," she says. "I'm Greek. Are you going back to the motel or are you going into Lowell? I live in Lowell. Oh, that's cute. The pens in your pocket. What were you doing in Tucksbury?"

"I was visiting my great-uncle's grave."

"Oh, that's so nice. That's cute," she says as we motor west, then north, past drive-in banks and stop-and-go food marts. Her hair is tar black like Blau's, her skin is milk white, legs long in faded blue jeans and remember, she's barefoot. Slender. "Do you like this music? I like the classics. Barry White. That's what you want to play when you're with your woman, right? Hey, you really have piercing blue eyes. Where do you live? Near here?" I tell her Buffalo, New York. "Buffalo? It gets really cold there. What are you going to Lowell for?" I tell her. "Oh, that's so sweet. You're going to his grave. Do you want to be dropped off at your motel first? I can do that."

Maybe she wants an invitation to my room, the Beast is thinking. A tease, more likely. What would Blau do? I decide to go straight to Lowell, to Edson Cemetery, and when we come to a parking lot to turn around because Angela has driven too far, has passed the street, I put my hand on her wrist as she stops to look both ways. I lean toward the woman to kiss her. Like an old widow, she offers me her right cheek.

"Oh, that's so sweet. You tried to kiss me," she says as she takes a right on to Gorham Street. Tried. Another sister. "That never happens to me. I'm shy."

"I can see that."

"No, really. I am. I've only been with four men my whole life."

"Well, they're four lucky men."

"Oh, that's sweet. Thank you. How cute. I'm a single mom. My kids are four and two." We arrive at what looks like the cemetery entrance. I lean over to kiss her again and, once again, she offers her right cheek. More sister than lover. I pick up her right hand and kiss it. "You're sweet. I'll be at my mother's for a while," Angela says as I get out of the passenger seat. "But if you need a ride back to your motel, call me, okay?"

"Okay. Thanks so much."

As Angela drives away, I look at the entrance gate to the cemetery, but a sign there reads 'St. Patrick's Cemetery.' I stop into an Italian pizza place, eat a slice with anchovies, then walk back out toward the graves. Edson, a stranger says, is down the road just a bit. I have with me, a map of the cemetery and have highlighted Lot 76, Range 96, Grave 1. 'Entrance at 3rd Avenue and Gorham Street,' it reads and the grave's easy to find under imperishable old and young oaks, poplars and evergreens. *Ti Jean. He honored life.* His widow's haiku. There are three pens stuck into the dry soil surrounding the headstone, a red pen, a white one and a blue one. There's a quarter and a dime in the lower left-hand corner, a handwritten note with a rock placed on top and a yellowed cigarette is at the upper right on top of a bottle cap. I don't kneel. I kind of want to kneel, but for some reason, I don't. Suddenly, I remember the pine cone in my coat pocket, the one I'd found at Tom's grave. I take the phallic pine cone, like the ones of myth, take it out of my pocket and place it at the upper left hand corner of Kerouac's tomb. One should honor the sanctity of the moment with complete silence—no one knows this better than I, one who has walked among the dead—our deeds are the soil upon which the dead stand, doncha know—but instead, I call Esmé. Not home. I try Josh Moses again. Voice mail. Again. I call Blau. No answer. Somewhat impulsively, I call the Brown-Eyed Belle of St. Mark, maybe because the Gallic feel of Lowell, the Frenchness of it, reminds me of the Belle's Jacqueline Bouvier hair and eyes. She picks up.

"I can't wait until someone asks me 'do you ever hear from O'Brian?' That happens from time to time," she says, "because I'm going to say 'the last time he called, he was standing at Jack Kerouac's grave!'" Her laugh is like leaves rustling.

"I'm glad I got you," I say.

"You know, I had a gig in Cambridge not long ago and I stayed in Lowell," says the Belle who's a video artist. "It's becoming kind of like Brooklyn, a place for artists to live cheaply." Her voice, as always, radiates a cool intelligence. "How are you?"

"Good."

"How's Esmé?"

"Good. How's Elliott?"

"We got married," says the Belle. "Just two weeks ago. We did it for the kids. My mother is ecstatic that her grandkids are finally legit. We had a small ceremony, family only. I'll send you pictures. My mother is delirious. Well, you know. I'm a Sacred Heart girl. And now, I'm married to the *ne plus ultra* SoHo guitar genius." I'm a little surprised at how unwelcome this news is. Am somewhat crestfallen. The Belle's husband once played guitar behind Ginsberg at a reading and that makes me jealous, too. "How is it there? In Lowell?" she asks.

"It's beautiful, the cemetery is. It's a beautiful day. It's warm."

Someone else would have asked why exactly I made the trip to Kerouac's grave but not the Brown-Eyed Belle of St. Mark. Honeysuckle and ginger. I miss the days when I'd call her up and say 'wear that pretty little black top I like, okay?' Star and crescent.

It may take you twenty years to find true love again . . .

"You know, nobody ever called those guys, Ginsberg and Burroughs, on their misogyny," says the Belle. "I'd see them all the time here in the Village. Burroughs said that women are a mistake of evolution. Ginsberg says at an East Village gig, 'I'm sorry. I just can't remember women's names.' Cursing mad Naomi and her scent. Their penchant for boys. They were like priests. Nobody ever called 'em on it."

"You're right. Like priests."

"While you're in Lowell," she continues, "go to this place called the Four Owl Sisters. Something like that. Owls . . . you'll see the four sisters there; they all look like the same woman in different stages of her life. It's funny. Are you there?"

"Yes."

"Hey, you're breaking up. Let's get together next time you're in New York. Call me, all right?"

"Yes, I will," I say. I dial Esmé. Again no answer. I dial Archie's number and he's home, thankfully.

"You're in Lowell now?" he growls. "How did you get there? Drive?"

"No, I took a bus. Greyhound to Hartford. Peter Pan the rest of the way."

"Well, aren't you the authentic American." Ever the lingo surgeon, Archie dissects the word 'aren't,' using two syllables: "are-*ent*."

"My car is shot. It's over." I don't tell him about hitting my head and passing out at the seminary.

"Yeh, I thought so. Now, listen: Johnny says you owe him some money. He's kind of pissed."

"Johnny? Shit. I forgot." I close my eyes and lightly touch my brow.

"Just kidding," says Archie, "well, I exaggerate. Look, I took care of it. I lent him some more. I'm just too kind for my own good. Too pure." Archie laughs that rough tobacco-throated laugh. You have to love his voice, dig his voice, the way Kerouac loved the deep authoritative hum of Ginsberg's.

"You'll be getting that scratch back soon, I'm sure," I say sarcastically. "Lent it? You just *gave* him some more money. How much?"

"Hey, I don't care. He does good work. And look, I'm sorry about the other night. I guess I did exaggerate, as always. I . . ."

"Forget it, Archie. You're a good friend. Forget everything else. I should be apologizing to you. You're a motherfucker."

"Gee, thanks."

"No, really. You're a true friend."

"I appreciate that. So, your car is history, eh? The Pontiac?"

"Probably. I'll be all right. Don't worry. I'm not even going to try to drive down to New York in that thing. I'll take a train, maybe."

"Call me when you get back," Archie says. "Let's all get together. You, me, Aidie, Sandra. Franklin, Ginny, Martin. Okay? We're going to have a *seder* here. Downstairs."

"At your house?"

"Sure. Sandra knows the whole ritual. So does Aidie. But, if you go to New York, have a great time."

"Thanks."

"How long you gonna be in Lowell?"

"I'll leave tomorrow morning. I have to teach at the Native American school for the rest of the week. Eighth grade science."

"You know, pal," Archie starts. "I hope you're not offended but I never cared much for the Beats. They seemed like lost young men with no older man as a mentor. And who did they go to for initiation? William Burroughs. You're going to be brought into the larger world of adulthood, of manhood, by William S. Burroughs? I don't think so. The artist has gotta be the sane one. They were lost young men, Holden Caufields, with no older man to bring them into manhood like Bly says. And

Kerouac ended up burning crosses on his front lawn, acting like a redneck, like a fucking Klansman. He should have revised himself, man. Doranne lived where Gregory Corso lived, ya know. Lived in the same house."

"In Buffalo?"

"Yeh. On West Ferry. She said Corso was a mess. Arrogant. A junkie. Combative. Then, they became friends and Doranne had to cradle and rock him like a baby when he was in withdrawal. A kind of piéta. Kerouac died in his mother's house, ya know."

"I know. Listen, Archie, I have an offensive question."

"There are no offensive questions, my friend, only offensive answers."

"What are you, Harry Truman? Believe me this is offensive."

"What?"

"It's been said that Mary, the Virgin Mary, conceived in her ear, the immaculate conception."

"The Immaculate Conception refers to Mary's conception not to Christ's."

"I know, but didn't Mary conceive in her ear? That's what I read. That means she heard something, right? It doesn't mean that the Paraclete *came* in her ear, obviously."

"God, you're profane." As with Blau, I can hear a smile in the great man's voice, the smile of someone who's seen it all. "Actually, you're right. It means she heard something. What one hears is more powerful than an image. Have you heard of the forgotten song?"

"Hell, yes."

"It has something to do with that," Archie says with slow-moving Toronto-like elegance, like brandy being poured. "Hey, I heard you hit your head. Are you okay? When did this happen?"

"The other night. I'm okay, though. How did you find out? Who told you?"

"Martin spoke to Esmé. When did this happen? When you were here?"

"Yeh."

"Watch yourself, pal. Take it easy and drink a lot of water. You gonna be back in town tomorrow night? Call me this week, okay?"

"Okay. I will."

"Now, go and sin no more."

THREE

The Grotto

"I want to work in revelations, not just spin silly tales for money."—Jack Kerouac, letter to Father Armand "Spike" Morissette

I walk away from Edson Cemetery, having bid adieu to *Ti Jean*, wanting to believe that my work is done here, finished—my bones are tired, I feel almost spent, my left leg hurts as does my head—but something I can't see or hear urges me onward, pushes me—the Divine Dameoiselle?—to explore Lowell and find Merrimack Street, the Grotto by the river, and find the bridge where the man with the watermelon died. ***Lowell . . . Howl . . .*** There's some assonance here. I walk half-heartedly on Gorham Street and a woman with a Spanish accent says that Merrimack is only a few blocks away ("that way, you can't miss it") and I can see that Gorham Street, or the one that continues in a straight line and becomes a cobblestoned street after the curve in the road here, ends at Merrimack which is perpendicular to it. Two French women in a café near Middlesex Street say that the Grotto is on Pawtucket. I see, in the distance, only one red brick smokestack and the river, always the river. You can't step twice into the same river.

"Just keep walking on Merrimack for two or three miles," says the more talkative one, "and look for Pawtucket and the Franco-American Orphanage, built by the Oblate fathers."

If you were walking on Merrimack, you'd pass the Jeanne d'Arc credit union, a couple banks, a nightclub called El Rancon, and come to the Jean Baptiste Church at Merrimack and Decatur where Kerouac's funeral took place in 1969. *Ti Jean* had been an altar boy there, too.

"Blessed are the dead," said Father Spike in his eulogy. "They shall rest from their labors, for they shall take their works with them."

Still farther up at Pawtucket is the bridge extending over the Merrimack River (you'd have passed a Concord River bridge earlier) and if you turn left on Pawtucket, at St. Joseph's Hospital, you see on the right, finally, a sign that reads "Our Lady of Lourdes Grotto" which points to the orphanage parking lot—well, it's not actually a parking lot but a paved area, blacktop, complete with a dumpster, but the fourteen Stations of the Cross are memorialized here. (Didn't Bernadette Soubirous meet the Blessed Mother in a dumping ground, too?) Logically, you'd follow the fourteen statues, each contained in a 6 x 4 or thereabouts white house with a plexiglass window, to the grotto reproduction and the grotto is far more impressive and awe-inspiring than I thought it would be. Just beyond my imagination's vanishing point. *Mad, vast, religious.* Not Mr. Hefner's grotto, nor even Bernadette's, but Lowell's grotto, the People's grotto, Jack's grotto. There's a spiral notebook set on a table to the left of the altar where pilgrims and penitents have made entries: *I've been sober for a year but my life is still hard . . . I'm sorry I missed a day, Jesus, thy will be done . . . I'm so sick, Lord, please remember me . . .*

When an arm or leg is broken, it's temporarily cut off from the stream of life and becomes a part of the dead material world, prey to sullen gravity. You know how it is: you can feel as though you've been broken and cut off for years. Bloodless like an undertaker. I sit by the altar, reading the supplications and confessions. (Remember: no confession, no communion. No state of grace.) Addiction, lots of addiction. Dependencies. A sparrow flies into one of the nooks under the curved ceiling of the grotto. Two sparrows fly in and perch, settling frenetically on one or two of the clinging vines. Then, a white dove flies in and perches. This is life. *Je suis.* I am. Always merry and bright. Say 'I am' and the cops and yuppies fall to the ground. Walls come down, too. The rest is fiction. I get up and walk to the right side of the altar and light a candle, then place the lit candle on top of the altar or platform. I put three dollars into the collection slot. The Oblates of Mary Immaculate built the Grotto in 1911, the year after Father Tom entered the Tewksbury novitiate. I walk the thirty or so paces to the Stations of the Cross and peer through the plexiclass cases at the burnt red waxy figures, entangled in drama and passion. Each station is titled in French. ***Jesus est condamne a mort, Jesus est depouille de ses vêtements, Jesus meurt sur la croix (Il a dit, 'c'est finit,' non?), Jesus est mis dans le sepulchre . . .***

Mary, don't you weeeeep!

Again, I puncture the sanctity of the moment by calling Joe Valentine once more—I can see him struggling to get to the phone in his Long Island home—and I say, "Joe, the Grotto. It's all about the Grotto. You have to see it. I can't really talk because my phone's running out of juice and I'm gonna have to call a cab, but you've got to come here some day."

"Yeh, yeh," he says, still sounding like Bogart, "call me when you get home."

Just as I'm putting the phone back in my pocket, a white-haired woman appears in the grotto carrying a bundle of flowers or something that looks like flowers, roses, and seems to be moving in complete silence, like falling snow, as she drops a coin into the collection box, lights a candle, places the flowers at her side, then kneels and crosses herself at the altar. I walk toward her, trying to be quiet, and watch her as she prays silently. She finishes rather quickly, crosses herself again, lays a red rose down at the altar, and as she stands up, she notices me walking toward her. We both sit on the bench by the altar, sit at the same time.

"You look like a searcher," she says to me with amicable authority. "A seeker. Did you find what you were looking for? Here at the grotto?" Her face is child-like. Her skin is as smoothe as glass.

"I'm not sure," I reply. "I came here because my great-uncle died in Lowell. He was a Catholic priest and I wanted to know if he heard Jack Kerouac's confession. I wondered for a long time, then I decided to come here."

"I knew Kerouac," the woman says softly, brushing strands of white hair from her forehead. She's wearing a white pull-over sweater and a black blazer. A small silver crucifix around her neck. "God, he was a drunk. A sweet guy. A very sweet man, but a terrible drunk. Well, I guess he was in anguish."

"You knew him?" I say in disbelief as I kind of slide closer to the woman, inching my way nearer to her like a woolly bear caterpillar.

"Well, I met him two or three times. No. Only twice. I was just a kid. A teenager."

"When did you meet him?"

"Let's see. I was born in '33. He was at least ten years older than me. I met him for the first time during the war. I was quite young. Everyone was in uniform, then. He was drinking with my brother, but they weren't really friends, you know. Just tying one on, I guess." Her voice is gentle like flowers. "He'd already moved away, but I did meet him again after the war. This was about 1947." She's stymied for a quick second and looks up at the clear sky. "Yes, it would have been '47, because I was fourteen and had just been confirmed. Do you want to hear the story?"

"Oh, God, yes."

"I saw him, Kerouac, right here in the grotto. I used to come here as a child. I was a very devoted little girl and I used to bring my spiritual offerings here, you know, my spiritual bouquet as we used to call it. My worries, too. I had a tubercular lung as a child and when it was healed, I felt obligated. One day, I saw him sitting right . . . pretty much where you're sitting now." The woman smiles wide. It's a knowing smile, though. Weariness around the lips. "He was drunk. And he was crying. And he said—I'll never forget this—he said 'little girl, will you bless me?' I said 'what?' and he said 'can I put my sins in your basket?' I used to carry a little wicker basket with sandwiches and my flowers and other things. He said 'please, give me your blessing. I hate my life and I want to die. I just want to die.' It was terrible. He reeked of booze. It was that sweet, almost honey alcohol smell that you smell on people's breath when they're drunk. I wasn't afraid because I knew people who'd grown up with Jackie. That's what we called him then. He kept saying 'I want to die. I'm dying in my sins.'"

"Really?"

"Yes. *Really*."

"That was the year Kerouac went out on the road. 1947. That's just before . . . everything."

"Kerouac said 'everyone thinks I'm happy. The life of the party,'" she continues. "He told me what a great football player he had been; how popular he was, but that ever since his brother Gerard died as a boy, he wanted to die, too. He said *je suis malade* with a country accent, then he said 'bless me, Terry.' I was surprised he remembered my name. Then, he told me he was a writer but stuck; that he had a hundred stories in his head but couldn't get them out on to the page. Couldn't make sense of them. Now, remember, I'm only fourteen years old." Terry laughs and clears her throat. "He also told me that after his first confessional, he heard a voice telling him that he would die in pain and horror, but that he'd find salvation in the end. He was confessing to me, you might say, and wanted me to, you know, give out the penance. I didn't know what to say. Fourteen years old . . . Then, a voice came to me or spoke through me. I don't know how. I just heard myself say 'there is nothing to do but give praise.' That was it. Give praise. That was my penance. No Hail Marys or Our Fathers. I can't remember how long we spoke, but at some point, he kissed my hand." Terry lifts her left hand, blue veins under her skin like battery wires, and stares at it. "And I never saw him again."

Who is *this woman?*

"Were you surprised when he became famous?" I ask Terry. "A legend?"

"Surprised? Not really. I knew something was up with Jackie. He was deep. Had the most beautiful face I've ever seen. A beautiful man. His eyes were on fire. But by the time his books came out, I wasn't really paying attention. I was in the convent, you see. I was a Carmelite. A Carmelite nun."

"A nun?"

"Yes. It had something to do with my bad lung. My parents. They cried real tears over me for years. They were worried to death. But, you know, I knew I'd be healed. I just knew that because I had the desire to be well, the desire would be realized."

"But you left the Carmelites . . ."

"Yes. In '57 or so. That's a long story, though."

"Do you ever regret leaving?"

"No, not really." Terry begins touching, probing the petals of one of her roses. Only now do I notice her deep brown, almost black eyes. "Would you like a rose?" she asks me.

"Yes, I would, but . . ."

"But, what? They're free. No charge."

"No, I mean, where do you find red roses this time of year?"

"I have a place," Terry replies. "A little place." She hands me a fully bloomed red rose, then speaks again. "Is your mother still alive?"

"Yes," I say. "But, she's sick. Quite sick."

"I'm sorry," Terry says with a frown. For the first time, she looks old. Then, she takes my hand, my right hand. "Stay close to your mother," she says. "You're going to have to help heal her. Just keep your thoughts clear. She'll be fine, eventually, but she still has a lot of suffering to undergo. There will be many tears. I'm sorry for that."

Terry lets go of my hand, stands up, bundle of flowers in hand, then tells me she has to leave. Her silver-gray slacks are loose-fitting. Ice-white hair is almost shoulder length. Black deck shoes. It's spring.

"Why did you leave the convent?" I ask her. "How come?"

"That's a long story. I don't have time."

"You left, though," I say, still clutching the single rose in my left hand. "There must have been a reason."

"Yes, there is," Terry says, smiling. "I fell in love."

As if to say 'the rest is none of your business,' Terry turns around and leaves the grotto as silently as she entered it. I'm more or less in a trance as I walk up the steps on the right side of the grotto and look straight up at the huge, gruesome crucifix, the gigantic cement statue of the crucified, dying Christ over the grotto. It's not nearly summer yet, but flies buzz around the wounds and the crown of thorns, the Merrimack River bleeding in the background through a thicket of branches just budding. I walk back to the altar, lay down Terry's red rose, and for the first time in ages, kneel down and hear, playing softly in my inner ear, all the rhythms: road rhythm, silence rhythm, rhythm restores order to the world rhythm, the light of the song rises in the soul rhythm—the ghost dance for a nearly destroyed people, the music of the rosary, lullabye for the soul, the camaraderie and love of the beatniks tuned to A=444—RHYTHM, not Reagan's rhyme, not an eternal star wars, not insolence, no adolescent meanness, but the **BEAT** heard 'round the world.

The Revolution.

So, this is where The Road begins . . .

I have the power now. I can grab that snake and use it as my staff, my Saint Paddy crozier, my pen, and make that silver-tongued devil work for me; inscribe every fact, every feeling, every heartbeat, every smell, into the virgin Book of Life, fertilize it, make the world a work of art, *and heal Gabby, gotta heal Gabby, then my mother,* but have to leave the small self behind if you want my opinion: have to beware of hubris, the downfall of gods and men.

And goddesses.

Angela'd given me her phone number, so I dial her up but she's not in, or she's not answering. Probably with hubby. I call a cab, which arrives in about fifteen minutes—drives up in front of the orphanage where I'm sitting. Teen couples walk by on the sidewalk like a chain of train cars passing. Cab driver's a man of about fifty, named Patrick and he, too, is open and talkative.

"Kerouac was that famous?" he says, his accent as Boston as the Red Sox and the Kennedys. "You know what they say about him around here? He was just a drunk. I know guys in their sixties who drank with 'im. I could introduce you to 'em. Maybe tomorrow morning if you're still here. I'll still be working this shift. Hey, you wanna see Lowell High? You wanna see where he played football and banged up his knee? Got benched. Look, there's his high school." We cruise for another minute, then pass more charming New England homes, assymetrical cobblestoned streets, gardens, remnants of the shopkeeper's republic, before the serpentine industrial beast was completely unleashed.

"There's the Cosmopolitan. Used to be a strip joint. He got thrown outta there a lot. Used to be a strip joint but now Lowell is on the upswing. People from Boston are coming to buy homes here. There's the *Lowell Sun*. Good paper. Have you been to Kerouac *Pock*?"

"No, I haven't."

"You haven't been to Kerouac *Pock*? I'll take you. Look, I gotta get some coffee. I'll leave you at the *pock* and I'll come back in five minutes, okay?"

Kerouac Park, like the grotto, fills me with unexpected awe and solemnity, heart leaping up to freakin' empyrean, no drugs, no smoke, and yet awareness is heightened, because there are eight russet-red granite columns here, each inscribed with Kerouac's words, passages from *On the Road*, *Maggie Cassidy*, and from his journals. Writing was a duty to him, chronicling life "whether it really happened or not." The dead speaking to the living. *This story is my skull, my world, my gift to the living and the dead . .* It's not about the so-called reality of what is written, it's, rather, about the sponteaneous creative act, at the moment you put your pen to paper. A body in motion. Leaving town. You don't ask 'did it really happen?' and yet you want that feeling: ***Yes. It really happened***. The Lou Reed model. ***How could I have been so dumb?*** *It's all about revision.* Ti Jean *revised the world. This trip to Lowell has revised* me.

Am thinking of that passage from *On the Road*, the one at the end in which Sal Paradise refers to "the coming of night that blesses the earth, darkens the rivers . . ." *Ti Jean* was so much sweeter and kinder than I am. More respectful. What did he tell Steve Allen on TV? 'Beat' means 'sympathetic.' Again from *The Dharma Bums*:

What did I care about the squawk of the very little self, which wanders everywhere? I was dealing in outblowness, cut-off-ness, snipped, blownoutness, putoutness, turned-off-ness, nothing-happens-ness, gone-ness, gone-out-ness, the snapped link, nir, linl, vana, snap! 'The dust of my thoughts collected into a globe', I thought, 'in this ageless solitude,' I thought, and really smiled, because I was seeing the white light everywhere, in everything at last.

And now the night does indeed come as I get back into Patrick's cab. Who's the architect here? Don't know. Go to lowell dot com slash kerouac hyphen park and see it. His work's alive, I'm saying to myself as we drive away. Kerouac's work. It breathes. Sanity, intimacy and . . . what was the last one? *Ti Jean* in the promised land. Jackie set free. See it now . . .

The Oblates' Provincial office in Washington, D.C. says that Father Tom didn't teach at St. Joseph's Parish on Merrimack Street. His obituary reads, however, that he did "serve as a Knights of Columbus chaplain to the armed forces at Portsmouth and Norfolk, Virginia during the Great War. In 1935," the obit continues, "he was assigned once more to Tewksbury as Assistant Novice Master, succeeding to the office of Novice Master two years later." Back to the tonic chord. Coming and going. Eternal circle. Later, I pore over articles and essays and find nothing about Terry from Lowell. But, we've all heard Jack Kerouac's confession: *Leave the small self behind . . .*

"Call me in the morning," Patrick says. "I'll still be workin'. I'll take you around to meet some of Kerouac's old cronies. I'm sure a couple of 'em will be having breakfast at one of the diners. I'm workin' a 12-hour shift. I only do it once a week. Hey, come back to Lowell some time. Spend a few days. I'll probably still be here."

As I come nearer to the motel on Main Street, riding east in the back of the cab, I reach up to feel my bruised crown. On my forehead, I feel two small horns coming out of my forehead. In the back of the cab, right here and now, red-brick textile mills and black window shutters racing by, I make a vow. ***I will never hate this life again. Never. I will only honor it. Praise it.***

There's nothing to do but give praise.
My work here is done. Complete.
It's finished.

FOUR

E-mail from Esmé

Beast,

Why didn't you tell me you were going to Lowell? By bus??? I could have lent you my neck pillow . . . you know, that pillow? You just disappear and don't call? How's your head? And your leg? Archie?

My new floors look good. They're still a little sticky but should be fine in a couple of days. Come over tonight. We won't be able to walk around upstairs, but we can order out or maybe you can make some of your tempeh and coconut oil.

Have to be in court in an hour. Call me later. I'll put some hot ointment on your leg. Remember, you always have a home in Willoughby. You're like a brother to me.

P.S. Had a dream I was pregnant! And I'm late this month.

FIVE

Fundamental & Astounding
(Jack Kerouac's Confessor)

"You worship what you do not know; we worship what we know, for salvation is from the Jews."—John 4:22

A week passes and Joshua calls. He asks me to come see his mother because she's fading fast. Off life-support. No food, no water. No resuscitation. He also makes a remark that goes elegantly to the heart of another matter.

"Don't bother trying to be objective about your trip to Lowell," he says. "There's no such thing as objective journalism."

Wait. Hadn't Mo said that decades ago? About my Peter Gabriel story? Putz still thinks he's my editor, that he can revise my writing. This is a man who would revise the Declaration of Independence and leave out the slavery for a boost in his ratings. If you follow my meaning. *Revise* this, *Mo*. You know I'm being, again, playfully antagonistic and yet, despite the miracle at the grotto, despite meeting Kerouac's gentle and mysterious muse, even with the healing heart, the black and white arts, and my shillelagh made of red oak—even though we both fucked Dustin Hoffman's old girlfriend who looked exactly like Claudia Schiffer, swear to Invisible and Almighty God—even in the dream within the dream—I still harbor some resentment and I'm not entirely certain this can be remedied, although, obviously, this is hardly the time for a showdown between The Beast and The Genius. It's not the 1980s. It's not even the 90s. I'm here to heal Gabby, not to fight.

"But don't go overboard, either," Moses continues. "The real story is probably rich enough as it is. No need to gild the lily."

Gild the *lill-ee*?? Jesus Christ, does anybody talk like this anymore? Yes. People with the metabolism of a hummingbird. I leave town immediately; driving a rented car on the thruway and on the Taconic, and make it to the Moses house in under seven hours, where Marly, Josh and Mim's younger daughter, is doing last-minute preparation—reading *haftorah* and reciting Hebrew—for her bat mitzvah, which is still two weeks away. Hebrew words and sounds hum dirge-like from their second floor, lifting up the house with some magnetic force. Josh and I drive to Long Island together. Miriam and three of the kids are driving down later and Ellie the oldest, finishing her senior year at the University of Maryland, will take a train up to meet her family in the evening.

"So, what was Jack Kerouac's confession, anyway?" Joshua asks when we get to the Whitestone Bridge. "I did blow Gore Vidal after all?"

"Huh?"

"Gore Vidal claims that he and Kerouac slept together and that Jack publicly said 'I blew Gore Vidal'."

I'm kind of pissed that he'd say this especially as he hasn't asked anything substantial about Lowell since my return, not even once (he's been kind of smug about it, too), and in addition to playing the role of editor, he always says, 'I'll be your agent. No, really. I'm your biggest fan.'

Judge the state, *not the man who inhabits that state*, the hasids said . . . *say the healing, praising, word . . . unforgiveness burns like fire in the souls of the departed . . .*

"No, that's not it," I say. "Jack Kerouac's confession is that he did revise his work. But he didn't get to . . . I don't know. Mental health. It's a confession to the Lady . . . "

"Can you prove it?" Moses asks with a laugh, voice squeaking.

"Yeh," I say. "Absolutely. Never be spontaneous."

"The *lady*," gripes Moses as he brakes at a stoplight. "Even Dylan said that the goddess doesn't exist."

On the Long Island Expressway, JoMo's unusually eager to talk about his mother and his Aunt Cecile, who, perhaps because she's a retired psychiatrist, has taken it upon herself to dictate to the family ("with the ferocity of a Faulkner matriarch," according to Mo) how they should mourn and grieve, what should be done about executing the will, how services must be handled, and everything else, and it's weighing on Joshua as are most things, as the big boss in London has yet to make him a wealthy man, his job is a source of unmitigated stress (he's an independent contractor now: no benefits, no vacation days) and his debts are now more titanic and terrifying than ever before. Josh and Miriam are set to put their house on the market. Josh looks even thinner now. He's not eating, and, of course, his mother's often on his mind, too.

"What is it, do you think?" Joshua asks as we speed along the turnpike. He's wearing his Nguyen Cao Ky fatigues and is sniffling often.

"Power? The need to control? I would never tell anyone how to mourn or grieve but, you know, no one stands up to Cecile, not even her husband. I tell you, Slick, I'm really afraid for our country. No one stands up to the powers and dominions anymore. We're becoming a nation of sheep. Servile, blind sheep, sacrificial lambs, cheering and encouraging the shedding of blood. The blood of the innocent. Which is why I love Roth so much. He said Bill Clinton should've fucked Monica up the ass and that would have kept her quiet. Would have guaranteed her loyalty. I mean, he said it through one of his characters. Oh, God, *oy vey*, you've got me cursing again. You're a demon. A dybbuk. Well, so what? If Clinton had fucked that little JAP up the ass, she'd have been loyal but the Clintons, Roth says through one of his characters, were 'insufficiently corrupt.' Isn't that great? Insufficiently corrupt. Not perverse enough. It's all about power. You're surprised by my candor and stridency, aren't you, Slick? You thought I was naïve. Delicate. After all these years. It's about power. I'm not so naïve. You're either a slave or a master. That's what I think."

Traffic on the expressway is unaccountably thick. It's spring. No crowds trekking out to Jones Beach or to the Hamptons, but the ride takes longer than the usual hour. Normally, Josh would be lighting a bowl to make the ride easier, but not today. He has no money. No, seriously: this is his mom.

"So, what do you think?" says Mo. "Look what's happened right out of Blau's beloved Chicago. The city of the big shoulders, city of the blues. Look what's happened. Barack Obama."

"You think he'll win?"

"Yes, I do."

"I think it's going to be Gore."

"Nah, he won't run. It's too late. He'll never enter the primaries. Obama's going to be the first beatnik president. Attaches 'man' to the ends of his sentences. If only Hubert could see it. And Ted Kennedy . . . Obama has silenced these ice-cold intellectuals with their talk of the doomed black underclass and South Chicago. At least for now. They've been drowned like Pharaoh's army. Like Ahab. 'Barack' means 'praise.'"

Joshua's words feel hot like pine needles burning on a summer night, yellow and gold sparks flying out of the fire before being consumed in the cool rational night air.

"You know," he says, "I like the Jewish billionaire, he puts it all out there, no pretense. He started with soft porn and is moving into entertainment rags, but there's no pretension or loftiness. You know what? I'm getting really sick of these little goddam reform Jews from the suburbs holding forth about Hitler and the camps and again with the camps, because no one who went through that, no one who lived through that, talks about it in stark terms, ever notice? They know it's not about good and evil. It's more complex than some Sunday school lesson. If you were a 14-year-old kid, a yeshiva boy, and you had to punch your father, your beloved papa, to get him to work faster because if you didn't, your brain would become a puddle, you'd stop seeing the world in numbingly simple terms."

"You'd realize that yer capable of pretty much the same thing," I say. "It wouldn't be absolutely impossible for anybody to become a

Nazi. Even a Jew. That's why God gave us Henry Kissinger."

"Exactly. That's it, exactly. Ask Blau, he'll tell you. Ask his dad, ask Zollie. They know about the *kapos* and all that. They're not going to cover it all up with the dress of moral indignation like some suburban *hava nagilah* Jew."

"You'd have done well at Auschwitz," I say.

"Yeh, right."

"In the early days, you'd have been able to play music. Start a jazz club like your dad. Sorry. A rock 'n roll club. You could supervise poker night, play pinochle, hold forth on every subject under the blank and pitiless sun."

"Anything for science," Josh says.

"That's good. That's a rap. For science. That's good."

"Thank you, mon Slick. There are dimensions to yours truly that have yet to be plumbed. I mean, I never knew—hey, what the hell is coming out of your forehead?"

"What?"

"It's like you've got horns coming out of your head," JoMo says, mouth open. "What the . . . ?" Behind his bible black glasses, Josh's eyes narrow as he looks toward me, then, back at the highway. "My eyes are going bad."

"Must be the time o' day," I say with a shit-eaten grin.

The hum of the car's engine doesn't quite harmonize with our voices. The sound is like a third person's commentary. Outside are viaducts, bridges, road signs, diners, little money-laundering fronts that look like plastic hotels on a Monopoly board.

"What did Hubert used to say?" Mo continues, trying to stop a sneeze. "'Something about the intellectual and the fascist, right?"

"Yeh. He said over and over, 'the intellectual will always sell out to the fascist. It's just the old church in a suit and tie. They're not human; they're reptilian. Children of the serpent. Ritual killings of children. Moloch! Moloch! But I'm not sad. Nope. Not sad. We're a nation of laws, not of assholes.' That's what he used to say."

"Down in the South Seas, it was what?" says Josh with a frown. "With Melville. Cannibals, right? Cannibalism. God. But, in the end, was slavery any different from cannibalism? Is it? I don't think so. I mean, 'Call me, Ishmael'—he's saying right from the start that he's the child of slaves."

"Next, you'll be crying for the ducks in Central Park," I kid.

"I never cry," Moses asserts. "As God is my eyewitness."

"But, you're an atheist, Mo."

"So what?"

"Fuck!"

"What? What is it? I have no right to be an atheist?"

"No, no. I forgot to bring a present for your mom. I had a rose. A red rose and I forgot it. On the thruway. At one of the rest stops . . ."

"Don't worry. She can't see."

"Yeh, but she can smell. She's alive. You told me she can still hear and smell."

"Listen, don't worry about it. Just showing up is enough."

"Well, okay. Hey," I start, "were the Beats a bunch of intellectuals, too? Did Kerouac sell out to the fascist? He got to be pretty right-wing and all that."

I open the passenger window.

"Please close that, okay?" Josh says.

"But . . ."

"My eardrums freak out if the window is open. Close it, okay? Fresh air. Who cares? Fresh air is overrated." He winks at me. "Kerouac wanted to canvass all of North America, the roads and highways, the port towns, the diverse peoples. He left town but rarely did he leave the goddamn country. He didn't even leave the city very often. Because he took on the whole country, he had to atone for the whole country, ya know what I'm sayin', Slickeroo? Had to atone for slavery, the slaughter of the Indian, for Hiroshima, all while the Cold War raged. He was a martyr and that's why he stayed drunk his whole life. So, there was his alcoholism, too, and his attachment to his mother. It was an atonement. Can't get away from the agenbite monster." We ride over a rough patch of road and the whole car vibrates like someone gargling with mouthwash.

"But the Beats were pretty open, right?" I say. "About all their vices and obsessions, yes?"

"Ginsberg was open about all that, not Jack. Kerouac thought of himself as a right American novelist and a good Catholic. 'I'm not a beatnik, I'm a Catholic,' he said. Remember? He wasn't Whitman, you know, 'candor ends paranoia.' I think he became a drunk anti-Semite and a racist, you know, a right-wing crank angry at the hippies and at the Eastern establishment and at the Jews because of some weird interpretation of atonement, like, his bigotry was kind of an inverted love or perverse atonement . . . and he never harmonized with women, not really. If you can't get away from your mother, you'll never be able to really love a woman. But, his confession is his work. I think we all know that. Now, what about the penance?"

A hot sharp steely feeling of dread pierces the middle of my chest. It's as if I'm being judged, too.

You didn't meet Jack's muse, I'm thinking. *You don't know anything. You didn't hear his confession, therefore, you can't give out the penance . . .*

"What?" I say anxiously. It's getting hard to breathe in this car. "What was it?"

"Never-ending restlessness. That was his punishment," Josh points with his right index finger again, then waves his hand dismissively as if swatting a fly. "He sought freedom on the road but he never got free. He'd have to *stay* on the road. For eternity. A wandering Jew, never at peace, a voice crying in the wilderness, atoning for America's original sin, even for our debts. A slave. Kerouac could yearn for a new life, he'd be able to see sanity, to hope for it and maybe even describe it and inspire a feeling of freedom and sanity in others, but he would never attain it no matter how much he meditated or studied the lotus flowers. Home with your mama isn't really home. He had no resting place, no rest, like a junkie in withdrawal. Like when your body contains so much anxiety, you want to die but can't. Personally, I liked *The Subterraneans*. That's the Kerouac I like."

"Isn't it a myth?" I start to say, "in fact, it is a myth that he never edited or diagrammed or re-wrote anything."

"The real truth is in fiction. But 'fictional' and 'fictitious' aren't the same thing. He could have told a happier story. A more triumphant one."

GodDAMMMMMMMmn! *There's nothing to do but give* ***praise*** and yet I'm getting pissed off, real pissed off, because it feels as if Moses has taken the daylight out of the afternoon and put it in his shirt pocket. I'm chary. Suspicious. He's damn insightful, and acts as if he's my best friend, my confidant, my editor, my Revisor, then he pounces, or withdraws, and what's this sudden concern for truth? He hasn't asked one authentic question about the Lowell trip. Not one. Not 'what was the town like?' ' How was the trip? Did you feel like you'd arrived at Parnassus?' 'How was the weather?' 'You stood at his grave? How did that feel?' Nothing. But what should I care? He's not my goddamn lover; he's my erstwhile editor.

"Don't be so friggin' harsh," I say after some thickened silence. "What are you saying? He had no imagination? He was incomplete? Caught in some fucking purgatorio? You sound like one of those lit-crit critics that I hate."

"Don't hate," says Josh. "It's never worth it. Not even Hitler. Hate's a mythology." He looks at me. "Hey, you seem perturbed. What's up?"

"Well, Jesus Christ, Josh, I was standing at fucking Jack Kerouac's grave a little more than a week ago. Standing at his tomb! Do you understand that? Jack Fucking Kerouac! My great-uncle, with my last name, spelled with an 'a,' is buried nine miles away from him and you don't even ask me about the journey. You just yammer on about this and that. This is my story, man. It's not some discourse, not an academic thing. I appreciate your insights, but I was *there*, you understand? It *happened.* I was there. I met his muse. Passionate *Mercy*." I'm contemptuous.

"What do you mean you met his muse?"

"Some other time," I say. "Let's just say that I heard Jack Kerouac's confession directly from the source. From his confessor."

"Okay, sorry. Please . . . . I'm sorry. It's been very tough for me. I've been kind of selfish, I know. I apologize. But, listen, I *have* thought about your project and your Uncle Tom. I'm just preoccupied, okay? I'm up against it. I'm broke. I'm rent asunder, you dig? I'm goddamn Sisyphus, all right? Not everyone has a goddess protecting 'im."

Moses smiles and his eyes all but disappear behind his black-framed glasses as he signals and charges into the left lane like Dean Moriarty, like some mad Ahab at the wheel and he's stopped his sneezing and sniffling, too.

"Let me finish what I was going to say, though. I don't think Kerouac's in some kind of purgatory, all right? Let's put it this way. Let's be imaginative. A mean priest like your Uncle John, an inquisitor, a prick, would have sentenced Jack to eternal damnation on the road. A long sentence of restlessness and repentance for his sins. That's the dead we can't speak to. Or hear. A good priest like your Uncle Tom would have let him off the hook, would have remitted the debt. That's why Tom is probably off the hook, wherever he is. And Uncle John? Well, who knows where he is. He's dead, I guess. When you're dead, you're dead."

"Unless . . ." I say.

"Yeh, right," Moses says. "Unless."

"Sooo, you have been thinking about this whole thing, after all," I say.

"Well, of course. You're surprised? You seem to want to think the worst of me."

"This is your first other-than-casual statement about this project in a year. A year! Anyway," I continue, "I wouldn't opt for either Uncle John *or* Uncle Tom. You have to be an angel and a beast, too. At the same time. Sure. And Jackie had a pure heart, maybe too pure. I have no problem with Ahab in some respects. I'd strike the sun if it insulted me, too."

"You would, huh?"

"Not before I kiss the sky, though."

"How's your head feel?" Josh is a little short with me. "You'd strike the sun, eh? Tell me, how does your head feel after it's been struck? You might have to come down to earth a little, Slick. Just a little bit. And lose the anger."

Josh drives his van off of Route 25 and into a space in the suburban parking lot. The two of us walk to the front door of Gabby's complex enveloped by a warm spring breeze. Soon, I'll be going to the Blaus for a Passover *seder*. With a full and brazen moon lurking somewhere behind light, we'll be playing b-ball and breathing in the peppermint that wafts in the air near the Bronx botanical garden, Zoltan Blau's Hungarian-accented voice underscoring the freedom celebration like a Mingus bass line. Moses's jeremiad had surprised me. Always was a contradiction. Rhymes with 'fiction'.

"Oh, one another thing, ass*hole*," Mo says. We stop walking. What the hell is this? "You think I don't know that you and Miriam made out at the Statue of Liberty party? When everyone was doing the ecstasy and the fireworks and you had to have a ticket to get in?"

"Well, I . . . . did she tell you that?"

"Did she *tell me* that? Did she?? You're incredible. Yeh, I know, it was over twenty years ago and I wasn't exactly faithful, either . . . ."

"I'm sorry."

"Sorry. *Sorry*." Mo's words are like bullets. "I don't want to hear it. As far as I'm concerned, the matter is closed, Slick, but I have this one request: cease and desist from the moralizing and patronizing. Okay?"

He turns his back to me and I follow him into the building.

Listen: I'm here with my horns and staff to bring the walls down and heal Gabby and, JoMo's rebuke notwithstanding, that's what I'm going to do, but I don't know: Should I feel guilty? Kissing Miriam was really no big deal and I'm not one to make a big deal out of a *big* deal, let alone a little one; about something that happened in Reagan's first term. ***No, I won't feel guilty***. Maybe I shouldn't have kissed auburn-haired, long-nosed Mimi that night, Mimi with the liquid eyes, as Henry Miller would say; it was real quick, like sweet wine kissing, and maybe I'll only complicate things if I even think about saying something wildly inappropriate to poor Gabby after all, something like "I always wanted to *schtup* you, to fuck you; I'd rather fuck you than Phil Rizzuto's widow"—by making an obtuse connection between 'erection' and 'resurrection, then again, why be polite? Aaron's Rod, the World to Come, the forgotten melody's dominant chord is the woman's orgasm . . . like *being blinded* . . . So, I decide to not feel guilty and to put Aaron's Rod to good use, to be perfectly profane, and prick and praise the lady back to life. Metaphorically, of course.

Was half expecting to see Harry and Shira and even Cecile there in Gabby's room but she's alone with the TV on and looks as if she's already been laid-out like at an Irish wake but she looks better than I thought she would, except that her mouth is wide open and her hair, which used to be that brassy golden calf hue, is now snow-white, skull-white, dove-white, white as a lamb, white like the full moon, white as Moby Dick and Orval Faubus, as white as the lines on the lost endless highway, and she's wearing brown shades, too—blue eyes covered up—and lay motionless, filled with a massive dose of morphine and other painkillers; buried alive in the darkness, in a sterile, efficient and life-hungry facility that looks exactly like all the other retirement-old folks facilities across the nation where 85-year-old women in wheelchairs yell out "I want my Mama!"; where the room smells of iodine and feces, the lingering scent of The Greatest Generation. And the staff, the nurses and orderlies, are condescending. Patronizing. They talk to the old folks like children, in that revolting sing-song. *Now, you take this little pill, Mrs. Moses . . .*

She's getting stronger spiritually, I'm thinking. That's supposed to be the secret. The best is yet to be. Right? What else do you at this stage of the game but dream about the better world? Beautiful dreaming, right? On a bed stand next to Gabby is a bowl of fruit, two apples, a pear, an orange. Only one of the apples isn't rotten. I still love her, though . . . still love Gabby, more than I love her son. The real woman is alive somewhere, living within this arrangement of skin and hair and unreachable stillness, hidden like the sun at midnight.

"Ma, look who it is," Joshua says walking toward the bed. I want to take her hands in mine and kiss them but hers are coiled up under her chin like a chipmunk's. Josh and I both stroke her hair.

"Gabby, it's me," I say, just above a whisper. An ocean of silence lay between the two of us. "It's Bob." She doesn't make a sound. I look for signs of life behind the shades and sightless eyes but can find nothing. Only four years older than Archie, Gabby looks ancient, but did she have time to build her ship of death? At this point, you'd have to become especially conscious of the breath coming out of her open mouth.

Breath.

"Remember when Jay and I told you we were going to start meditating and stop smoking pot and the next morning you found roaches and a pipe in the living room and said to Jay, 'you're a bullshit *ahtist*! You were smoking pot all night long! Isn't that for kids? When are you going to grow up?'?"

Josh and I laugh and I think I can see something brighten up at the corner of the woman's mouth, so, she must've heard. Judge Judy holds court in the background but I'm convinced Gabby can hear us and JoMo even said that, as far as he knows, there's nothing wrong with her hearing.

"Ma," Joshua starts again as he brushes his mother's hair back with his hand, "everybody hates the war now. You'd be so happy. Everyone sees it for the failure and the imbecilic venture that it is. The emperor has no clothes. Finally!" Joshua kisses his mother's forehead and smiles. He seems taller than normal. His voice and form fill the room. "Maybe you'll be appointed to the Supreme Court now." Gabby's breathing becomes heavy but quickly returns to its normal rhythm. In a minor key. The two of us stand at Gabby's bedside for ten or twelve minutes, stand in silence as we watch weightless, precious, intangible and goddamn *honorable* life seep out of her like smoke rising up from dampened logs. Somewhere on I-90, I'm thinking, somewhere on the thruway, a red rose is dying from a lack of care.

"Listen," I say, breaking the silence, "I'm going downstairs to get some coffee. Do you want coffee? Anything?"

Joshua says that he doesn't need anything, and as I walk downstairs to the first floor, I look out for a moment, out one of the windows at the poplars and willows just as they're beginning to bud and bear fruit. These assisted-living complexes are generally located in the rural areas, built on top of old Indian burial grounds like the novitiate-retirement home in Tewksbury. Here on Long Island, you can actually hear the voices of the Poospatuck and Mohegan, the susurrus of the old dead souls. Years ago, Josh talked about Gabby's father, as a kid running from the Cossacks in Czarist Russia; running with his family, all holding hands, and when one of the little girls was shot, they just let her drop to the ground and kept running. The father, the husband, Gabby's grandfather, had sailed to America first and when his family arrived at New York harbor later without the little girl—she was about Marly's age at the time, ready to be bat mitzvahed—he understood immediately what'd happened. Didn't need to be told. Poor little thing. Poor family. Poor little goddamn planet.

I fill up a styrofoam cup with coffee and suddenly feel impelled to commit the profane yet healing deed, a loving and profane deed that'll hopefully bring the Grotto to Gabby, bring her back to life, you know, strike the first note, fuck her into the orgone, the spiraling World to Come: she might as well come while she's getting gone. No, seriously . . . I want to embrace her, coax her back to life. Heal her. But you've gotta have the right rhythm, the right note. 'G' for grace. Am starting to feel giddy, even feverish.

What does it take to heal someone? I mean, to actually heal? *Do you attract the Lady's grace by awakening the inner King? Is that it? Is that the Bright Morning Star? Let's get real* GONE *for a change . . .*

Who wants to be a square, a schoolteacher; fearfully symmetric and trapped in the mother's realm, in *Memere's* world? Too cowardly for your calling, the mind technology of the 21st century, and for that whole new theory of literature? Sweet & angelic? *I don't think so.* We've got a *real* healer here. I take a few sips of my coffee, then dump the rest out into the sink next to the coffee-maker and head back upstairs.

I approach the third floor and walk toward Gabby's room, having decided to confront death directly because what good was the journey to Lowell if you don't use your horns and staff, the staff with 'I am' written on it? No guilt. The woman language. Pierce the veil. What ails thee, motherrrr?

Infectious beat. Gabby laughing, cursing, opining, smoking, even. Entreaties written by the old crusader, the letter-writer, the civil disobedient, written in the penitent's book at the Grotto in Lowell, written, no doubt, with one fist raised at the self-conscious sky. *Heal me or I'm calling my fucking lawyer!* I run my right hand over my left leg and try to convey some warmth to the damaged tissue. *Crawl up the staff for me and for Aesculapius just like you did for Pixie, Lyla and maybe Tatiana. Now here's Gabby. Rise up. I'm in love. I'm a healer.* Emperor Jones beat. Spiral up, spiral Up. Dance to the tune.

THIS WOMAN IS HEALED.

HEALED! Spiral Up. Upppp . . .

I get to the doorway of Gabby's room and am flabbergasted to see Joshua kneeling at his mother's bed. He's crying softly but tearfully. In our twenty or so years of acquaintance, I've never seen Joshua Moses cry. Or kneel.

Look at that lady. Will you look at that lady . . . *!*

"Ma," he whispers. "They all say you're suffering, but you're at peace, right? Can you hear me? You're not suffering anymore, are you?" Joshua falls silent for about ten seconds, then begins talking again. Softly. "You're at peace. I can feel it. Don't be afraid. But I wish we could talk like we used to. I'm so sorry for what you've been going through. So sorry. God. Don't be afraid, Ma. Don't be afraid." Josh pulls out a handkerchief and wipes his eyes and nose. His color is a soft gold as he feels, must feel, life exiting the woman who'd given him birth.

"I know I never said it, Ma, but I love you," he says. "I would give my life up right now if it would help you in any way. Please tell me you're no longer in pain. Please make a sound. Can you hear me, Ma? Can you hear?" He kisses her on the lips, on her open mouth, and Gabby puckers a bit.

Now, here is the real genius. He cancelled the debt. Free at last.

Fundamental & astounding.

I feel like a selfish—a disgracefully selfish and fucking self-involved—unmentionable. Vain and insolent and without any grace. Josh puts his head on his mother's breast and closes his eyes. He lay there, a figure of yellow and gold, for something like twenty seconds, sobbing gently, then looks up quickly. "She's stopped breathing," I hear him say quietly. He puts his hand over her heart. She's not dead, she couldn't be. You could hear a faint death rattle, like the sound of a French racecar's engine, but no intense labored breathing. Her hands are coiled up, claw-like, so Moses reaches for his mother's jugular, but there's no pulse. Gabrielle Moses has, indeed, left the sad, hurting, misbegotten earth. Gabby is gone.

SIX

Kaddish

(The Forgotten Chord)

Gabby's cremated and there's no *Shiva* call, but a service is held one week later at the assisted-living complex in Jericho. Never knew the name of the place. The religion of their fathers. Poppy seeds and pastries. If you'd heard Harry play "Goodbye," Benny Goodman's theme song, on his clarinet—his hands shook just a little from Parkinson's as he blew his horn—you might have felt like the rest of us: like we were back home but not behind walls. Like this is too deep for tears. Too deep. The breath. Harry. The threnody. Like a question being answered. The Will. Fate. *Adieu, Gabrielle. Sweet love to you.* Afterwards, Esmé kissed Harry on his right cheek and said "we'll be back for Marly's bat mitzvah, okay, Heschel?" The old man likes it when Esmé calls him 'Heschel.'

"We'll see you then, darling," Harry said, his sort of plangent-gentle voice an approximation of his horn. "Thank you so much for coming."

Is it sentimental to propose that the living, heeding the dictates of a hidden rhythm that can defy entropy and make you sane, are able to breathe life into and awaken the dead? Is it true that only the living can bring life to the static, sightless and dying world?

Willing to be seen? Wanna be famous? Or maybe like the bishops and Father Spike said: *We will keep alive the memory of our deceased . . . for they shall take their works with them . . .*

Works of art.

Outside, in the parking lot, Josh hugs me, then Esmé. Still has more enthusiasm about life and death than it's hip to have or display.

"Thanks for coming," he says.

"So long, Jay," I say. "And thank you. For everything. I'll call ya."

"Adiós," he says. "See ya soon." Josh is alone in the lot as we all wave goodbye. It'd rained earlier. Everything's sort of wet but the sky's partly clear now. Clouds like puffs of cigar smoke. Look at Josh. He's grown, don't you think? Physically, even. Still skinny, still way pale, but bigger, it seems. More gold than yellow. Power's been released. 'Passionate mercy' as he says and . . . **WAIT**: are those little horns coming out of his forehead? Yeh. Indeed. **Look**: Two thin beams of gold and yellow light, like tiny moon crescents, are radiating from Mo's brow, from his skull. As the car pulls away, I look again at the thin figure in his black suit and blue silk tie. Black glasses. Mustache. Damn, he's looking more and more like Melvyn Douglas. But with horns. Josh smiles slightly, waves again, then becomes smaller and smaller before he and, finally, his faintly radiating, spiraling, horns disappear.

While driving home on the Jericho Turnpike in Esmé's black Honda, my left leg begins to bother me. I'm taking fish oil daily, in capsules, and putting balm on the leg but it itches a little. My head throbs a mite. Maybe it's the horns. Esmé looks straight ahead, at the long, seductive road by the ocean, and is silent.

"Ezzie," I say. "Don't you think Josh looked . . . different?"

"Yes," she says still looking ahead at the road and its motion, her hair dirty-blonde like the ocean sand. "He's changed. Everything's changed. And I keep having dreams that I'm pregnant." She looks at me. "Can you believe that? And I told you that I'm late."

"Did you say you're late?"

"Yes. I told you . . ."

"What? You got another boyfriend?"

A solitary black crow takes flight and I imagine it's a bald eagle. Will we be able to see water on the horns of a reticent spring moon? A train whistle can be heard in the distance and I think of Zollie Blau and the unspeakable train ride to Auschwitz. Some things just can't be revised.

Can I wake up now?

And admit impediments?

Have You Build Your Ship of Death?

Have ye?

Your greatest Work of Art . . . ?

I'm thinking about my Uncle Bill coming home from Okinawa, about the kids from South Buffalo coming home from Iraq in body bags, and about Hubert, Joe Valentine, Terry from the grotto, my mother, and the ghosts of Tompkins Square—and about Jack and Neal and Allen and Naomi and Teddy Kennedy, too, the last brother—then I just know I have to look out my window and try to praise the strip malls and deserted industrial plants of Whitman's Long Island; praise a hurting and burdened land of ashes and dust and meds and debt and hope, the Jericho that Gabrielle Moses'll never see again; the Babylon where the lady's in chains—*build your ship of death, o, build it for you will need it*—the America that my father's father's father never even saw or knew.

SEVEN

Unless . . .

Printed in Great Britain
by Amazon